Steve lives in rural Oxfordshire with his wife, Sarah, and golden retriever, Evie. Being awarded a fifteen-yards swimming certificate at age nine and a prize book token for writing an essay about the Sun at secondary school were life-changing moments. These achievements led to a degree in Maths and Astronomy, and a fulfilling career in teaching and lecturing.

Steve has had a lifelong passion for all things space-related and has thoroughly enjoyed writing his first novel *Empire of Mars*. He is currently working on the sequel.

To Sarah and Evie

Stephen Darnell

# EMPIRE OF MARS

AUSTIN MACAULEY PUBLISHERS™

LONDON • CAMBRIDGE • NEW YORK • SHARJAH

A CIP catalogue record for this title is available from the British Library.

ISBN 9781398477711 (Paperback)
ISBN 9781398477728 (ePub e-book)

www.austinmacauley.com

First Published 2023
Austin Macauley Publishers Ltd®
1 Canada Square
Canary Wharf
London
E14 5AA

# Table of Contents

*When it comes to controlling human beings there is no better instrument than lies. Because, you see, humans live by beliefs. And beliefs can be manipulated. The power to manipulate beliefs is the only thing that counts.*

Michael Ende, *The Neverending Story*

*Never attempt to win by force what can be won by deception.*

Niccolò Machiavelli, *The Prince*

*Since mankind's dawn, a handful of oppressors have accepted the responsibility over our lives that we should have accepted for ourselves. By doing so, they took our power. By doing nothing, we gave it away. We've seen where their way leads, through camps and wars, towards the slaughterhouse.*

Alan Moore, *V for Vendetta*

# Chapter 1
# Preparations

Aka-mas stood up to address the House of Elders.

'But we have evidence,' he said, clearly exasperated by his lack of progress. 'Our probes have indicated that there is life on Earth. Not intelligent life, granted, but life nonetheless. We should tell the public now. We are not alone in the universe.'

He sat down to await the response.

The five elders sat in a row on a platform adorned with the imperial symbol, a golden circle with five "rays of light" emanating from the centre. They were all dressed in their pure white robes of office, with the same symbol emblazoned on the left shoulder. El-bas, the chief elder, turned to his colleagues. They all nodded their agreement.

'There is no real proof,' he began, crossing his slender fingers as if in prayer. 'Our probes have indicated conditions might be suitable for primitive life forms, but that is all.'

'But that's not true,' Aka-mas blurted. 'We know that vegetation exists, as do seas. We have evidence that life forms exist in the seas and—'

'The emperor believes we should not be too hasty in making unnecessary announcements to the public,' El-bas interjected. 'It is quite likely that some mechanical malfunction in the probes has led to incorrect readings being taken. We need further corroboration before we inform the public.'

He stared at Aka-mas and his voice hardened.

'There will be no announcements at present. Is that understood? The emperor forbids it.'

With that, the five elders stood up. Aka-mas and the other scientists present did the same. The meeting was over.

'Why are they so against a public announcement?' Aka-mas pondered as he turned to fellow scientist and friend Am-ral.

'They don't want the competition,' his colleague replied. 'The emperor is supposed to be a god, and we are created in his divine image. Mars is unique as an abode of intelligent life, or so the story goes. If word gets out that the universe is teeming with life, we lose our unique position; and more to the point, so does the emperor.'

'You're right, I suppose,' said Aka-mas gloomily. 'But it's ridiculous in our day and age. Here we are, an advanced technological civilisation, sending space probes to explore our celestial neighbours, and at the same time believing that our emperor is an omnipotent god. It's just wrong.'

'Don't let anyone else hear you say that,' Am-ral warned. 'You could get into real trouble. The emperor's lackeys are everywhere.'

As they walked out into the street, the group of scientists dispersed. Aka-mas continued on his way home. In two days' time it would be Emperor's Day, and everywhere the imperial symbol fluttered from flagpoles and the balconies of buildings great and small.

The streets were already being cleaned in readiness for the great procession, when thousands would line the route as the Imperial Guard escorted the god emperor on his way from the palace to the House of Elders, where the annual address would take place.

Of course, no one would actually see the emperor. He would be cocooned in his imperial orb, which would hover above the ground as it made its way to the House. Citizens would hear the words of the emperor, but he was never seen by mere mortals.

It was said that he was handsome beyond belief. A perfect specimen of Martian manhood. But he was a god, after all. It was good enough just to hear his words of wisdom, marvel at the brilliance of the orb, wave a flag and cheer. Nothing else was expected, or encouraged.

Aka-mas felt downhearted. *How could people be so gullible? What had the emperor ever done for the Martian people? He gave out orders which were obeyed without question, and he made the odd "appearance" such as at the Emperor's Day parade. That was all. Martians are an intelligent race, taking their first steps into space. Why should they still adhere to the preposterous notion that their leader was a god? Why had no one ever seen him? Surely things would have to change*, he reasoned.

But, as Aka-mas looked around him, he wasn't so sure. People really seemed to enjoy the preparations for Emperor's Day. They liked the party atmosphere, the flag waving and the cheering. Admittedly, a day off work was not to be sniffed at, but it was more than that. Emperor worship was a religion. It was accepted as being natural, as it always had been. *Perhaps people really aren't bothered by the lack of political freedom after all*, mused Aka-mas. *Perhaps they are happy being treated like children, with no say about their future, or being told what to do and what to think, with no chance of voting their political masters out of office. People are generally content with their lot, and contented people don't normally cause trouble.*

As Aka-mas walked into his house, he was greeted by his wife who was arranging flowers in a large vase.

'It's for the Emperor's Day Eve party,' she announced. 'I've invited some of our friends and neighbours around. You don't mind, do you?'

'Why do you want to celebrate Emperor's Day?' asked her husband.

'You know that I don't approve of all this fawning of the emperor. He's just a man, you know.'

'You do talk rubbish.' Mrs Aka-mas laughed. 'We always celebrate Emperor's Day. It's a tradition, as you well know. Everyone is so excited. It'll be such fun.'

She continued to arrange her flowers, humming to herself contentedly, and ignoring the complaints of her husband.

Aka-mas gave up. It was no use berating his wife for her beliefs. It was he who was in the distinct minority, not her. He would no doubt go through with the charade of the festivities, just to keep her happy. *One day things will change*, he thought to himself, *but not yet.*

He turned to the communications console to hear the latest news. Plenty of items about the forthcoming Emperor's Day festivities. Interviews with smiling, excited individuals eulogising about the greatness of the emperor and of his love for his people. People reminiscing about past parades and holding images of the imperial orb. *Of course*, thought Aka-mas, *no one will be holding an image of the emperor himself.*

Then, a brief item about a skirmish at the city gates. Apparently, a group of Antis, large insect-like creatures who roamed the plains surrounding the city, had tried to break in. Nothing serious; it happened all the time. One of the Antis was killed and the others escaped. Hardly news, really.

Fed up with the incessant news coverage of the great emperor – someone was now giving a detailed summary of his great and holy actions of the last year, including curing a small boy of a fatal disease and ending a drought in the Ellas region – Aka-mas switched off. *This is madness*, he thought, *sheer madness*.

The city felt claustrophobic to Aka-mas. Everyone seemed to be involved in some way with the preparations for Emperor's Day. It was the only topic of conversation. Families were preparing celebratory meals. Best clothes were being cleaned in readiness for the big day, and yet more flags and bunting were being erected. It was a tradition to give small presents to family and friends on the day itself, so the shops were heaving as people searched for the ideal gifts. Young and old, rich and poor, everyone was caught up in the festive atmosphere of the Emperor's Day preparations.

Aka-mas had to escape. He had to leave the confines of the city, even if only for a few hours. People were free to come and go as they wished, as long as they informed the officials at the city gates of their departure, proposed destination and expected time of return. This was mainly for safety reasons. There was always the possibility that individuals, and even small groups, exploring the countryside, or "Outside" as anywhere beyond the city boundaries was known, would be ambushed by the Antis. If you did not return to the city when expected, the authorities would send a rescue party to find you.

Aka-mas felt the need for some company on his excursion, and found his son Aka-des lounging in his bedroom. Aka-des was a student at the Central College in the city and had inherited some of his father's rebel instincts, although not so blatant. It was not so much emperor worship that annoyed him, but the treatment of the Antis. Aka-des had studied the history and culture of the Antis race at college, and believed that they had every right to share the planet with his own people. The Antis were intelligent, too. They had family groups and although a nomadic race, they had a hierarchy of authority which in many ways operated as a far more democratic system than that of the Martians.

But the Antis felt threatened. Their way of life was under attack as the Martians grabbed more and more land for their expanding city. Antis tribal lands were being confiscated with no thought for the consequences. This, Aka-des believed, was the reason for the supposedly warlike behaviour of the Antis. They were being pushed into a corner, so had no option but to fight. If only both sides could negotiate, everyone – Martian and Antis – could live together in peace.

'Fancy a walk Outside?' asked Aka-mas.

'Sure, why not,' replied his son. 'Nothing else to do.'

Father and son walked through the streets to Povas Gate, the nearest exit to the Outside. A beautiful, stone-built structure intricately carved with scenes depicting events from Martian history.

They both filled in the necessary forms and handed them to the bored-looking official sat at his desk. The official glanced fleetingly at the forms and then waved the two men through.

Aka-mas and his son started to walk out into the stunningly beautiful Martian countryside.

# Chapter 2
# Outside

Aka-mas and his son stepped into the bright Martian sunshine. There was barely a cloud in the sky as the two men set off on their walk. The route they took was a familiar one; a ramble through local woods down to the fishing village nearby, a small settlement on the banks of a vast lake.

The day was warm with a slight breeze, an ideal time to escape the confines of the city. Aka-mas found that he increasingly needed to get away from the regimented and ordered life in the metropolis. The Outside was his escape valve, a different world where the dictates of petty officials held no sway. Admittedly, there was always the possibility of an ambush by the Antis; but in his experience, the insect creatures weren't really interested in lone walkers. Their hatred was aimed at the city and all it stood for.

In fact, some Martians chose to live permanently outside the safety of the city. Small settlements such as the fishing village they were now aiming for were springing up all over the place. Perhaps Aka-mas was not alone in wanting to escape the stifling atmosphere of city life after all.

'Why do you get so bothered about these things?' asked Aka-des.

'So what if people want to dress up and wave a few flags. It is a holiday, after all. You don't have to take part.'

'Technically you are correct,' replied his father. 'But if you don't get involved, it is noticed. Someone will mention it and word soon gets around. You will be marked as a troublemaker, someone who is disloyal to the emperor. So-called friends will start to avoid you, cancel meetings with some lame excuse. You will become ostracised, an outcast. Colleagues will start to pick fault with your work. Suddenly, you are selected for "retraining" and sent away from home for months, even years, at a time. Perhaps never to be seen again. It's happened before, you know. Choice? Oh yes, we all have a real choice.'

Aka-mas spat out the words bitterly.

'Then why be a troublemaker?' queried Aka-des.

'You have a comfortable life. A job you enjoy. A nice home. Do you really want anything more?'

'That's good coming from you,' Aka-mas retorted. 'Mister eco-warrior himself. You're the one who wants to make friends with a bunch of insects. Don't tell me about living a comfortable life.'

'But that's different,' replied his son. 'The Antis are misunderstood. The way we treat them is clearly unjust. We don't own this planet; we share it with them and with all the other species, too. Mars is, or should be, about all of us sharing what this world has to offer. There's more than enough to go around.'

Aka-mas laughed.

'Bold words, my son, but you're not really in any better position than me. People ignore my concerns about the direction our society is heading, and they ignore your concerns about the Antis. To most people, the Antis are a bunch of bug-eyed, brain-dead insects. Little more than animals. A nuisance – nothing more. People certainly won't see any need for some form of coexistence between the races.'

'People will learn,' countered Aka-des. 'If we explain to them the benefits of a truce with the Antis. If people understand their culture and their concerns. It will happen one day soon I hope.'

'Wishful thinking, I'm afraid,' replied his father, softly.

The pair continued on their way along a well-trodden track leading down to the lakeside. The countryside around them was lush and green. Wild flowers, a myriad of colours and sizes, edged the path. Large trumpet-like blooms in shades of red and orange swayed in the breeze, giving off an intense scent as anything brushed past. Nearby, a small vivid yellow bloom was in full flower at the top of a long, ridged stem. If an insect landed on the bloom, it would immediately snap shut, and the stem would retract into the ground. Once the meal had been digested, the stem would again reach up into the air and the yellow flowers would open once more. This was happening all around, stems moving up and down, blooms opening and shutting, as if some macabre dance were taking place.

Father and son now entered the wood. Everything was quiet, apart from the rustling of leaves in the velvety breeze. Occasionally, a small animal would dart across the path and disappear into the undergrowth, as if returning home from some undercover operation. Perhaps bringing food to quell the hunger of a growing family, hidden from the attentions of Man.

Mars was a planet teeming with all forms of life. A Garden of Eden, a near-perfect world. But could this last forever? Did man deserve this beauty and bounty? Could he handle it, or would greed and ignorance destroy nature's inheritance?

Through the trees, Aka-mas could see the water of the lake glinting in the distance. They were getting close to the village of Meroe, a settlement of some five hundred souls.

'Fancy living here' Aka-des enthused.

'All this beauty. To be a part of nature, living off the land. Surely these people have got the balance right. Largely left to their own devices, they aren't bothered by the petty concerns of city folk. They make their own laws and live their lives as they see fit. We have a lot to learn from them.'

'It seems idyllic, granted,' Aka-mas pondered. 'But how many of us would really give up our home comforts to come and live out here. These people eke out a living as farmers and fishermen, but what of all the modern conveniences we take for granted in the city? Restaurants, theatres, shops, hospitals, schools – the list goes on and on. These people have made a conscious decision to live as they do. Surely, we couldn't all live like this?'

'I think I could,' said Aka-des, deep in thought. 'It's an honest life, doing real work, and getting a sense of satisfaction from it.'

'Rather you than me.' Aka-mas smiled. 'I suppose at heart I am still a city person. I like to come out here from time to time, but I know that after a few hours I can return to all my home comforts. It's not really living in a city I loathe, but the type of city we have created.'

Lake Qarun was vast. It was impossible to see the far-side shoreline. All that was visible was a shimmering sea, stretching out into the distance. The rocky beach, which the two men had now reached, met the lapping waves at the water's edge. They were still some distance from the village, but a few fishermen sat on large rocks talking while others mended their nets or tended to their boats.

Aka-mas approached one of the villagers.

'Good day to you,' he said as he greeted the young fisherman. 'A good catch today?'

'Not bad,' replied the other. 'A good catch of quivvel. That's something, I suppose.'

Aka-mas looked down at a large tray where about fifty quivvel were still squirming in the warm sun as their life ebbed away. Quivvel were a delicacy, and restaurants in the city would pay a handsome price for a catch like this. A combination of sea horse and small squid, quivvel were a peculiar sight. Roughly six inches long, the sea horse body merged with a nest of tentacles, much prized by city gourmets. The delicacy would be held by the head as the diner first sucked away at the tentacles – somewhat chewy but very filling. Next, the flesh of the body would be eaten, gnawing at the soft meat down to the bones. Some would even eat the eyes of the creature, considered an aphrodisiac, before discarding the bones on the side of the plate. Eating a quivvel in company was certainly an art in itself.

Aka-mas had never really taken to quivvel. Somewhat conservative in his tastes, he found many sea and lake creatures just too much for his delicate system. Too many eyes, tentacles and slimy bits for him. Give him a nice steak from the pig-like snoller any time.

Next to the tray of quivvel, Aka-mas noticed a basket full of blind narchus. These strange creatures were almost transparent. They had no eyes, but sensitive pimples on the head which acted as organs of touch. They were also able to create an electric field around their body as they swam. Any solid object entering this field would bend the lines of force, and this would tell the narchus to alter course to avoid an obstacle. Larger than the quivvel, and more abundant, the narchus provided a tasty dish for a family supper.

Looking out at the lake, Aka-des noticed a fishing boat in the distance, trailing a large trawl net behind it, dragging it along the bed of the lake and scooping up yet more fantastic creatures of the deep. *Not a bad life*, he thought. *Not bad at all.*

Aka-mas and his son continued along the beach until they came to the village of Meroe. The houses were built into the cliff face, one layer above the next, with winding paths connecting the higher levels to the lower, and finally to the beach itself. Aka-mas could see children amusing themselves by throwing pebbles into the lake, and small groups of mainly women sitting and talking, darning clothes or preparing ingredients for the family meal. The sun was shining on the stone buildings at an angle so that the windows and doors stood out in relief. There must have been over a hundred such dwellings perched like a pack of playing cards, one above the other. It seemed as though if one house were to collapse, the others would follow, tumbling down the rock face, one domino after another.

'It must have taken ages to build this village,' Aka-mas commented. 'It's a real work of art.'

Aka-des nodded.

'They probably built it like that to provide protection in the case of an attack by the Antis. Certainly, if you lived on the upper levels, you should be fairly secure. The whole village would know what was happening before the insects reached up there.'

Aka-mas looked at his wristband to check the time.

'We should think about returning. We don't want to be late and then find a safety patrol coming to meet us. They don't like false alarms, and we could end up with a hefty fine.'

They made their way back up to the wood, taking another path which skirted the edge of the village. The two walkers continued for some time in silence, each absorbed in their own thoughts. Suddenly, they both heard a scratching noise and came to an abrupt halt.

'Look down there,' whispered Aka-des, grabbing hold of his father's arm. 'Antis.'

As they peered down a grassy slope to a clearing below, they could see a group of about a dozen Antis busily working away at some task.

The insects stood at about seven feet in height, with head, thorax and abdomen in the same greenish hue. Their eight legs were segmented and covered in fine hair. Their antennae were waving in all directions, perhaps a form of communication between members of the group. Some of the Antis appeared to be digging with their mandibles, scooping out soil, while others were carrying away the dirt in their mouths.

'It looks as if they might be building a new nest,' said Aka-des quietly. 'They must be the workers. Different types, or castes, of Antis do different jobs. Look at the couple over there.'

He pointed to a pair of Antis standing some way from the main group.

'Why are their abdomens so swollen?' asked his father.

'They are repletes,' replied Aka-des. 'Their job is to drink as much water as possible so their abdomens swell up like a balloon. When another member of the group is thirsty, it strokes the replete, which then gives up a quantity of water. And look at those.'

He pointed to two larger Antis standing by the workers.

'They are probably doorkeepers. They look after the entrance to the nest to make sure only other Antis can enter.'

'I can't see any sign of a queen,' said Aka-mas.

'She'll be along soon,' replied his son. 'Once everything is ready, she will take up residence. The soldiers will escort her, and heaven help anything that gets in their way, or threatens the queen. They can be a very nasty piece of work.'

'I don't really want to be part of the welcoming party.' Aka-mas shuddered. 'Let's leave. These insects give me the creeps.'

Both men crept slowly through the woods until they were well away from the Antis nest. By the time they reached the outskirts of the city, the sun was just starting to set. In the sky above you could see the first bright stars heralding the start of night. Except these weren't stars at all. One was the moon of Mars. Much smaller than Earth's moon, many believed it was really a rogue asteroid which had been captured in Mars's orbit millions of years ago.

Then Aka-mas noticed a greenish star appear low down near the horizon. Earth. *I know there is life there*, he thought to himself, *and somehow, I'm going to prove it*.

# Chapter 3
# Mars, the Abode of Life

The planet Mars was indeed a Garden of Eden. Although barely half the size of its nearest planetary neighbour, Earth, Mars was large enough to support a huge diversity of life forms. The planet itself had oceans, lakes and rivers, teeming with a multitude of bizarre creatures, large and small. The climate was largely temperate, with a countryside of green fields, forests and a variety of agricultural crops. Wild flowers grew everywhere, in every colour imaginable. Huge blooms which gave off an intense scent, and plants that visibly moved in line with the sun. Others changed colour within seconds should any living creature come too near, while the amerot plant actually emitted a faint humming noise, a natural song of Mars. There were mountainous areas, too, with snow-capped peaks and lakes of water ice. Indeed, Mars had the highest mountain in the solar system, more than three times as high as Mount Everest on Earth, and its own Grand Canyon which dwarfed its terrestrial counterpart.

The atmosphere of Mars then was similar to Earth's today. Slightly thinner perhaps, but basically the same mixture of nitrogen and oxygen, and perfectly breathable. The Martian sky was a pale blue in colour, contrasting with the green of the fields and the reddish orange of the rocks and hills.

Inhabiting this world of plenty were two intelligent races; the humanoid Martians and the insect-like Antis. The Martians were seen as the dominant race. From beginnings as farmers and hunters they had, over the years, become a largely urban people. They built a huge city which became the centre of their civilisation, as well as satellite towns and villages across the vast plains of Mars. The city grew and grew, and was now home to over forty million people. Over the years, the Martians had largely overcome illness and disease. Wars between different Martian factions were also a thing of the past, something to be read about in schools and discussed in colleges. The Martians were now a truly global race, without nations and petty squabbles between nation states. The people were well educated, and both science and the arts were well developed. In areas such as medicine, engineering and the natural sciences, the Martians were centuries ahead of current human development, and both philosophy and psychology were studied with a passion.

The Martian people, particularly those living in the city, the cultural and economic heart of their civilisation, were obsessed with fashion. Men and women would vie with each other to be seen in the most up-to-date clothes and to have the newest gadgets and accessories. The current fads included intricately carved helmets made of gold and encrusted with jewels, decorated with huge feathers and shimmering fabric, which also covered the eyes of the wearer. Small slits emphasised the blood red of the Martian eye, but even these could be closed by the wearer craving peace and solitude. These helmets were worn both by men and women, and ever more bizarre designs were sought as testimony to the wearer's social status, whether perceived or not.

Pets were another fad at present. The "must-have" companion now being the squillert, a small birdlike creature which would hover inches above the owner's shoulder. The creature was covered in multicoloured feathers and its two heads would sing to each other, creating a beautiful harmony to soothe and entertain. People would seek out the most colourful and vocal birds, which could also be taught to sing songs of the owner's choosing.

People dressed in loose, flowing garments of exquisite fabrics, similar to the togas worn by citizens of ancient Rome. Fine jewellery of gold and silver was worn by everyone.

The Martians themselves were humanoid and generally taller and thinner than their earthly counterparts. They had no body hair at all, and the stunning features of their faces were the large red eyes, contrasting with the greyish hue of their skin. They had no obvious ears, and a small nose and mouth. Each had six fingers on each hand, and four toes on each foot. The Martians spoke in a soft, lilting voice, although some were experts in telepathy and communicated through thought transference instead.

Although the Martians were a sophisticated race in many ways, politically they were rather naïve. Political parties were unknown and elections unheard of.

The Martian people were ruled over by an omnipotent emperor, a ruler who was never seen in person but was treated as a god by his subjects. The emperor was assisted, nominally, by the House of Elders who provided advice and, in theory, a link between emperor and the governed. However, the elders were hand-picked by the emperor; their sole role was to agree with the emperor's every word.

The fact that ordinary Martians had very little say in the way they were governed did not unduly worry most people. They had never known any different way of life. Emperor worship was a global religion and was seen as being entirely natural. The emperor was a god. He kept his people well fed, prosperous and safe. If these needs were being satisfied, why cause trouble? It must be said, however, that a small number of people were unhappy with the current political system and wanted change. Many saw these troublemakers as misfits, and shed few tears when they were carried off to correction centres to learn to reintegrate with mainstream society. The fact that these misfits were rarely ever seen again did not seem to concern most people.

The other intelligent race on Mars was the Antis. These huge insect-like creatures largely kept to their own tribal lands. They were a nomadic race, moving around in groups or hives, each group under the control of a queen. Each hive tended to live a separate existence, resulting in little contact with other groups of their own kind. In many ways, this was the weakness of the Antis. They lacked any real sense of racial identity, treating other hives in much the same way that they would treat a group of Martians: as a threat to the existence of their own colony. Yet within their own group or family, the Antis exhibited a true sense of community. Each member of the hive would have a predestined role to play, whether as a soldier protector of the group, as a collector of food and water, or as a servant of the queen, attending to her every whim. The servants would feed their queen, clean her and keep her comfortable. If they failed in their duties, they would pay the ultimate price.

The Antis did have their own language, and communicated in a series of what sounded like high-pitched screeches. However, they were also masters of telepathy, and would tend to use this form of communication in preference, the swaying movement of the long, slender antennae of the creatures being the only visible sign that communication was taking place.

Although the Antis tended to keep to themselves in their tribal lands, making nests and raising their young before moving on to explore new regions when resources became depleted, life was becoming harder for the creatures. The urban Martians were expanding their city and towns to house a growing population, and were gradually eating into Antis lands. The insects tried to move on and keep out of the way of their humanoid neighbours, but eventually some hives felt they had to try and stop the encroachment. Skirmishes would develop between Martian incomers and exiled Antis. Occasionally, the Antis would be successful and drive out the humanoids, but more often than not it would be the insects who would face defeat, as yet another stretch of ancestral land would pass from their control, to become a new suburb of the city, or a new settlement entirely.

Many Martians were oblivious to the problems of the Antis, caring little for their predicament. Most humanoids considered the insects to be little more than wild animals, a nuisance to be dealt with as the authorities saw fit.

Some, however, thought differently. Some, like Aka-des, were concerned that the Antis were being forced from their lands, and believed it was time to make amends. He and others like him believed that the Antis would become more of a threat if their needs continued to be ignored. After all, if you are forced into an ever-shrinking corner, there is only one thing left to do – namely, retaliate. Aka-des was worried that different hives of Antis might eventually decide to work together to overcome the Martian invasion of their lands, with swarms of warrior insects fighting to regain what they saw as rightfully theirs.

Aka-des and others of his persuasion wanted to communicate with the insects to try and find a mutually acceptable solution, but this was still very much a minority view. As always, most would bury their heads in the sand, get on with their daily lives and leave discussions of interracial harmony to those with time on their hands.

# Chapter 4
# Project MARS

Tom Fisher had always wanted to go to Mars. He had looked up into the dark night sky as a young boy and been awestruck by the reddish point of light, glinting amidst the myriad of stars visible from his garden. The planet seemed to be calling to him, urging him to find a way to journey the millions of miles needed so that he could experience Mars first-hand. When he bought his first telescope and was able to see the Martian polar caps and detect the greenish-grey markings on the surface for himself, his mind was made up. He had to go to Mars.

At school in his native Oxfordshire, Tom had excelled at science and maths. He had chosen to study astrophysics at university, and on graduation had gained a place at the UK Astronaut Training School based in Cambridge. Competition for the few places available each year was tough, but Tom had always fought for what he wanted in life. His father had been a fleeting presence in his childhood, having left home when Tom was a young boy. His mother had brought up her three children on her own. Times had been hard, but they had survived. Tom and his brother and sister had always been close, his younger siblings looking up to Tom as a father figure in the family.

He had almost relished the early responsibility handed to him. Tom liked being treated as an adult, and his mother had depended on him more and more as he moved into his teenage years.

Astronomy had always been a passion of Tom's, and he worked hard at weekends and during school holidays to save enough money to buy his first telescope. Having decided to study astrophysics at university, he then worked to help fund his way through the course. While a student, he took every opportunity to learn and gain experiences that he thought would be useful in his future career. He developed a real friendship with one of his tutors, Dr Alex

Barton, a world-renowned astrophysicist, who was instrumental in securing Tom a recommendation to join the Astronaut Training School course. Tom's drive, ambition and sheer determination to succeed impressed staff at his interview, and he was offered a place as a trainee.

After he had successfully completed the course, he moved to Melbourne, Australia, to start his career as part of the UK Space Programme.

Since the union of Great Britain and Northern Ireland with Australia, Canada and New Zealand in 2047, the new federal United Kingdom had been a major player in space. In the latter part of the twenty-first century, there were a number of players actively involved in space exploration apart from the UK. The USA, EU, China, India and Brazil all had space programmes of varying degrees, and all had contributed to the establishment of a permanent Moon base in 2066.

Tom had eventually been posted to the Moon as part of the UK contingent, and had been involved in a number of projects, such as the capture and examination of comets and asteroids passing within the vicinity of Earth's orbit. It was thought that these celestial bodies could in the future provide a useful source of minerals to supplement the dwindling stocks available on Earth, and plans for mining operations were at an advanced stage.

Although the world's population seemed to be stabilising after the phenomenal growth in the twentieth and early twenty-first centuries, there was a seemingly inexhaustible need for raw materials, as formerly Third World countries in Africa and Asia sought to catch up with their counterparts in the West. New cities were being built across the globe to replace the teeming slums of yesteryear.

The UK was also involved in planetary exploration, and a number of unmanned probes had been sent to the planet Mars to try and establish whether life had ever existed there, and whether it still did. There was also interest in the possibility of establishing a permanent base on the planet, so work was being undertaken to try and pinpoint a suitable location. Since the discovery of huge reserves of frozen water beneath the Martian surface, and large deposits of iron ore, copper and tungsten, the prospect of using these resources to help build and sustain a base made the idea much more viable. Results concerning the discovery of signs of life had initially proven inconclusive, but the recent Mars Prospector probe had discovered something while trekking across the bleak Martian desert, which had caused quite a stir at the UK Inuvik tracking station, north of the Arctic Circle in Canada.

The UK federal premier, Angela Minton, from New Zealand, had been advised to draw a cloak of secrecy around the findings until more facts could be established. Project MARS had been set up to coordinate government reaction, and a team of eminent scientists from across the UK gathered in Oxford to plan the response. Few outside the project understood the true meaning of the innocently sounding acronym for its name.

Although no manned landings had so far taken place on Mars, Tom had been involved in various simulation exercises based in the Australian outback, and he had been chosen to be part of the first UK-manned flight to the Red Planet planned for 2086. The spacecraft for the journey had already been built on the Moon, named New Endeavour, and it was capable of transporting six astronauts on the six-month voyage to Mars.

New Endeavour was the most sophisticated spacecraft ever built. Its construction had to overcome the problems of living in zero gravity for months on end, which causes the wasting of muscles and loss of calcium in an astronaut's bones. The result was to build the ship like a large doughnut, rotating once every minute to create 1g, which is equivalent to Earth gravity, in the outer rim of the structure. Moving towards the centre of the craft meant that gravity would be gradually reduced to zero in the central core. On reaching Mars, the entire ship would land, providing a home for the crew during their stay.

The crew would carry out a range of experiments on the Martian surface before returning home, bringing back samples of rocks for analysis. The long-term aim was to establish a base on Mars, and a successful first mission would lead to longer-term landings in preparation for building a new permanent settlement on the rusty soil of the planet.

The decision taken by the Project MARS scientists in the light of the recent discovery on the Martian surface had brought forward the plans for New Endeavour, and take-off was now scheduled for 23 April, in three months' time. Tom and his crew mates were notified of the early departure, but they were not informed of the exact nature of the new discovery. The view taken by the authorities was that the less people who knew the facts the better, and the less likely leaks would occur. The astronauts would be told about the true nature of their mission when arriving on Mars.

# Chapter 5
# Arrival

'Come and look at this,' Martin Robson called as he stared out of the large porthole in the side of New Endeavour's rim. Martin was a stocky Scot, and the only other member of the crew from the "original" UK. He was an engineer by profession and had been an astronaut for nearly ten years.

The other members of the crew stopped what they were doing and joined him at the viewing platform. Angela Trike, the New Zealand astrobiologist, was first to arrive.

'What a view.' she gasped. 'Just look at the detail.' Stretched out before her was the vast looming presence of Mars. The reddish-ochre disc clearly showed the huge gash of Valles Marineris, an immense canyon system which made the Grand Canyon on Earth seem like an insignificant crack. The enormous extinct volcano Olympus Mons, three times larger than Mount Everest, gave the impression of a one-eyed Mars staring at the uninvited intruders now making their way towards the surface.

The icy white polar caps broke up the barren redness of Mars, otherwise relieved only by some wispy blue-white clouds which hung in the thin Martian atmosphere. To one side of the planet, the tiny dark grey potato-shaped moons of Mars, Phobos and Deimos came into view, like two shy children emerging from behind the skirts of their protective mother.

'Just think,' Jason Lombard, the Canadian medic, responded. 'We'll be landing down there in a few hours. Perhaps time for a stroll before dinner?'

'We might be able to find a nice pub nearby. I could sink a few pints without any problem,' joked Robert Franks, the gutsy Australian geologist.

'Good idea,' piped up Frances Downes. Frances was a chemist and a compatriot of Robert. 'You can pay for the first round.'

Tom was last to arrive; he stared open-mouthed at the view unfolding before him. He thought back to his childhood, taking those first glimpses at the tiny disc of Mars through his telescope, with half-imagined details observed through the turbulent atmosphere of Earth. *Here I am*, he thought to himself. *At last, we're here. A dream come true.*

The atmosphere of Mars is painfully thin, with temperatures averaging -60 degrees centigrade. Mainly carbon dioxide, the air is unbreathable; and with no magnetic field, the surface is bathed in deadly radiation from the sun. Although often referred to as the most Earth-like of the planets, the fact remains that Mars is a very inhospitable place. Astronauts need to wear protective spacesuits when working on the surface and also to carry their own supply of oxygen. Without this protection, death would occur within seconds.

The crew of New Endeavour were told that a significant discovery had been made on Mars by the rover Mars Prospector, but the exact nature of the discovery was not explained. Their job was to locate the probe and report back their findings before receiving fresh instructions. All very hush-hush, but that was the nature of space exploration.

'When do you think we will be told exactly what we are supposed to be doing here?' asked Angela.

'It all seems very odd to me.'

'Perhaps we are ambassadors,' Robert retorted. 'We are going to meet a real-life Martian and say, "Take me to your leader."'

'We'll find out soon enough,' Tom interjected. 'The main problem now is to land this thing safely and get ready for our first trip outside.'

# Chapter 6
## Emperor's Day Parade

The day of the parade had arrived. The sun shone brightly in a clear blue sky, mirroring the imperial orb symbol fluttering in a soft breeze on a thousand flags across the city. Aka-mas had woken early and breakfasted on a plate of muskies, large pink grubs which oozed a sweet honey-like substance when broken into, and washed them down with a glass of warm mistal juice, freshly squeezed from the slug-like creature of the same name. This proved to be a very satisfying meal. From his window, Aka-mas could see the preparations taking place in the streets below.

Many people were already out and about buying provisions for their Emperor's Day picnic, or hanging garlands, bunting and flags from their houses and apartments. Children were playing as their parents chatted, marching in line pretending to be soldiers of the Imperial Guard.

'You're early.' Aka-des yawned as he stretched his arms upon entering the kitchen. 'You must be keen to get a good vantage point to watch the parade,' he teased.

'Juice?'

Aka-mas reached over to pick up the squirming mistal from its glass container.

His son nodded while reaching for a loaf of tissal and a knife. Tissal was a mix between a bread and a cake, and his mother was an expert baker of this Martian diet staple. Loaves could be bought from the local shops, but they weren't as good as the home-made version in the eyes of Aka-des. His mother always added some special ingredients to the mixture. This time it was ninchos, tiny worms which, when roasted before being added to the dough, gave a wonderful crunchy texture to the tissal. He cut himself a thick slice and covered it with a layer of jasa, a type of fruity jam, which his mother had also made.

31

'Are you going to the parade later on?' he asked his father while happily munching his way through his breakfast.

'Of course,' replied Aka-mas sarcastically. 'It is expected.'

'I may not bother,' said Aka-des as he slurped his juice. 'I've got other things to do.'

'But you must go,' Aka-mas countered more seriously. 'It will be noticed if you don't. Just go for the main parade. You don't need to stay for the party afterwards.'

Aka-des licked his fingers and took his plate and glass to the dishwasher. He put his crockery inside the unit, which was built into the kitchen wall, and closed the door. He waved his hand above the dial and waited a few seconds. Opening the door again, he retrieved the sparkling clean plate and glass and returned them to the cupboard.

'We'll see,' he said nonchalantly before returning to his bedroom.

'You should have woken me!' cried Mrs Aka-mas as she breezed into the kitchen. 'I've so much to do before the parade.'

'We've plenty of time,' said her husband as he refilled his glass of juice.

'No, we haven't,' snapped his wife. 'I need to prepare food for the picnic, and I haven't decided what to wear yet. Mrs Bar-bel has bought a new dress for the occasion. Her husband has just been promoted at work; you know. They can afford such luxuries.'

Aka-mas sighed as he returned his empty glass to the table.

'You are always buying new clothes. You'll look wonderful in whatever you decide to wear,' he added, hoping the compliment would help to diffuse the situation.

Mrs Aka-mas grunted and dashed off to the bathroom, leaving her husband alone in the empty room.

*I wonder what the emperor really thinks of the parade*, thought Aka-mas. *Does he honestly enjoy the occasion? A chance to meet his people. But then, he won't actually meet the people, and the people won't meet their emperor. He'll be cocooned in his golden orb as always, and that's all we'll see. A funny old world*. With that, he collected his empty dishes and moved towards the dishwasher.

\*\*\*

In the Grand Square crowds were already gathering, although it was at least another hour before the official parade commenced. At the far end of the square, a huge platform had been erected in front of the House of Elders, with seats set out for the elders and other senior officials to each side. In the centre was a large dish-shaped structure of pure gold, topped with a canopy of gold mesh festooned with symbols of imperial power. At each corner of the canopy, flagpoles inlaid with precious stones held aloft flags of yellow and white, which fluttered in the warm breeze. All around the edge of the platform were garlands of lush greenery, with flowers of every imaginable colour. Huge scent-filled blooms and tiny buds of exquisite hues were interwoven with a brilliant green foliage and vibrant yellows and oranges. On arrival, the emperor's orb would hover above the golden dish on the platform while he addressed his people.

In front of this spectacular stage, a troupe of court musicians entertained the waiting populace. Wearing tailored suits of shimmering yellow and white, they played their instruments with relish, a medley of tunes wafting into the Martian sky. Folk tunes celebrating famous events in Martian history and legends passed down through the ages were performed, interspersed with songs dedicated to the god emperor.

Some musicians were playing flute-like instruments, fashioned from the hollow branches of the banyul tree, their melodies attracting groups of children who sang and danced as the musicians serenaded the crowd. Darting between the throngs of people were the bright blue tinskist birds. Their tuneful song added to the spectacle, and the perfumed air they expelled as they flew wafted amidst the people, leaving a delicious fragrance which gradually dissipated in the Martian air.

Food vendors moved amongst the gathering crowds selling everything from small sticky lemox grubs, wrapped in the edible, orange-coloured leaves of the cabax plant, to hot slices of snailey, a type of eel found in the numerous freshwater lakes of Mars. These were cooked in a spicy broth and served in the upturned shells of the baticcs fish. People were laughing and talking, enjoying their holiday and waiting in growing anticipation for the arrival of their emperor.

'I knew we should have left earlier,' Mrs Aka-mas complained as she took her place in the crowd with her husband and a reluctant Aka-des. 'We won't be able to see anything from here.'

'We've got a perfectly good view,' replied Aka-des. 'We can see the platform and will be able to watch the procession as it arrives. Stop worrying!'

Aka-mas's wife was wearing a fashionable mask, adorned with bright yellow stones to match her yellow dress and shawl. The golden mask glinted in the strong sunlight, and the white feathers of the peacock-like trumly, which protruded from the sides of the mask, brushed against Aka-des as he stood beside his mother.

'Do you have to wear that thing?' asked her son grumpily, moving beyond the reach of the ticklish feathers.

'It's fashionable,' replied his mother. 'Look around. Many people are wearing masks. We should all look our best to greet the emperor.'

Suddenly, a great fanfare of trumpets announced the arrival of the imperial procession, and all heads turned as people tried to catch a glimpse of their god king. The scene was spectacular. First came the Imperial Guard, resplendent in their golden armour, marching in step as they moved their heads in unison from left to right, as if watching what the crowds were doing. The guards were completely covered in armour. There was no sign of the person underneath, not even a glimpse of their eyes in the narrow slits of their gleaming headwear.

*It sure must be hot inside those suits,* Aka-des mused.

'My son joined the Imperial Guard last year.' enthused a purple-clad woman standing next to him and sporting a large ecxylltot feather in her hair. 'He was chosen to enlist at last year's parade,' she reminisced. 'I'm so proud of him.'

'Is he here today?' asked Aka-des as he watched the rows of guards take their place at each side of the ornate platform.

'Oh, I don't know,' she replied. 'I haven't seen him since he joined. He must devote himself completely to the service of the emperor from now on.'

Aka-des detected a touch of sadness in the woman's voice. She recovered her composure quickly, however, and beamed at the young man beside her. 'But we are so proud of him,' she repeated. 'What better life than one of service to our beloved emperor?' She waved a flag at the group of guards passing by. 'Long live the emperor!' she shouted enthusiastically.

After the contingent of Imperial Guards came the elders. Dressed in their formal state robes, and each wearing a mitre of gold and white, they looked like a gathering of bishops at an Easter Day service. Some of the elders looked remarkably old to Aka-des, with no spark of life in their tired eyes. Each of the elders carried a scroll in their left hand, and a tall golden rod in the other topped with an imperial orb covered in priceless jewels. They slowly took their allotted places at the front of the platform.

Next came a number of other key officials from the imperial household. They were dressed in garments of pure white, each wearing a band of gold like a tiara on their heads. The officials wore a sash over their shoulders, the size and colour of which indicated the importance of their role in the imperial palace.

After the officials came a band of imperial musicians. The crowd roared as they heard the well-known patriotic anthems being played with gusto. Some of the musicians carried the huge trumpet-like stems of the large econvy plants, which emitted a symphony of different sounds depending on how the player stroked its warty surface. Others carried the shells of the enormous vazadoos. These creatures, similar to snails but roughly the size of a small pig, lived in the warm Martian seas. Their flesh was a prized delicacy at the best restaurants, sliced thinly and served with a good chilled local wine. The shells made magnificent musical instruments, sending out a booming sound of haunting beauty when blown into by a skilled practitioner.

A huge cheer erupted from the crowd as the emperor himself finally arrived. A dazzling light filled the sky as the imperial orb moved towards the platform, hovering a few feet above the ground. The globe was surrounded by members of the elite imperial bodyguard, a section of the Imperial Guard reserved for those who had served the emperor with distinction in the past.

Aka-mas looked around at the cheering crowds.

'What are they doing this for?' he asked himself.

'What has the emperor ever done for them?'

But he knew it was hopeless. The people had never known any other kind of life. They were well fed and most lived in comfortable homes with jobs for life. The fact that they did not control their own destiny seemed irrelevant to the vast majority. Aka-mas turned to his son, who was watching intently as the emperor moved ever closer to the platform.

As the orb passed by, Aka-des caught a faint smell of something unpleasant. It was gone in an instant, but he could not banish the thought that the smell had originated from the orb itself. Blasphemy, he knew, to even consider the possibility, but he couldn't help it. He secretly smiled to himself as he pondered the likelihood that the people had a pongy emperor!

The orb came to rest above the disc-shaped structure on the platform beneath the canopy, which fluttered gently in the warm breeze. The music suddenly stopped and all eyes were fixed on the god emperor. The brilliant glow emanating from the orb seemed to dim slightly; the crowd stood in silent expectation.

Aka-des was sure he heard a soft gurgling sound as the light dimmed, but he put it down to his rumbling stomach. *Surely it must be time to eat soon*, he thought just as he glimpsed something move briefly inside the orb. *A trick of the light, surely?*

Then the emperor spoke. His voice was strong and measured; a voice to give confidence to the adoring masses. The voice you would expect a god emperor to have.

'My people,' boomed the emperor. 'It hardly seems like a year since I addressed you last. This year has been a good one for all our people, who have benefited once again from the wise counsel of the government. Employment is standing at record levels, and homelessness has been banished from our streets. We are producing more food than ever before, and none of our citizens are going without nourishing meals.'

Aka-mas looked at his feet. *It's true that everyone seems to have a job, and you never see people begging on the streets. But if anyone admitted to being out of work or without a home, they would suddenly just disappear. The authorities wouldn't tolerate such failure.*

The emperor continued with his list of magnificent successes achieved over the past year, and the people seemed to be lapping it up.

'Long live the emperor!' someone shouted excitedly from the crowd. Cheers immediately rose from the assembled masses.

'Doesn't he look handsome?' whispered the woman in purple standing next to Aka-des.

'A fine specimen of manhood. He looks younger every year!'

Aka-des looked at her with a mixture of astonishment and amusement. *How can she tell what the emperor looks like?* he mused. *All we can see is that orb hovering above the platform. She's mad.*

Mrs Aka-mas was clapping wildly, completely engrossed in what was enfolding before her eyes. She turned to her husband.

'What a wonderful day,' she gushed. 'We are so lucky to be ruled by such a kind, caring and charismatic emperor.' She sighed contentedly and turned back to gaze in admiration at the imperial presence.

'We now come to one of the most important and solemn parts of today's events,' said the emperor. 'We welcome the new recruits who have this year been chosen to enlist in the Imperial Guard. Such an honour only falls on those of proven character, who will doubtlessly serve their emperor and people with distinction. Their families should be proud that their sons have been chosen in this way to serve at such a high level, upholding imperial laws and protecting our communities from the dangers which exist in the Outside.'

'They don't get a choice,' Aka-mas muttered to himself. 'Serve the emperor or disappear. Also, no mention of the fact that these recruits will be lost to their families forever. Never to be seen again.'

A fanfare of trumpets rose into the sky as a group of twenty-four young men marched onto the platform. They were all tall and strong looking, dressed in the novitiate uniform of a loose flowing robe in pure white. The recruits stood in line and bowed to the emperor. The light emitted from the orb appeared to brighten temporarily; the soft gurgling sound grew slightly louder.

A massive cheer rose from the crowd as the twenty-four new members of the Imperial Guard filed silently from the platform, led away from their former lives by two praeceptors with special responsibility for novitiates.

Aka-des looked at the group aghast. Included in the line-up was his good friend Beta-vac. He had only seen him a few days ago, and no mention had been made then of him joining the Imperial Guard. Admittedly, Beta-vac had certainly never been a troublemaker, and had never made any disparaging remarks about the emperor or the government. On the other hand, his friend had never expressed any desire to join the military in any capacity, let alone join the elite Imperial Guard.

*He must have been forced into joining*, thought Aka-des. *Now he is lost to us forever. It's just not fair.* Aka-des felt a rising anger well up inside. He was usually a fairly placid person by nature, but he did not like to see unfairness in any shape or form. Hence, his sympathy for the insect Antis fighting for their lost lands in the Outside. In his view, this was just another case of a dictatorial regime caring nothing for those it was supposed to serve.

Aka-des was snatched from his thoughts by another loud trumpet blast. The formal events had come to an end, and the emperor was preparing to leave the platform. A contingent of Imperial Guards were first to leave, leading the procession and making way for the emperor through the crowds. They were followed by the elders, raising their imperial staffs of office in salute to the emperor as they left the platform.

The emperor himself came next; the golden orb surrounded by the elite imperial bodyguards as it moved through the assembled mass of cheering people. Many were throwing flowers as the orb passed, while others waved flags and clapped enthusiastically. For some reason Aka-mas got the distinct impression that the crowd was being watched carefully by whoever sat in the orb. A presence who was anything but benign and looking for something which might indicate a possible threat to the so far unchallenged imperial power. The people were irrelevant, mere cogs in the wheel of state. If they did as they were told and served their emperor without question, there was no problem. However, if they moved out of line, even slightly, they would be spat out and ground into the soil like inconsequential insects.

'Why don't people see things as I do?' he asked himself.

'Why do they actively support this charade? No one has ever seen the emperor in person, or any other member of the imperial family come to that. Yet no one questions why this is so.'

He shook his head and moved off with his family as the crowds began to disperse. In the near distance, the imperial orb was entering the State Carriage, a huge white globe emblazoned with the yellow sunburst emblem of imperial authority. As the door slid shut behind the emperor and his immediate entourage, the craft lifted off and silently rose into the brilliant blue sky, like a balloon being cut loose on a windy day. It quickly moved towards the imperial palace compound on the outskirts of the city.

Another large crowd had gathered around the carriage to wave off the emperor, but once the imperial presence had departed, everyone started to move off to enjoy the rest of the holiday.

Some headed to the restaurants and bars of the city to celebrate with family and friends. Others went to one of the many parks to enjoy a picnic, and yet more simply went home to hold their own festivities or watch the events being repeated on the state-run media.

Mrs Aka-mas had determined that this year the family would have a picnic together, and she had invited their neighbours, the Rel-do family, to join them. The food and drink had already been prepared at home and was placed in a large metallic canister in the kitchen. Once they had reached the spot selected for the picnic, all Mrs Aka-mas had to do was press a button on her wristband and the canister would appear before them.

*Isn't technology wonderful?* mused Mrs Aka-mas as she started to remove the lid off the canister to survey the feast contained within. *Yet another gift to the people from our ever-loving emperor.*

The Rel-do family would also know exactly the spot selected by their host for the picnic by using their own wristbands. These would detect the coordinates of the chosen site and lead Mr and Mrs Rel-do directly there.

'So wonderful to see you both,' Mrs Aka-mas gushed as she welcomed her picnic guests. 'Do come and join us.'

Rel-do was a rather small man, with a rather large opinion of himself. He was a lawyer in the city and held in high regard by his contemporaries. But he was not a very pleasant individual and did not enjoy social occasions. His wife, however, was very different. Mrs Rel-do was a social climber who would do anything to improve her standing in the local community. A tall, rather plump woman, she dwarfed her husband physically, and her booming voice could be heard for miles around. Why his wife had invited this pair to the picnic, Aka-mas could not understand. He did not like Rel-do at all, and only agreed to come to keep Mrs Aka-mas happy.

Aka-des didn't care who came to the picnic as long as the food was handed out quickly. He was starving.

'Do try one of these,' said Mrs Aka-mas as she handed around a dish of small wriggling weally grubs. 'Freshly caught only yesterday.'

The weally grubs were similar to small bright green caterpillars, each sporting a unique pattern of tiny orange spots. When bitten into, the first sensation was a distinct perfumed aroma, followed by a soft meaty texture tasting of smoked chicken. Weally grubs were not cheap to buy, but were considered a real delicacy, and a must for any celebratory meal.

'Wasn't the parade wonderful?' roared Mrs Rel-do as she munched her way through her fourth weally grub.

'The emperor was absolutely stunning. Those beautiful deep red eyes of his just send a shiver down my spine.'

Aka-mas, who was pouring glasses of a thick yellow fizzy drink for his guests, looked at her in amazement.

'But we never saw his face,' he replied. 'All we ever see is the orb.'

Mrs Rel-do simply laughed and pushed his arm.

'You are a tease.'

She chuckled while picking another writhing weally grub.

Aka-des, lying on his back and staring at the cloudless sky above, sucked on his grub. He rose slightly and took a swig from his glass.

'I thought I saw Beta-vac today in the parade,' he mentioned. 'He was one of the novitiates being led off to join the Imperial Guard.'

'Oh, what an honour!' Mrs Rel-do squealed.

'Yes,' agreed Mrs Aka-mas. She turned to her son before adding, 'It's a shame they never pick you. How proud I should be.'

'Thanks,' Aka-des muttered. 'Nice to know your parents can't wait to get rid of you.'

'If you were a bit more enthusiastic about life,' said his mother, 'they might pick you. Instead, you fill your mind with silly thoughts such as befriending those hideous Antis creatures. Carry on like that and you'll never bring honour to your family.'

*Long may it last*, thought Aka-des before taking another swig of the thick juice.

Mrs Aka-mas now brought out the next course from the cylinder. First came a bowl full of cold grula legs. The grula was a centipede-like creature, but much larger. Its legs were similar in size to chicken legs, but with a taste more like pork. Then came a mixture of salads and home-made bread. Finally, small pots of various dips and relishes completed the meal.

'I thought we would open a bottle of vishto wine to go with the food, as it's a celebration,' said Aka-mas, with a tone of sarcasm in his voice.

Rel-do, who had remained remarkably quiet until now, raised his glass ready for a share of the fruity liquid.

'My favourite,' he spluttered. 'No celebration would be complete without a few glasses of this stuff.'

*Shame you didn't bring a bottle yourself, then*, thought Aka-mas, biting his tongue while topping up his neighbour's glass.

'How is work going?' asked Aka-mas, more out of politeness than any real interest.

'We have a big job on at the moment,' replied Rel-do. 'We are dealing with all the legal work relating to the new extension to the city on the Bolan Plain.

Big new housing project, together with a lot of commercial property. It will be huge once it's completed.'

'What about the Antis?' queried Aka-des, suddenly becoming interested in the conversation. 'I suppose they will be pushed even further away from their tribal lands.'

Rel-do took a drink from his glass before offering the near-empty vessel to Aka-mas for a refill.

'We must make sure those insects don't cause any trouble while the building is in progress. We will need to construct secure defences around the site to keep them out. It all adds to the cost, you know. They're a damned nuisance. Exterminate the lot of them, I say!'

'But it's their land,' argued Aka-des, anger rising in him as he spoke. 'What right do we have to confiscate their home from them? We're heading for trouble – just mark my words. The Antis won't put up with this for much longer.'

'And what will they do?'

The lawyer sneered.

'We could wipe out the lot of them in a few days. Just let the Imperial Guard loose. Problem ended.'

'Unbelievable,' Aka-des retorted.

Just then, his mother quickly interjected.

'Now then, you two,' she said softly but firmly. 'Don't let's argue over a few insects today. We are celebrating. Anyone for cake?'

Yet another dish appeared from the canister.

'I made it yesterday. Filled with jamora fruits and coated with a layer of ground farssi seeds. It's Aka-des's favourite.'

Her son had to agree, and his anger dissipated as he munched his way through a large slice of his mother's cake.

As the afternoon wore on, the small party finished their meal and chatted about matters of general interest. In fact, it was Mrs Aka-mas and Mrs Rel-do who dominated the conversation. The men sat back and merely grunted here and there, as appropriate, as the two women became ever more excitable.

'You'll never guess who I saw yesterday at the garden centre,' quizzed Mrs Rel-do, making room for one last morsel of cake. 'It was only Mrs Mes-la, of all people!' she shrieked loudly, slapping the shoulder of Aka-des, who had the misfortune to be lying right next to her.

'Ouch, that hurt,' hissed the young man.

Mrs Rel-do ignored the comment and carried on.

'I don't know how she has the nerve to be seen in public after what she did,' she huffed.

'I thought she had moved out of the city and was living in one of the new settlements along the river,' said Mrs Aka-mas, slightly confused at this amazing revelation.

'No, no, she never went, more's the pity,' replied Mrs Rel-do, her headdress of safoli feathers and diamonds shaking precariously on her head as she became more and more animated.

'What dreadful deed did she carry out?' asked Aka-des, trying desperately not to laugh.

'She made a very disparaging remark about our dear emperor,' she spluttered in total disbelief and disgust. 'She actually said at the women's meeting last month that she thought the annual parade was a waste of time because no one gets to see the emperor in person! Can you believe it?'

*At last*, thought Aka-mas. *Someone with a bit of sense. Perhaps I'm not alone after all.*

'I know she was barred from the women's group after her comments.'

Mrs Aka-mas recalled.

'And I was sure she was leaving with her husband.'

'Poor man.'

Mrs Rel-do tutted, her headdress now perched at a very odd angle on her head.

'Fancy living with a woman like that. I don't know how he puts up with it!'

Aka-des's eyes were watering and he had to smother his mouth with the palm of his hand. This was not totally successful, however, as the odd whimper managed to escape as he fought valiantly to stop erupting into gales of laughter.

Mr Rel-do busied himself with his toothpick, trying to remove the odd bit of meat from a grula leg which had become stuck between his teeth.

'Perhaps we should take our leave,' he announced before chewing the offending morsel of food released by the toothpick. 'We don't want to outstay our welcome.'

'What a good idea,' Aka-mas grumbled silently as he helped to gather up the empty dishes and glasses.

'Just put them back in the canister,' said his wife. 'I can then send them home.'

Once everything had been replaced, Aka-mas sealed the canister and, with one touch of his wristband, the object disappeared. Seconds later, it would reappear in the kitchen, with the crockery cleaned and dried, ready to be packed away when they arrived home.

The two families said their goodbyes, and Aka-mas walked with his wife and son through the park, watching members of the public enjoying their holiday. Some were picnicking like themselves; others were taking rides on the lake in small wooden boats and others were flying kites made of the skin of a wasrus.

'I must just pop in to see Mrs Fel-por,' said Mrs Aka-mas. 'She is making some alterations to a dress of mine.'

'She asked me to call in if I was passing today so we can have a fitting. You two carry on home, and I'll see you there later.'

With that, she rushed off down a side street, leaving her husband and son on their own.

'Thank the gods that's over,' Aka-mas said to his son. 'Why did we have to waste the day celebrating?'

'And why did Mum have to invite the Rel-do family, of all people?' added Aka-des.

'That man is a complete bigot, and his wife is even worse. Does she never shut up?'

Aka-mas smiled.

'At least it's only once a year. Could be worse.'

'Don't you believe it' reminded his son. 'There's the emperor's birthday coming up soon. Yet more fun and games.'

The two men walked on without talking until Aka-des broke the silence.

'I was surprised to see Beta-vac at the parade. Seems as though he's joined the Imperial Guard. He never mentioned it to me when I saw him recently.'

'I don't suppose he wanted to join,' said his father. 'People don't get a choice when they are honoured like this.'

There was a distinct bitterness in his tone.

'I can't just leave him,' Aka-des pleaded. 'What can I do to help him?'

'You can't,' replied his father bluntly. 'Just accept that he has gone.'

'I can't do that,' said Aka-des. 'I must do something.'

The two men continued on their way, each deep in their own thoughts.

Aka-des was trying to hatch a plan. *I must try and reach Beta-vac as soon as possible,* he decided. *If I can get to him soon, I may be able to persuade him to abandon his training in the Imperial Guard and come back to his family and friends. A long shot, I know, but I have to at least try. The only problem is that I need to get into the imperial compound without being seen. It's not going to be easy.* Aka-des also toyed with the possibility that Beta-vac would reject his pleas to return home, even if he could be found. *Perhaps he really did want to join the Imperial Guard after all,* he considered, but quickly dismissed the idea from his mind. *Beta-vac has never expressed any interest in the military. He has always been interested in environmental issues, and was considering applying for a course on land management at the university before this happened.*

Suddenly, Aka-des noticed a bakery with a sign saying "Cru-lem and Sons" above the door. Underneath was another sign saying "By Imperial Appointment" next to a sunburst symbol. The young man immediately had an idea but didn't want his father to know what he was planning. *He will only try and talk me out of it,* thought Aka-des. *Better keep this a secret.*

'Dad, I'm feeling a bit peckish,' he announced to Aka-mas. 'I'll just pop in here and buy something to see me through until dinner. You carry on and I'll see you at home.'

His father laughed.

'You can't still be hungry. You've eaten enough weally grubs, grula legs and slabs of cake to last a week.'

'I won't be long.' promised his son, before entering the shop.

Cru-lem was well known in the district. His breads, cakes and pastries were a firm favourite with everyone, and it was no surprise that he should have received the coveted imperial warrant. Aka-des's weakness was dikka bread, with a soft doughy texture, but with the added bonus of a crunchy crust provided by tiny insects known as dikkas. These were similar to ladybirds in appearance, and when roasted produced a tasty snack on their own, or a delicious coating to breads and cakes.

*A nice slice of that with a dollop of bela honey will go down a treat,* thought Aka-des, licking his lips in anticipation, surprising himself that he really did still have room for yet more food.

'I'll have a loaf of that please,' he said, pointing to the item on the counter.

44

'Certainly, sir, will that be all?' asked Cru-lem as he wrapped the still warm loaf in a few tillus leaves and bound the package with string.

Aka-des nodded.

'That will be fifty pillu,' said the shopkeeper as he handed over the bread.

'Thanks.'

Aka-des moved his wrist towards the payment pod at the end of the counter. His wristband beeped, confirming that the required amount had been registered.

'Nice shop you have here,' said Aka-des. 'I notice you have an imperial warrant too. You must be proud.'

The proprietor beamed.

'Oh yes, we've had that honour for many years. The munificence of our dear emperor knows no bounds.'

Aka-des noticed a small tear well up in the older man's left eye.

'Do you make regular deliveries to the palace?' he enquired nonchalantly.

'Indeed,' replied Cru-lem. 'I take a delivery twice a week to the compound in my van. I have to unload the goods just inside the gates, and the delivery is picked up by palace staff later on. Same procedure every time. I leave here at about six-thirty in the morning on the dot. In fact, I'm taking another load up there tomorrow. That reminds me, I must start to get things together. Only the best for our beloved emperor.'

The shopkeeper wiped the tear from his face and smiled at Aka-des. 'Enjoy your bread,' he added.

Aka-des thanked Cru-lem once again before leaving the shop with his purchase.

*That's it*, he decided, squeezing the loaf in his hand. *I'll stow away in the back of the van tomorrow morning and sneak into the compound when the delivery is made.* With his mind made up, he walked the short distance to his home in what was admittedly a desirable part of the city. The houses were fairly large by urban standards, with pleasant, if rather small, gardens, and the streets were lined with numerous trees and flower beds. *All very civilised and middle class*, thought Aka-des. Yet he couldn't help thinking that this civility was merely a façade. *Underneath this veneer of respectability lies something much darker and very unpleasant, I'm sure of it. Crack this shell of normality and who knows what you will find inside. Perhaps I'll find out more tomorrow.* With these thoughts churning in his mind, the young man entered his house.

Inside, his father was busying himself putting away the already cleaned crockery from the canister they used at the picnic.

'Find anything to eat?' he enquired with a degree of amusement.

'Just this loaf of dikka bread,' replied his son. 'Fancy a slice?'

'Not for me,' said Aka-mas. 'I've got things to do. I have a meeting of the council at work tomorrow. Some papers I need to get in order before then.'

Aka-mas knew that as a senior member of the Earth Observation Team at the observatory, which was attached to the Imperial University, he had to report back concerning his earlier meeting with the elders. This had related to the discovery of evidence of life on their neighbouring planet. The elders had been adamant that nothing should be made public for the time being, so where did the team go from here? Without the support of the government agencies, funding for any further research was likely to dry up, and with it Project Earth itself.

Just then, the door flew open and in breezed Mrs Aka-mas.

'The daughter of Mrs Fel-por has recently had a baby girl,' she announced, reporting back on her session with the dressmaker. 'A very pretty little thing.' She added, 'They are holding the citizenship ceremony at the local temple next week. We've all been invited. What do you think?'

Before Aka-mas had a chance to reply, his wife butted in.

'I've said we would love to go. I can wear my new dress, once Mrs Fel-por has finished the alterations.'

Every child born had to undergo the ceremony during the first few months of its life. The official aim was to welcome the new-born child into the community, and to formally recognise that the infant now benefited from imperial protection as a citizen of the state. There was no choice about it. The ceremony was a legal requirement, and officials from the Department of Citizenship would soon come calling if the event had not been organised by the parents within the permitted time period.

The highlight of proceedings was when the officiating priest presented the child with the Egg of Imperial Splendour. This tiny golden egg, no bigger than a grain of sand, was inserted into the neck of the infant using a syringe-like apparatus. It symbolised the integration of the new life into the imperial family to which all citizens belonged. Everyone had the egg within them. Once inserted, most simply forgot it was there.

Mrs Aka-mas sat down and poured herself a glass of a thick greenish juice from a jug on the table next to her. Suddenly, she let out a piercing shriek.

'My ring, it's gone! What shall I do?'

'What ring?' asked her husband quietly, trying to calm his hysterical wife.

'My square-topped gold ring,' she wailed. 'The one with the row of diamonds across the centre. I've had it for years.'

She started to cry and covered her face with her hands.

'When did you see it last?' questioned Aka-mas, trying to be rational but sympathetic at the same time.

'I was wearing it at the picnic,' she responded, trying hard to think. 'I definitely had it on when we were packing up, just before Mr and Mrs Rel-do left.'

'Did you notice it when you were at Mrs Fel-por's for the fitting?' asked her husband. 'Perhaps it fell off when you were trying on the new dress.'

'I suppose it could have fallen off,' Mrs Aka-mas agreed. 'I will contact Mrs Fel-por at once. But if she can't find it, you will have to go back to the park and look for it.'

With that, his wife left the room so she could make her call in private.

'It would be like looking for a needle in a haystack,' said Aka-des to his father. 'What chance would you have of finding it even if you looked? It could have been lost anywhere between the park and Mum arriving home. It's insured, isn't it?'

'Oh yes,' agreed Aka-mas. 'But that won't stop your mother. She'll be like this until we find it, or die trying!' he added with a dark sense of humour. 'Let's just hope Mrs Fel-por found the wretched thing at her house.'

***

It was so dark that Aka-des could not see anything around him. Suddenly he felt a cold metal hand grasp first his left shoulder and then his right. The hands tightened on his skin, like being held in the unyielding grip of a vice. As his eyes became more accustomed to the darkness, he noticed three other shapes move in front of him. The outlines of men, but very tall, and moving with a slightly cumbersome gait.

The figures were wearing armour. Imperial Guards. Aka-des was shoved forward by the soldier holding his shoulders, and then he felt a pinprick in his neck. Then nothing.

When he awoke, he found himself lying on a long metal slab in a small room devoid of any other furniture whatsoever. A small but brilliant light shone from the ceiling, dazzling his eyes as he tried to regain focus.

'Where am I?' he slurred groggily, his mouth feeling dry and slightly numb.

. Then a concealed door slid open and an elderly man wearing a yellow toga-like garment walked in, accompanied by two Imperial Guards.

'Come with me,' ordered the man, indicating for Aka-des to follow him.

The young man rose unsteadily from the cold metal slab and staggered while trying to balance himself on his still shaking legs. The two guards grasped his shoulders and led him out of the room, with the elderly man in front. They walked along a long corridor without seeing any other signs of life. The corridor was completely bare and lit by a row of lights similar to the room where Aka-des had been kept. The floor was also metal, and Aka-des was aware of a regular clanking noise as the Imperial Guards marched ahead, their synchronised movements echoing throughout the cavernous tunnel they were progressing along.

At the far end another door opened, and the youth was shoved ahead. The room they entered was very different from those he had seen so far. It was sumptuously decorated in gold, with a stage at the far side. On this stage was an enormous throne, encrusted with diamonds and with a large sunburst symbol emblazoned on the back of the seat. There was a large canopy above the throne in yellow and white, held in place by four columns of gold, with exquisite carvings of fabulous creatures, flowers and imperial emblems. At each side of the throne stood an Imperial Guard, their bodies motionless, but their eyes following Aka-des's every move. He felt as if those eyes were burning right through him, and he suddenly felt sick.

'Prepare to meet your emperor,' said the man in yellow, and Aka-des was pushed down to a kneeling position by the guards at his side.

There was an intense flash of light, after which Aka-des had to look away. When he returned his gaze to the throne, he saw that it was no longer empty. A tall man of middle age was sitting in the chair, wearing a golden mitre with the largest diamond Aka-des had ever seen set at its centre. The god emperor was dressed in a suit of gold mesh and he wore a white sash covered with symbols of imperial authority. His features were as Aka-des had expected. A perfect skin with a healthy complexion, blood-red eyes and a chiselled jaw. The divine presence stared at Aka-des, who felt as though he was about to faint.

'My guards found you hiding in the palace grounds. You know it is a crime of the utmost severity to enter the imperial estate without appropriate authority. What do you have to say for yourself?'

'I… I was looking for a friend,' replied Aka-des feebly. 'I meant no harm, your majesty. He joined the Imperial Guard recently, and I wanted to speak to him, that's all.'

Aka-des realised this sounded utterly pathetic, but it's all he could think of to say.

'Members of the Imperial Guard are not permitted to fraternise with outsiders, as you well know,' the emperor snapped. 'You have violated imperial laws, and therefore must suffer the consequences of your actions. There is only one sentence for such a heinous crime, and that is death.'

The emperor's eyes locked onto Aka-des and his lips curled into a snarl.

'Death to those who defy my rules. Death to those who defy me…'

Aka-des felt weak and about to pass out. Just before he did so, he smelt the same unpleasant fishy vinegary smell he had experienced at the parade. The last thing he recalled before he lost consciousness was a soft gurgling sound…

# Chapter 7
# Stowaway

Aka-des sat up suddenly in a cold sweat. He was in his own bed, safe. Daylight was dawning and he could hear birdsong greet the new day. As his eyes became accustomed to the semi-gloom, he made out the familiar features of the furniture in his room. His panic began to subside.

It was only a dream, he realised. Or a nightmare, more like. Then his thoughts turned to the task ahead. *I need to get up and make my way down to Cru-lem's shop quickly. Otherwise, I'll miss his delivery to the palace.* His stomach churned as he considered how dangerous his mission was. *What if I am caught and brought before the emperor?* he considered. *Will death actually be the sentence?* Doubts began to creep into his mind. *What are the chances I will actually find Beta-vac anyway? Even if I do find him, what happens if I can't persuade him to leave? What if he really doesn't want to come home?*

These thoughts began to make him question the viability of the job ahead. *Perhaps I should just stay here in bed and forget the whole thing.* He was on the verge of surrendering to his doubts, but then changed his mind. *No,* he decided, swinging his legs out of the warm bed. *Beta-vac is my friend. I have to at least try and make him see sense. If I fail, I can console myself with the knowledge that I did my best.*

His mind made up, Aka-des quickly dressed and tiptoed through the silent house, quietly opening the door. He looked around at the still deserted street and stepped out, closing the door behind him. He walked on towards the bakery of Cru-lem, mindful of the fact that the van was due to depart at six-thirty, in roughly half an hour's time. *Should be enough time to get to the shop, find the van and hopefully sneak inside and hide without being seen by Cru-lem*, he reasoned. *Without being seen is the difficult bit.*

As he walked on, deep in thought, life was beginning to stir. A few hardy souls were already out and about. Aka-des noticed one man out walking his pet dougril. These six-legged furry dog-like creatures were a great favourite with many people in the city. Totally devoted to their owners, there was a sort of psychic bond between pet and master. Never needing to be on a lead, one of the three eyes each dougril possessed was always trained on its owner. Any instruction transmitted to the creature by thought from its master would instantly be carried out by the obedient pet, without hesitation. However, if the owner died, so would the loyal dougril, at exactly the same instant. Once the bond between the two had been created, the poor creature could not exist without its master.

There were also a couple of joggers out enjoying the early morning air and a few people setting off for an early start at work. As Aka-des neared the shop, he saw the van parked outside. A van in the city consisted of a bubble-shaped capsule where the driver sat, with a cylindrical tail end where the goods for delivery were stored. There were doors at each side of the cylinder, which could be opened and closed from a control panel in the bubble. In fact, the driver had very little to do in terms of actually driving the vehicle, which would automatically find its way to the specified location once the relevant coordinates were input using the same control panel. The solar-powered vehicle required no fossil fuels in order to operate, so was environmentally sound, as well as being extremely quiet. The Martians had eliminated pollution almost completely from the city centuries ago, and new developments in technology were mopping up any small areas of activity where environmental improvements could still be made.

The physical delivery of goods to a location was gradually being phased out now anyway. The same technology used by Mrs Aka-mas to transport the canister holding the picnic at the parade was being developed so that much larger deliveries could be made in the same way. In a few years' time, it was envisaged that delivery vans would be consigned to history. There was even talk of transporting people instantly from one place to another as well, eliminating the need for roads, cars, railways, aircraft and all the other modes of physical transportation, together with the associated infrastructures.

Cru-lem liked his van, however. He saw no need to change a method of delivery that had served him well over the years. He also liked the contact with his customers which personal delivery required. Many of the individuals and firms he delivered to had been his customers for as long as he could remember, counting some of them as firm friends and not just business colleagues. He wouldn't change over to any new-fangled method of delivery until he was forced to. With any luck, he would be retired before then anyway.

*Of course, the palace is another matter altogether*, he thought while carrying another crate of bread to the vehicle. *I never see anyone when I deliver there. The place is like a ghost town. To be honest, it gives me the creeps. I would be quite happy to press a button and transport my bread and cakes without actually having to visit the place myself.* Cru-lem deposited his crate in the van and returned to his shop to pick up the final tray of cakes.

Aka-des saw his chance and made his move. He quickly darted over to the van and jumped inside the open cylinder. In one corner, he saw a pile of sheets used to cover the crates when deliveries were being made. Aka-des, hoping these sheets were surplus to requirements for this delivery, slid under a particularly large one. He held his breath as he heard the shopkeeper return with his cakes.

'That's it, ready to go,' said Cru-lem as he positioned the tray, checking that all was in order.

When satisfied, he entered the bubble and settled into his seat. The coordinates for the palace were already stored in the control panel's memory, so all he had to do was press the relevant pad on the console and the doors of the vehicle closed.

The van moved off so silently that Aka-des wasn't sure if they had started the journey or not. His heart was beating at such a pace that the young man was convinced he could hear the blood flowing through his veins. *What have I let myself in for?* he agonised. *Still, too late to do anything about it now.*

Cru-lem sat in the bubble surveying the scene around him as the vehicle moved effortlessly through the city streets. More people were out and about now, starting their day in a variety of ways. Dougril walkers made their way to one of the parks to exercise their pets, some chatting as their animals sniffed each other as a sign of curiosity or friendship, or licked their lips in anticipation of the walk to come. One eye of the dog-like creatures would invariably be fixed on their owners, while the other two darted from side to side, interested in everything going on around them.

Shopkeepers were starting to open up their stores in readiness for a new day of trading while other people were walking to work or waiting for public transport to whisk them to their offices or other places of employment. Many people worked from home these days and only occasionally needed to travel to their office for an important meeting, when it was deemed necessary or desirable to have the physical presence of those involved.

In the past, many shops had closed their doors as a result of a growing trend for customers to buy their goods from the comfort of their own homes, to be delivered at a time of their own choosing. However, this trend had reversed somewhat over the last few years as people began to miss the social contact with others. Being able to run your life without ever leaving your home had its advantages, but it could lead to feelings of isolation and loneliness. Shops, latching onto this feeling, had developed more as social centres where people could meet one another and socialise as well as buy their goods in the traditional way. Many shops now included cafes and restaurants, and even medical drop-in centres for the treatment of minor ailments. Others included "pay as you stay" crèches for young children, legal advice centres, and day centres for the elderly. All of these developments had helped foster a renaissance in traditional town centres and everyone, young and old, seemed to benefit from the increased social interaction.

The imperial estate was located on the outskirts of the city, separated from the homes, offices and shops where ordinary people lived by a huge area of parkland. The outer regions of the parkland could be used by the public, but the closer you got to the palace the greater the restrictions on access. No one was allowed within a mile of the imperial compound, and this area was regularly patrolled by members of the Imperial Guard. Anyone found in this forbidden zone would never be seen again by family or friends.

However, Cru-lem was on official business, so he was permitted access to the imperial seat of power, or at least the outer limits of the compound. The road to the palace was lined with enormous zaspi trees, their branches swaying gently in the light breeze. These trees had large waxy leaves, and at this time of the year they were covered in deep yellow trumpet-shaped flowers with an intense perfumed scent. They looked stunning, backed by the rich green grassland of the surrounding park. At the end of the flowering season, the flowers would detach from the branches and glide gently down to the ground, emitting a soft whistling sound as they did so. As thousands of the flowers followed suit, the haunting "Lullaby of the Zaspi Trees" attracted crowds of people who came to watch and listen to the magnificent symphony of nature.

As the van got nearer to the imperial compound, Cru-lem could see the familiar sight of the palace glimpsed through the dense foliage of the trees in the parkland. The sight of this impressive structure never ceased to amaze him. An enormous pyramid of gold, and seemingly completely featureless, it sat at the centre of the imperial estate, glowing with a warm intense light as it reflected the rays of the rising sun.

There were many other buildings in the compound, although Cru-lem had no idea as to their use, but it was the palace itself which stood out as the physical embodiment of imperial power. Anyone gazing upon this glittering spectacle could be under no illusion. The emperor was all powerful and all knowing. Anyone who defied him would be crushed mercilessly. No excuses and no exceptions.

The entire compound was surrounded by a high wall, as featureless as the palace itself, and finally a wide moat of crystal-clear water separated the estate from the surrounding parkland. Flocks of multicoloured pruken birds swam in the water, some calling out in their unique high-pitched song, as if warning any would-be trespassers that they should go no further. About the size of a large swan, these birds were considered to be the most beautiful creatures in existence, with their bodies covered in feathers of the most intense colours. When a pruken bird took to the air and its wings expanded to their full extent, the sight was one to quicken the heart. A kaleidoscope of rainbow colours, the birds would swoop up and down, like kites being blown around in a stiff wind. Each bird had two heads sitting at the end of long slender necks. The heads would appear to sing to each other as the bird danced across the sky, their purple beaks opening and closing as the creatures mouthed the words of their haunting song.

Although the body pattern of each bird was unique, the one feature each pruken bird had in common was the huge blood-red tail feathers, which fluttered like an explosion of hand-held fans as the creatures soared into the Martian sky. So beautiful were these birds that they were all deemed to be imperial property, and as such were owned by the emperor himself. It was illegal to capture or interfere with the birds in any way whatsoever. Although the feathers could be used for imperial decoration, anyone else sporting a pruken bird feather would be dealt with severely.

Cru-lem was now approaching the walls of the estate, crossing one of the bridges spanning the moat. He did not need to announce his arrival, as a gate set in the wall opened automatically, giving him access to the hallowed ground inside.

Within the cylinder containing the goods to be delivered, Aka-des was unsure whether the vehicle was still moving or if it had arrived at its destination. He was still covered with the sheet, straining to hear any noises that might indicate where they were. Suddenly, the doors on each side of the container slid open, flooding the storage area with light. Aka-des knew he must make his move now or he would be found by the shopkeeper or, even worse, by the Imperial Guards.

Cru-lem peered into the cylinder and picked up a couple of the crates. As he disappeared again temporarily, Aka-des took his chance and leapt out of the other door. He stopped momentarily to get his bearings and noticed that they had arrived in a small square surrounded by tall buildings. There were some enormous columns at the far end of the square and what looked like a narrow alleyway in one corner. He looked around, fearful he might be spotted, but luckily there appeared to be no signs of life.

As Cru-lem was busying himself unloading his deliveries, Aka-des sprinted across the square and hid in the alleyway. His stomach was churning and his legs felt like jelly. *If I'm found now, I'm done for*, he thought, taking deep breaths to help calm his nerves. It was then that he became aware of the unpleasant smell once more, but this time it was stronger. It reminded Aka-des of vinegar, but there was something else mixed in as well. *Something like decaying fish, perhaps?* He wasn't sure what it was, but he felt bile rise up in his mouth. *I can't be sick now*, he resolved, fighting the bile back down his throat.

Cru-lem finished unloading his van and checked the pile of crates stacked nearby. He silently counted the number of crates and, happy that all was in order, he got back inside the vehicle and shut the door. He looked around, but the square was completely deserted, as always. *Strange*, he thought as he started up the van *this place is like a morgue. I've never seen anyone during my deliveries. Not ever.* He shrugged his shoulders and prepared for his journey back into the city. *Still, as long as I get paid, I suppose it's not a problem.* He knew that he was always paid on time, and the amount due for the current delivery was no doubt already deposited into his account. With one final look around he moved off towards the gate, which was still open. He sped through, crossing the bridge spanning the moat. As soon as he left the compound, the gate closed behind him.

Aka-des watched as the van disappeared from view. *What now?* he thought. *All alone, with no escape route.* He was still crouched in the shadows of the narrow alleyway pondering his next move when he suddenly heard a noise from the other side of the square. Two Imperial Guards marched across the stone floor towards the pile of crates recently left by Cru-lem. Their movements were in perfect synchronisation, the metallic *clunk* of their feet echoing around the otherwise empty square.

'They even march like this when they're not on public duty,' whispered Aka-des in amazement.

*Do they wear their armour all the time? It must get really hot in the summer. Perhaps they then have a special lightweight uniform with air holes for ventilation.* He sniggered at the thought, imagining the guards as a sort of walking tea strainer.

He continued to watch the guards as they approached the crates. Instead of picking them up as he expected, one guard raised his arm and pointed it at the pile of food. A beam of intense light shot from a device on the wrist of the armour, causing the crates to be reduced to a pile of cinders. There was nothing left apart from a few burning embers. The guards then turned on their heels and marched away again.

Aka-des stared in disbelief. *Why have they just destroyed the whole delivery of food?* he questioned. *It doesn't make sense. Why order a delivery only to obliterate it?* He felt his flesh creep as he tried to make sense of what he had just witnessed.

*There's something very strange going on here*, he concluded. *An emperor no one ever sees, Imperial Guards who seem to live in suits of armour, food which gets destroyed before being eaten, and that awful fishy vinegary smell. Will Beta-vac still be recognisable even if I find him? Not if he's already been encased in his metal outfit.* All was quiet once more, so Aka-des decided he needed to make a move. *No use me crouching down here like a rangool in headlights. I need to get inside and at least try and find Beta-vac.*

He then noticed a small window in a wall further down the alleyway that was ajar. Keeping to the shadows as best he could, he crept along the side of the wall and quietly opened the window further. Lifting himself up, he pulled his body through the opening. He was inside the imperial seat of power. *No turning back now*, he thought to himself as he landed on both feet as silently as he could, waiting for his eyes to adjust to the semi-gloom of his surroundings.

He then heard an ear-splitting screech, which turned his blood to ice and froze his legs to the spot.

# Chapter 8
# The Landing

The landing phase of the New Endeavour craft began when it reached the Martian atmosphere, approximately eighty miles above the planet's surface. Tom Fisher and the rest of the crew had taken their seats in the command centre of the spacecraft, and were now transfixed as the surface of Mars loomed ever closer.

Martin Robson checked the speed as the craft entered the thin atmosphere. 'Twelve thousand miles per hour,' he announced. 'All systems green.' The New Endeavour would use the tenuous atmosphere to assist with the deceleration procedure while the ground grew ever nearer.

Tom pressed a button in front of him on the control panel in order to move the thick heat shield into place, preventing the possibility of the ship being sandblasted by a Martian dust storm. However, this was merely a precaution. Luckily, there did not appear to be any storms brewing in the area. Another flick of a switch, and the small rockets placed around the outer rim of the doughnut-shaped craft roared into life, helping to control the descent of the vehicle towards the rocky surface.

The crew members were watching the descent in awe. They would be the first humans to set foot on Mars, and the enormity of what they were about to do was starting to sink home. Their destination was the huge Hellas Planitia, a vast plain located in the southern hemisphere of the planet. This roughly circular impact basin has a floor some twenty-three thousand feet deep and a diameter of roughly fourteen hundred miles. It was thought that the feature had formed roughly four billion years ago, when a large asteroid hit the Martian surface. As the basin is so deep, the atmospheric pressure at the bottom is more than double the pressure at the top. The plain also has a relatively flat, honeycombed terrain.

Robert Franks, the team geologist, knew the current theory was that this unique surface was caused by ice moving up through the ground in the region aeons ago. Large masses of ice were thought to have pushed up layers of rocks into domes, which were then eroded over time to give rise to the honeycomb pattern seen today. He was itching to start examining the rocks and carry out the experiments he was scheduled to undertake, according to his detailed assignment plan.

Angela Trike, the New Zealand astrobiologist, also knew that the higher atmospheric pressure at the floor of the basin made this an intriguing place to try and locate any Martian life which may still cling on in the harsh environment. Tests carried out by the Mars Prospector probe had proven inconclusive, and she had a number of further tests to carry out once they reached the surface.

Frances Downes, the Australian chemist, would be assisting her compatriot Robert, and Angela, with their tests and experiments, as well as carrying out her own research on the composition of the rocks in the immediate area.

Martin Robson would be responsible for the systems on board the New Endeavour, and was also due to carry out maintenance and repair work on the Mars Prospector probe, once they had located it. The small vehicle had operated superbly since it had arrived on Mars a couple of years ago, sending back important data to the lunar base and Earth. However, since its important discovery had been made, it had experienced power failures, and it was thought that the problem could be due to damage to its delicate solar panels, caused by sandstorms.

Jason Lombard, the crew's medical officer, was carrying out research on the impact of long flights in space on the human body, both physical and mental. As well as looking after the day-to-day medical needs of the team, he was also responsible for their general well-being. Each member of the crew had their own personalised exercise plan, which Jason had to ensure was being followed, and he was also responsible for running "wellness sessions" for the team as a whole. These would include team-building exercises and yoga classes, making sure the crew members gelled as well as possible on the long mission to Mars. One of the main problems that had been envisaged at the outset, when the manned journey to the Red Planet was being planned, was how to deal with the psychological impact on a small group of people being confined in a small space for many months. It was vital that any potential problems were nipped in the bud early on, or they could endanger the whole mission.

Tom Fisher was the official leader of the expedition. His calm, thoughtful nature had earnt him the respect of those in overall charge of the UK Space Programme. His easy-going manner also made him popular with his fellow astronauts, so this relatively young Englishman was an obvious choice to head up the New Endeavour mission.

As well as being in charge of the other crew members, it was his job to ensure the goals of the mission were met, reporting back to mission control regularly with updates on progress. As an astrophysicist, he also had research of his own to carry out, particularly with regard to the two Martian moons, Phobos and Deimos. These tiny satellites were mere specks of light as seen from Earth or the Moon, but their erratic orbits had been a matter of great interest in the astronomical community for many years. Being on the surface of Mars gave Tom the ideal chance to examine the movements of these minute companions of the Red Planet in much more detail.

The final stage of the descent involved retracting the heat shield, and releasing an enormous parachute to help slow the craft even further, as it continued to pass through the extremely thin Martian atmosphere. Numerous shock-absorbing legs were extended from the underside of the craft, and the on-board guidance software clicked in to take control of the final slowdown of the spacecraft, until New Endeavour came to rest on the barren rocky surface.

'We're here!'

Robert whooped, raising his arms into the air.

'Shall we crack open the champagne?'

'I think that will have to wait,' responded Tom as he ticked off the safety checks in his mind, both eyes fixed on the numerous dials, buttons and switches in front of him on the control panel.

Martin was also carrying out the same checks as a backup procedure. When they had both finished, they looked at each other and nodded.

'All fine by me,' said Tom.

'Agreed,' Martin confirmed. 'All systems still green.'

The technology used on the New Endeavour was, by nature, cutting edge, and in some ways the crew of the spacecraft were guinea pigs testing out the systems in case any modifications were required before further trips were made to the Red Planet in the future. The team accepted this. They were well aware of the risks involved in such a ground-breaking expedition before they had agreed to join the crew. These risks, however, had to be weighed up against the thrill and honour of being the first humans to touch down on planet Mars. Tom and his team were all passionate about space travel as well as the long-term benefits it could bring to the entire human race.

Earth's resources were dwindling and, although the population was stabilising, much damage had already been done to the planet's ecosystems. A concerted effort was being made to try and repair some of the worst damage, but it was a long and difficult pathway. Cleaning up pollution in the seas, reforestation of large tracts of land, eliminating all fossil fuels and reducing the amount of carbon dioxide in the atmosphere were not easy goals to achieve. They required the goodwill and determination of all countries. The ultimate success or failure of these measures was still to be determined, so it would be many years before scientists were able to say conclusively whether the outcome was favourable or not.

In the meantime, Earth still needed raw materials of all kinds. The Moon was one obvious source, as were comets and asteroids, but Mars was much larger and, in some ways, more Earth-like. It could be easier to tap into the planet's resources, particularly if permanent settlements were established and significant numbers of people agreed to move to the Red Planet.

One problem that had to be solved was how to provide the food, oxygen and fuel which would be needed for any long-term bases on Mars. The thin Martian atmosphere consists mainly of carbon dioxide and is unbreathable to humans. New Endeavour carried excess amounts of hydrogen on board, and the plan was to mix this hydrogen with carbon dioxide in the air. A state-of-the-art chemical processor would then convert these elements to create methane and oxygen to propel the craft during lift-off on the trip back to the Moon. The same processor could also generate oxygen, water and fuel needed for the crew's stay on Mars and for the flight home. On longer trips in the years to come, the water generated could also be used to grow crops to feed the inhabitants of the bases. It had been established for many years now that Mars also has large amounts of water trapped as ice beneath the surface, and this water could also be released to help sustain any full-time population of Martian colonists in the future.

Tom completed the first of his regular reports for the authorities back on Moon base, and then joined the others as they gathered in a huddle, staring in awe through the large observation windows of the craft, surveying the panorama spread out before them.

A desert landscape of harsh beauty welcomed them, seemingly completely devoid of any signs of life. Rocks of all sizes were littered across a surface of iron oxide dust with the consistency of talcum powder, reaching out in all directions into the far distance.

Although the surface of Mars appears reddish from a distance, because of the rusty dust suspended in the atmosphere, from closer up it was more of a butterscotch colour, with hints of gold, brown and green, depending on the minerals present in the rocks. The sky was a pinkish-red colour, apart from a few wispy bluish clouds moving slowly in the thin atmosphere. These clouds were mainly of water ice condensing on the dust particles in the Martian air.

'Might be quite a trek to the nearest pub,' said Robert, breaking the silence.

'It's so beautiful,' whispered Angela in a hushed voice. 'I know we've all seen plenty of images of Mars before, but nothing prepares you for this.'

'Stunning.'

Frances agreed.

'Literally out of this world.'

'Beautiful, but potentially deadly,' Tom reminded them. 'We wouldn't last for more than a couple of minutes at most out there, without the proper protection.'

'Spoilsport.'

Martin joked.

'I was just about to put on my shorts and trainers and go for a quick run before dinner.'

The others laughed.

'It will be a while before any of us makes a trip outside,' Jason, the team's medic, added. 'The sun will be setting soon, and the temperature will plummet.'

The small band of explorers continued to watch as the sky began to darken, adding a deeper pink glow to the Martian sky. However, in the vicinity of the setting sun itself, the sky took on a bluish tinge. The dust in the atmosphere absorbs blue light, giving the sky its normal pinkish colour, but the dust also scatters some of it into the area around the sun. The blue tinge only becomes apparent near sunset or sunrise, when the light has to pass through the largest amount of dust.

'I wouldn't have missed this for the world,' said Angela, finding it difficult to tear herself away from the view of the desolate but mesmerising landscape just outside their protective cocoon.

'Me neither,' Jason added in agreement.

'Well, I'm hungry.'

Robert butted in, once again breaking the reverential hush surrounding the group.

'And, as we can't find a decent pub within walking distance, we'll need to open up a few sachets of inedible muck to see us through the night.'

The stores of New Endeavour included sufficient pre-packed sachets of food to comfortably see them through the mission to Mars, even taking into account the enormous appetite of the Australian geologist. Separated into breakfast, lunch, dinner and snack meals, there was a sufficient variety of menus to avoid too much repetition, whether the diner fancied a traditional roast beef dinner, a vegetarian curry or a kung pao chicken dish. All that was required was to select the appropriate pouch, pop it into a microwave oven and tuck in.

The contents of the pouches did not look very appetising, but they actually tasted much better. If you closed your eyes while eating, you could almost imagine you were eating a breast of roast chicken or a fillet of grilled salmon. The food could simply be sucked from a tube in the pack if you were short of time, but Jason had decreed, in his role of medical officer, that whenever possible they should all sit down together at meal times, eating off proper plates and drinking from cups and glasses. He was convinced it would help with their emotional well-being, as well as enhance the close bond between the crew members required for a successful mission.

As this was their first night on Mars, it was even more important to have a proper celebration. A couple of bottles of non-alcoholic fizz were brought out of stores to be served in plastic champagne glasses so they could all toast their success so far and look forward to the challenges ahead.

'I wonder when we will find out what this additional task is,' Martin pondered while devouring the last of his beef stew and dumplings.

'All I know so far is that the Mars Prospector has found something unusual just below the surface, and we need to find out what it is,' said Tom, relishing the last spoonful of crème brûlée. 'We will be told more first thing in the morning, as I understand it.'

'What do you think the chances are that the old rust bucket has found an unopened crate of ice-cold beer?' asked Robert, smacking his lips at the very thought of downing a nice cold pint of lager.

'Much better than this fizzy lemonade,' he added with disgust as he emptied his glass of celebratory juice.

'Remember that Mars Prospector hasn't been working properly for some time now, anyway,' Martin added.

'She'll need a good old dust and polish to get her up and running, whatever else we find.'

'Yes, we've all got a lot to do tomorrow,' Tom confirmed. 'Probably best to call it a night.'

The others agreed and, after clearing away the dishes, they all retired to their bedrooms. Each member of the crew had their own room, which included a desk, storage for clothing and small personal effects, a comfortable chair and a small shower, as well as a foldaway bed. Again, it was considered important by the space authorities that crew members should have as many home comforts as could be squeezed onto the ship and personal space to escape to when needed.

By the time New Endeavour returned to Moon base, the crew would have been away for nearly a year. It had already taken them nearly five months to reach Mars, and so far, the team had gelled as well as could be expected. Jason was currently happy with the medical and emotional condition of everyone, and was adamant that this success would continue during the remainder of the mission.

As Tom crawled into his bed and turned out the light, he lay there thinking about the events of the day. He had succeeded in his lifelong dream of reaching Mars, and wanted to make the most of every second while he was there. He lay in the quiet, listening to the soft moaning of the Martian wind caressing the outside of the ship, just inches away from his head.

# Chapter 9
# Tellas Settlement

Although the vast majority of the Martian population lived within the walls of the city, a vast metropolis of over forty million people, an increasing number of families and individuals were moving out to the new settlements springing up at various locations in the Outside. The authorities were encouraging this exodus, as a way of dealing with the increasingly cramped conditions within the city. Imperial funds were being used to help finance the relevant infrastructures these settlements would need, such as schools, hospitals, roads and temples, and to provide grants towards the purchase of new homes.

One advantage of moving to the Outside was more space. Houses with large gardens were almost unheard of in the city, and only the very wealthy could afford a detached property. Most people lived in flats or rows of terraced housing, with the middle classes occupying the relatively few semi-detached houses available. The residential areas were fairly well laid out, however, particularly in the more modern neighbourhoods, with trees and public gardens, but a lack of privacy was an issue for many people.

As employers were increasingly being enticed to set up offices and shops in the new settlements, so the people began to follow. Small towns and villages started to grow along the shores and watersides of the many lakes and rivers on Mars to accommodate the exodus from the city.

However, these new settlements were not without their critics. Although few in number at the moment, voices were increasingly being heard questioning the wisdom of rushing headlong into a surge of new building. One problem openly being discussed in some quarters was the impact of the new developments on the Antis. There was normally little if any contact between the insects and the Martians, but as the new towns were encroaching more and more on their ancestral lands, the Antis were being pushed further and further out into the Outside.

There was always the danger that the insect race would start to retaliate against their treatment and begin to cause trouble for the Martian settlers. Martians were not allowed to carry weapons by imperial decree. Only the Imperial Guards could police the city and the settlements, but few if any of the guards had been sent to protect the incomers so far.

This meant that the people setting up homes and businesses outside of the city were mainly unprotected. Most towns and villages being built were surrounded by walls, which helped to keep out unwanted intruders, but whether they could withstand a concerted attack was, as yet, unknown. This had not been a significant issue so far, but with more and more settlements being constructed, there was always the concern that the Antis could only be pushed so far.

One such settlement currently being built was the township of Tellas. The developers' promotional literature made it sound like paradise itself. Aiming for a population of roughly three thousand by the time it was completed, the brochures presented a picture of a pretty, self-contained development, set on the banks of the large Vesula Lake. Complete with school, medical centre, a selection of shops, employment area, theatre and temple, it had everything needed for a thriving community. Situated only ten miles away from the city gates, it would be easy to travel back to the metropolis when needed, for a greater selection of shops, restaurants and entertainment venues, as well as access to hospitals for more urgent medical needs. However, it was also far enough away so residents would really feel the benefits of living Outside. Houses were to be much roomier than those in the city, with large gardens, and most with pleasant views of the lake, forests or surrounding countryside. Many of the houses would be detached, and the lower prices of housing stock in the Outside meant that many more people could afford the luxury of "detached" living.

The developers had decided against building the customary wall around the town as well, in order to open up the vistas from within the settlement and make it feel more like a place which fitted in with the surrounding landscape, rather than one that was simply imposed on its rural setting. Instead, an invisible force field would be switched on at night, or whenever danger threatened, using the most recent developments in technology. Metal poles would be positioned at strategic locations around the perimeter of the town and would be connected by invisible beams of plasma particles when switched on. Similar invisible barriers had been constructed on a much smaller scale already to protect farms in some of the more remote areas. When in operation, they provided an efficient physical deterrent to any intruders without causing any harm to the would-be interloper.

The force field was created by ionising gas into a plasma, heated to an extremely high temperature. The plasma was held in place by a magnetic field, and the particles in it had so much momentum that they repelled anything that tried to move through it, creating an impenetrable plasma field. The developers had also agreed to finance a small number of Imperial Guards, who would be stationed in the town on a full-time basis to give added protection to its citizens.

***

Klop-tra was in overall charge of the new development. An engineer and architect by profession, he had been involved in town planning for many years, and his team had built up an enviable reputation for designing high-quality buildings of an imaginative style. He had close working relationships with most of the major developers, and spent an inordinate amount of time on-site ensuring the work was progressing well, and in accordance with his detailed plans.

So respected was he by those involved in the new settlements, that they would plead with him to manage their developments, fighting to outdo each other in terms of the benefits they would shower upon the great man if he accepted their offer. He was, therefore, a very wealthy person, and could simply pick and choose which projects would benefit from his involvement. He was particularly interested in the possibilities presented by the new Tellas settlement, with its prime location and the enlightened vision of the developers. He played hard to get but eventually agreed to add this project to his already impressive portfolio of work.

Klop-tra lived in the city with his wife and family, and was one of the privileged few who could afford a detached property in a very desirable area. Having designed the house himself, he was very proud of his home. Located within extensive grounds, and shielded from prying eyes by a lush canopy of free-flowering trees, the house was light, airy and took full advantage of its position. The main living areas had jaw-dropping views over some of the most impressive buildings in the city, as well as benefitting from its close proximity to the parkland surrounding the imperial estate. Klop-tra had never met the emperor in person, but he had been advised by one of the elders that the divine leader took a great deal of interest in his work, and was well pleased with the progress he was making in promoting the expansion of settlements in the Outside. There was even talk of him being awarded an Imperial Service Medal in recognition of his achievements.

Klop-tra was just finishing his breakfast of trefu, a sort of thick yogurt made from the milk of the long-haired yarmul. This camel-like creature was farmed extensively in the Outside, and its milk used for a variety of dairy products. Klop-tra loved trefu, but was also very partial to the crumbly fargan cheese, and luscious aromatic creams, all produced from the same basic commodity.

He was whistling to himself as he cleared away his bowl, running through his busy agenda for the day ahead. He liked to take breakfast early on workdays so he could plan his schedule before the rest of the family arose. He would travel out to the Tellas site to begin with to check on progress. No one was living in the town so far, and building was still at a fairly early stage, but Klop-tra wanted to ensure that the general layout of the first phase was in accordance with his detailed specifications. If he got there early, he could wander around the site without interruptions before the builders arrived to start their day.

He collected his coat, as it was a chilly morning, and checked that there were no messages waiting for him on his wristband. Satisfied, he kissed his wife goodbye as she emerged from the bedroom to make a hot cup of fruity menwan juice.

'I have a number of site visits today, so won't be back until fairly late,' he warned her.

'That's okay,' she replied, filing her nails as she waited for the menwan seeds to fully diffuse in the boiling water. 'I'm meeting up with Mrs Pru-lek later on, and the children are staying for a sleepover with the Arn-fel family tonight after school. Mrs Arn-fel is picking them up after classes when she collects her own children.'

Mrs Klop-tra had never needed to work, having met her husband soon after leaving school. Always considered a woman of rare beauty in her youth, she had latched on to the young architect, convinced that he would provide the lifestyle she was looking for. Her initial conclusion as to his suitability had proven correct and as his career blossomed, she had been there at his side, urging him on to ever-greater, and more lucrative, achievements.

'I'll book a table at Marla's,' she announced. 'I want to try their new tasting menu. We can dine there tonight when you return.'

Marla's was one of the most expensive restaurants in the city, but Klop-tra was happy to indulge his wife, if it kept her contented.

'You do that,' he called back as he left the house. 'I should be back by sunset.'

Klop-tra clicked open his car and threw his coat inside. After settling himself in, he switched the vehicle on. He verified the coordinates for his intended destination, selected his favourite music and set off.

The journey to the Tellas site was only a pleasant half-hour journey at most, so as the vehicle took control of the driving, Klop-tra made himself comfortable and closed his eyes. Listening to the dulcet tones filling the interior of the car, he ticked off once more in his mind what he needed to accomplish by the end of the day.

He hoped the visit to Tellas wouldn't take too long, as he also wanted to take some time to chat to the developers of the nearby Windor village, now taking shape roughly fifteen miles further on. People had started to move in here, and he needed to check whether there were any teething problems as the incoming settlers started their new lives outside the city.

He had also planned a business lunch with his old friend Rel-do, the lawyer acquaintance of Aka-mas. Rel-do's firm dealt with a lot of the legal work associated with the new settlements, and the two men met up regularly to discuss developments. *Better not have too much to eat or drink*, thought Klop-tra, making a mental note. *Not if my dear wife is planning a blowout meal at Marla's tonight.*

The sun was rising above the buildings as the vehicle approached the city gates, a precursor to what looked like a glorious day of weather ahead. The monitor on the gate recognised his car, and the barrier swung open, giving access to the great Outside.

Klop-tra was a city man at heart, and could not understand why people would want to give up "civilised living" in order to move out here in the middle of nowhere. Still, their decisions to do so had proven extremely lucrative to him in the past, and had provided him with his envious standard of living. *Long may it continue,* he chuckled, looking around, taking in the scenery spread out before him.

Fields now took the place of the cramped city buildings, some filled with crops, others filled with flocks of yarmul, which provided the dairy products for city consumers, such as himself. The intense green of the surroundings were a joy to behold, even to a city lover like Klop-tra. *Wonderful to visit now and then,* he thought. *As long as I don't need to live here permanently.* The odd farm building gave perspective to the rural scene, and small woods and copses added further interest.

The vehicle sped on, with not much traffic about at this hour. Over to the left he noted the glistening waters of Vesula Lake, and knew that he was almost at his destination. Just behind the next copse of bluish eldo trees, with their orange leaves and purple fruits, was the new township of Tellas.

Klop-tra checked his wristband. *Twenty-four minutes door to door,* he noted with satisfaction. *Not a bad journey at all.* He parked his car on the outskirts of the site and then looked around. What he saw left him open-mouthed. Everywhere was utter devastation. The partly built walls of practically all the buildings had been smashed to the ground, with slabs of stone scattered like the site of a Roman ruin. Walls and fences were shattered, and glass panels stored in piles for later use were completely destroyed.

'Whoever did this?' asked Klop-tra, stunned at the amount of wreckage all around him.

He noted that the plasma field had not been switched on last night – whether by accident or design, he did not know.

As he moved further into the site, trying to avoid the debris as he walked, he saw that the entire site had been subjected to this wanton vandalism. Klop-tra then stopped in his tracks. In front of him was a view of utter sacrilege. The monument of the emperor had been toppled over, now lying broken in the mud surrounding its plinth. This he just could not comprehend. Every settlement had to have at its centre a monument to the god emperor. It had to be the first edifice to be completed, before any other building could even be started. The statue was a visible sign of the authority of the divine leader, which reached out to any settlement, large or small, where Martians were to make their home. The emperor's statue always consisted of the same imperial globe, resting on a plinth of gold, and decorated with images representing the god king's power and influence.

The fact that the statue had been desecrated in such a crude and blatant manner, hitting at the very heart of Martian civilisation, was an act without equal. Klop-tra could not believe what he was seeing.

Just then, another car drew up and the construction manager, Res-dor, alighted. A tall and rather stocky individual, he was very experienced in his job and had worked with Klop-tra on numerous projects in the past.

'What's been going on here?' he mouthed, turning to the architect for an explanation.

'You tell me,' replied Klop-tra. 'Why would anyone do something like this? It's unheard of.'

'It would have taken a considerable time to cause this amount of damage, even if there were a group of people involved.' Res-dor reckoned.

'What about security cameras?' asked Klop-tra, desperately trying to think what they should do next.

'Were they switched on before you left last night? And what about the plasma field?'

Res-dor sensed a change in the tone of the architect as he spoke, as if he were passing the blame for what had happened to the construction manager.

'The cameras are not operated manually,' he answered, trying to hide the anger and resentment welling up inside. 'They switch on automatically at sunset. I have no reason to believe the same wouldn't have happened last night. The same applies to the plasma field. It's activated automatically as well.'

'We'd better check, then,' replied Klop-tra, and they both moved off towards the site office.

Just then, Res-dor noticed something on the ground to his left and stopped, grabbing the arm of the architect as he did so.

'Look over there,' he said, pointing. 'Do you see?'

'What have you found?' asked Klop-tra, trying to focus on whatever Res-dor had spotted.

'I think it's a pile of Antis droppings,' came the reply.

As they both got nearer, they saw piles of soft, fibrous, sandy-coloured faeces, typical of the ant-like race.

71

'It's those bloody insects!' Klop-tra shouted. 'They've caused this destruction. But how did they get in?'

'They must have interfered with the plasma field in order to gain access to the site,' Res-dor reasoned. 'But how they did it, I haven't a clue.'

'Perhaps the cameras can shed some light on the matter,' came the brusque response as they quickened their pace towards the office.

However, as they turned a corner to face the building, they were met with the same destruction as elsewhere. The site office was no more, reduced to another pile of rubble. It was as if an earthquake had ripped through the entire area, with the contents of the office strewn about and the equipment smashed to pieces.

'It's like the aftermath of a tornado.'

Res-dor sighed.

'I don't think we'll find any answers here. They've really trashed the place.'

'But why here?' asked Klop-tra, his tone softening into one of abject despair. 'And why now?'

# Chapter 10
# The Tablets of Skothath

Professor Sep-lee was in a hurry as he was running late. He was a renowned expert in Martian antiquities and had a passion for the earliest period in the recorded history of the Martian civilisation.

It was well known that the Martian race had been in existence for many thousands of years, as had the insect Antis. In the earliest phase of the civilisation, the Martians had been nomads, moving around at will in small groups and setting up temporary homes wherever conditions were favourable. They were hunters primarily, living off the teeming wildlife which seemed to inhabit the entire planet. They also ate plants and fruit, but there was little evidence of any large-scale growing of crops to provide food.

Later on, the Martians began to settle in permanent villages, and turned to farming as well as hunting. They lived in small settlements of a few hundred people at most, growing what they needed, and tending to flocks of yarmul to provide dairy products, and woolly shestas for meat. It appeared that Martians and Antis coexisted quite amicably. Cave paintings had been discovered showing Martian farmers tending their fields, with groups of Antis grazing in the distance. Both races seemed to accept the existence of the other without seeing their neighbours as a threat. There was plenty of room, and food, for both Martians and Antis.

However, it was events said to have taken place about three thousand years ago which really interested Sep-lee, and this was what he was hoping to learn more about as a result of his scheduled meeting with his old friend, Chief Librarian Hak-tes, at the Imperial Library in the centre of the city.

His friend had been unusually reticent about the exact nature of the meeting when the pair had spoken recently, but Sep-lee believed it concerned the ancient Tablets of Skothath. These stone tablets had been discovered lying in a cave over a hundred years ago in the remote region of Skothath, some five hundred miles from the city. The area was now designated as an Imperial Sanctuary and, as such, no mere mortal could visit. It was said that the emperor would travel to Skothath periodically on an imperial pilgrimage in order to commune with the gods, but it was, of course, impossible to verify one way or the other.

The series of tablets, written in the ancient Martian hieroglyphics, were supposed to describe events of a divine nature that had had a great impact on the development of the Martian race. It was impossible to examine the actual tablets, which were apparently stored in the imperial vaults for safe keeping, although officially sanctioned transcripts were available for public scrutiny.

Sep-lee had, of course, examined these transcripts, but he had never been convinced that they told the whole story of what actually happened three thousand years ago.

The official version was that villagers had seen an enormous ball of fire appear in the sky, which lit up the area for miles around. The light was seen as a message from the gods, although the true meaning of the phenomenon was hard to tell. The view from the transcript was that the gods were displeased with the Martians for some reason, and had sent the ball of fire as a warning to mend their ways. The source of the light was said to have exploded behind some hills, causing the ground itself to tremble with fear over a large part of Mars.

The tablets then went on to explain that, in the days after the explosion, the gods themselves appeared before the villagers in the form of tall entities, glowing with a divine aura. The records also stated that, in the weeks and months following, a terrible plague descended upon the inhabitants of the villages, and large numbers of people were said to have died, or simply vanished without trace.

The scientific view was that Mars had been hit by a large meteor, causing the ground to shake with the impact as the celestial visitor crashed into the Martian surface. The plague could have been the result of radiation poisoning, caused by leakage from the minerals contained within the rocky debris as the meteor exploded.

Sep-lee had serious doubts about the validity of either the "religious" or the "scientific" explanations of those events of long ago, if they did actually occur at all. Personally, he did give credence to the occurrence of something quite dramatic, but without access to the tablets themselves, it was never going to be a matter which could be determined objectively.

As he neared the imposing façade of the Imperial Library, with its ornate columns of reddish stone, he noticed a sign advertising some of the classes available to the public within the building.

"Emperor Worship – The Way Forward".

"Being a Good Citizen, a Duty Not a Choice".

"Loving Your Home, Loving Your Emperor".

"The Temple as a Source of Inspiration".

Sep-lee smiled to himself, wondering who would waste their time on topics as bizarre as these. He knew he was in a distinct minority, and had tried hard to keep his rebellious views out of the public domain. The last thing he wanted to do was attract attention to himself. If he pushed the boundaries too far, he would certainly find himself out of a job, and probably a lot worse.

He had spent most of his working life at the Imperial University, working his way up to his current position as Professor of Antiquities. He was now officially carrying out research for his new book to be entitled *Man, Myth and Magic*, an exploration of the legends and myths passed down throughout history and their link to actual events. However, he needed to be careful not to step on too many toes as he carried out his research. None of his colleagues saw him as anything more than a pleasant, if somewhat out of touch, member of the faculty, and certainly not someone out to cause waves in the placid waters of academia. They were well aware that the university had imperial patronage, and they knew on which side their bread was buttered.

Sep-lee was quite happy with this state of affairs. It served his purpose that he was not seen as any sort of threat, as it meant no one paid too much attention to what he actually did. As long as he turned up for his few lectures each week and carried out a reasonable amount of research, which ended up being published in one or other of the obscure academic journals, which very few actually read, the university authorities were satisfied. This also meant that he had time to carry out research which, although not officially sanctioned, really interested him, such as the Tablets of Skothath.

Sep-lee walked up the steps and entered the huge library. The Chief Librarian, Hak-tes, had his offices on the top floor. The two men had been friends since their schooldays, many, many years ago. They had attended the same university as students, and both had studied Martian history. On graduation, Sep-lee had chosen to pursue an academic career, while his friend had moved into the Imperial Civil Service, before ending up at the Imperial Library.

As he pushed through the doors, Sep-lee entered the cavernous reception plaza of the building. He glanced up at the highly decorated ceiling, with its frescoes depicting the flora and fauna of Mars in stunning detail. The rich colours of the tableaux, with the gold leaf embellishments, presented an awe-inspiring introduction to the library. Sep-lee never failed to be impressed by the skills of the artists who had produced this national treasure hundreds of years ago, without the benefits of modern technology.

It seemed to him that few people today really appreciated the wonderful treasure trove of art which had been handed down from times long past. The Martian civilisation had created artists, sculptors and authors of great works of literature throughout the ages, but most people now were more interested in new advances in technology, rather than finding the time to really understand their past and appreciate what they had been bequeathed.

The historian sighed as he passed the obligatory statue of the imperial orb, placed in a prime position near the central staircase. A work of art in itself, with its gold railings and intricate ironwork, the staircase was another relic from a more gentle and aesthetic age. Few today would take the time to use the stairs to reach the upper floors. Instead, they would use the ele-pods discretely positioned in one corner of the plaza. The pods would silently transport you to whichever floor you desired, using anti-gravity fields. However, even these inventions were nearing the end of their lives, as technology continued to innovate. Within the next few years, it was anticipated that teleportation devices would replace the ele-pods, based on the techniques used with the canisters which transported the contents of Mrs Aka-mas's Emperor's Day picnic.

Sep-lee stepped out of the pod on the top floor and walked over to his friend's office. He stopped at the reception desk to announce his arrival, and was then ushered into the spacious room occupied by the Chief Librarian.

'Come in,' said Hak-tes, rising to greet his guest. 'Have a seat. Would you like a drink?'

Sep-lee noticed old-fashioned decanters of cut glass standing on a table in a corner of the room. In particular, he noted that one decanter held a bright blue liquid.

'Is that fendril juice?' he enquired, pointing towards the container, hoping he was correct.

He loved the flavour of a well-matured bottle of the juice which was extracted from the stems of the exotic fendril plant.

'Yes, I'll pour you a glass,' replied the librarian, moving over to the decanter. 'Few people drink it these days,' he bemoaned while filling two glasses with the blue nectar. 'Too strong a flavour for modern palates.'

He handed a glass to Sep-lee, who accepted it gratefully before closing his eyes in rapture as he took a sip of the precious liquid. He was in heaven.

'More fool them.'

He sighed, savouring the intensity of the drink.

'Well, what's all this about?' asked Sep-lee as he placed his near-empty glass on a small table at his side.

'What do you have to tell me?'

The Chief Librarian took another sip from his glass and cleared his throat.

'You are interested in the Tablets of Skothath, as I understand it.'

'Yes, of course,' came the reply. 'But my real interest is in examining the tablets themselves, not just the official transcripts.'

'Well, I may be able to help with your quest,' said Hak-tes, resting his hands together as if in prayer. 'I have a... device in my possession, which purports to show images of the tablets themselves.'

Sep-lee looked at his friend open-mouthed.

'You what? Are you sure? How did you get hold of this "device"?'

The questions came tumbling out of his mouth, one after the other.

'I thought the original tablets were held in the imperial vaults. How could someone simply capture images of them while under lock and key, and then walk out with no questions asked?'

The librarian smiled.

'As you know, there are a number of individuals like us – an increasing number, it seems – who, how shall I put it, "lack the enthusiasm" for the current state of affairs.'

He glanced out of the huge picture window of his office, watching people scurrying to and fro in the streets below.

'Like so many insects,' he mused, 'busying themselves with their humdrum day-to-day lives, totally indifferent to what really matters. It can't go on like this forever,' he stated emphatically. 'Sooner or later, things will have to change.'

'But why?' asked his friend. 'People lead comfortable lives in the main. They seem contented enough with their lot. Perhaps it is people like us who are the real problem, trying to rock the boat unnecessarily.'

Hak-tes went to refill Sep-lee's empty glass before returning to his seat.

'If you really thought like that, you wouldn't be here today. You would simply accept the transcript of the tablets, and that would be the end of it.'

He went on.

'No, increasingly some people are starting to question the official statements that regulate our lives. We are told what to do and when to do it, and are expected to comply without fail. The response to this from a small but, I believe, growing number of people is to say, "Why should we?"'

'And the images of the tablets. Where did they come from?' Sep-lee interjected.

'I obviously cannot betray my sources of information,' responded the librarian quietly. 'It would be too dangerous. We must be extremely careful what we say, and to whom. Suffice for now to say that I have known my informer for many years, and I trust him explicitly. He handed me the device containing the images, thinking that they may be of some use to our cause. Very few people now understand the ancient Martian language, but you do.'

Hak-tes stared at his friend and then reached down to a small drawer in his desk.

'If you can study the actual tablets themselves and interpret the messages they contain, we may have some useful ammunition for the future.'

He drew out a small package, about the size of a matchbox, and handed it to Sep-lee.

'Things aren't going to improve overnight. It is unlikely we can start a revolution by ourselves, as our numbers are too small. However, if we build up evidence that what we are being told by the authorities is untrue, and can drip-feed this information to the general populace, perhaps eventually things will start to change for the better. At least we have a duty to try.'

Sep-lee seemed unconvinced that this strategy would work, but he was certainly interested in what the images of the tablets may reveal. He took the package and carefully examined it. It contained a small metal box, five sides of which were a dull grey colour and the sixth a dark red. The sides of the box were completely smooth, with no buttons or switches of any kind.

'All you need to do is point the device at a suitable surface and gently press the red side of the box. The images will be transferred to the chosen surface one at a time. When you have examined a particular image, press the red side again and the next will replace it.'

'That seems easy enough,' said Sep-lee, nodding his head as he continued to turn the box in his hand.

'Yes, even you should be able to deal with this technology,' replied the librarian, a hint of a smile on his face. 'Just don't lose it, and bring it back to me when you have finished with it.'

Sep-lee said his goodbyes and left the office. He made sure the device was safely stored in his pocket before descending to the reception plaza of the library. As he moved towards the exit of the building, he noticed a small group of people congregating by the huge statue of the emperor, or rather of the imperial orb. Some were stroking the shiny surface of the globe, and one woman had tears in her eyes as she gently laid a single flower at the base of the statue.

Sep-lee shuddered as he considered the mountain people who thought like him had to climb, in order to change the perceptions of the general public. He was determined to view the images of the Tablets of Skothath as soon as possible, having waited for a chance like this for most of his adult life, and everything else would have to wait. He decided it would be unsafe to examine the images in his office at the university, so set off for home, where there would be fewer interruptions.

The historian lived alone in a fairly spacious flat in one of the less grand parts of the city. He had lived there for many years. It suited his purposes perfectly, being much larger than many of the newer flats being built, and it had far more character. Large picture windows gave extensive views of the surrounding area, and Sep-lee liked nothing better than to sit in his favourite armchair of an evening, looking out at the setting sun with a glass of something warming in his hand.

He had never married. He had been involved in a relationship in his early adulthood, and the couple had considered marriage at one stage. However, his intended was a keen archaeologist and had been offered the chance of being involved in a major expedition to the Hestral region of Mars, hundreds of miles from the city. Ruins had been unearthed of an ancient settlement, apparently abandoned thousands of years ago. She had jumped at the chance, even though the project would involve being away for many months at a time.

The couple had agreed to keep in touch, but Sep-lee never heard from her again. Whether she had found a new love interest on the far side of the planet, he never knew. As a result, he had decided to devote his life to his academic work, which had kept him fully occupied to the present day. He had a few close friends and numerous acquaintances, but was quite happy with his own company. He had his books, his music and his wine. In truth, he was content with his lot in life.

Sep-lee arrived home and checked again that the device was still safely stored away in his pocket before entering his flat. To say that he lived alone was not strictly true. He had a faithful pet purrdon, a furry cat-like creature with an extremely long tail, which he had owned for as long as he could remember. Purrdons had a lifespan of well over a hundred years, and he had originally acquired this fine specimen from an aged relative who no longer had the ability to keep a pet.

The person concerned had moved into a state-run community for the elderly, which did not allow pets. She had lived there happily in her twilight years, until deciding that she'd had enough of life, and therefore requested a Transference to the Bosom of the Sacred Emperor. Having been granted her request by the authorities, she had spent the last week of her life surrounded by family and friends, saying her farewells, before sinking into a deep and final sleep to the sound of her favourite music.

Sep-lee had named the purrdon Taya, after the name of his relative, Sep-tay. The two had bonded instantly and whenever he returned home, Taya would emit her distinctive whistling sound and curl her long furry tail around his arm. The same procedure took place as Sep-lee entered his flat on this occasion, and he happily stroked the animal's soft coat as he made his way to his desk.

The historian could hardly conceal his excitement as he reached into his pocket and placed the device on the desktop.

'Such a small object,' he marvelled while turning the metallic box in his hand.

'Let us hope that it can shed some light on the mysteries of the tablets.'

He pressed the dark red side of the box as instructed and then pointed the device at a blank wall opposite. Immediately, a blurred image appeared before him, which gradually cleared to reveal a stone tablet filled with the hieroglyphs of the ancient Martian alphabet. It was a three-dimensional image. Sep-lee rose from his desk and walked to one side in order to appreciate the true form of the tablet.

The monolith stood at about four feet tall and was a rusty-reddish colour. The symbols it contained covered the entire surface of the tablet, and some were worn and difficult to read. He knew that, by convention, there were four tablets in all, telling the story of those far-off events purported to have had such an impact on the Martian race.

Sep-lee settled back in his chair and started to examine the first tablet in detail. He was a renowned scholar of the ancient language, and as he began to interpret the symbols chiselled into the reddish stone some three thousand years ago, he started to take notes.

The first tablet seemed to tell of the lives of the Martians who lived in the Skothath region just before the monumental events took place.

'The people of the villages of Skothath lived a contented life, in peace and in harmony with their world,' he read.

'The gods provided a land of plenty. The rich soil produced abundant crops to feed the people, and hunger was unknown. They also provided lakes and rivers of the clearest, freshest water. The people tended their crops, looked after their livestock and gave thanks to the gods for their good fortune.'

*It sounds like a true paradise*, thought Sep-lee as he continued to read.

'The people were skilled, and made pots and jewellery of intricate design. They built homes of wood and stone, and traded with nearby villages. They understood the medicinal benefits of the plants growing in the fields and woods, and looked after the very old and the very young with true compassion. They studied the night sky, and could distinguish between stars and planets. The blue world, often shining bright in the sky, held a particular interest for them. It represented Eartana, the goddess of rain, the seas, rivers and lakes.'

This section of the story ended with the phrase, 'We are at one with nature, and take comfort in its grace.'

'Well,' said Sep-lee as he sat back in his chair and contemplated what he had just read. 'This paints a very rosy picture of rural life on Mars thousands of years ago. The people were relatively civilised, they understood basic science and medicine, could read and write, were socially developed, and were skilled farmers and artisans. Nothing so far to warrant hiding these tablets from public scrutiny.'

Taya, the pet purrdon, whistled gently as it stretched out its long tail on Sep-lee's desk, where it had taken up residence while he had been examining the tablet. The historian stroked the animal and turned back to the image projected onto the wall.

'Let's see what the next tablet holds, shall we?' he muttered, and pressed the device to reveal the second image.

As it came into focus, Sep-lee began to write his notes once again.

'The people of the villages of Skothath were celebrating a plentiful harvest. The last of the crops were being gathered as people sang the songs passed down through the ages while they worked.

'Suddenly, a bright light appeared in the sky above, brighter than the sun itself. The people stopped working and stood to stare at the vision before them. Some sank to their knees and prayed in response to this message sent from the gods. As to its meaning, they did not know. A wind blew up around them, even though the day had been calm and settled. The bright light moved slowly in the sky above and settled above the mountain of Rathkarn. It stayed silently in place for one whole day, providing such brilliance that even at night the people could see as clearly as if it were midday. The people gathered to discuss what the light meant, firmly believing it was a message from the gods themselves. Why they had been honoured in this way, they did not know, but they celebrated the arrival of the divine image with food and drink and sang their praises for being chosen in this way.

'After one full day, the light seemed to glow with even greater intensity for a brief time, before gradually descending from the sky, disappearing from view behind the peak of Mount Rathkarn. As it did so, the ground shook and the people became afraid. Then the wind suddenly dropped; all became calm once more.'

Sep-lee, quivering with excitement, carefully scanned the symbols etched into the stone tablet once again to make sure he had interpreted them correctly.

'Well,' he announced, looking at Taya as she curled her tail around his left arm, 'this is very interesting. It appears that the "ball of fire" mentioned in the official transcripts was instead a bright light, and rather than simply exploding behind some hills, it stayed in place for an entire day, before descending gradually to the ground. What natural phenomenon has the ability to hover in situ for such a time before landing in an apparently controlled manner? No, this implies that the light was not a natural occurrence at all, but was of artificial origin. But where did it come from, and why?'

By now the light was fading fast outside the flat, and people in the street below were hurriedly making their way home at the end of the working day.

Sep-lee stared momentarily at the bustling scene beneath him while he gathered his thoughts, before returning to the task of examining the tablets.

'Let's see the story unfold further, shall we?' he asked his pet purrdon rhetorically.

Taya stared at him with her large green eyes.

'Time for tablet number three.'

The image took shape as before, and the historian continued to read on.

'For three days after the light descended behind Mount Rathkarn, the people of the villages heard and saw nothing new. Continuing to work in their fields, they began to think that the gods had no further messages for them. Then, at the end of the third day, they were visited by messengers from the gods. A small group of three entities descended from the mountain and stood before the startled people. The entities were tall with burning red eyes. Their bodies glowed in the light of the setting sun; their faces featureless apart from those piercing eyes. The visitors said nothing, but pointed towards Rathkarn, at the exact spot where the light had descended three days ago.

'The people were afraid and did not know what was expected from them. Suddenly, one of the messengers moved forward and placed a hand on the shoulders of five villagers standing nearby, one at a time. The people selected were young men in the prime of their lives. They were all strong, tall and well built. As the entity placed its hand on each individual's shoulder, it pushed them forward towards the other two messengers.

'The entity then pointed once more at Mount Rathkarn and started to lead the five frightened men away from the village, without any explanation. The families of the chosen villagers were fearful. They did not understand why the gods had selected their sons, or where they were being taken. As the messengers departed, some people in the village began to cry.

'Gradually, the group ascended the side of the mountain, and were finally no longer visible. The remaining villagers returned to their homes and locked their doors tightly. They had no idea what would become of them in the days ahead, but the people were troubled. Sleep did not come easily to many on that fateful night.'

Sep-lee moved from his desk and went to pour himself a drink. Night had wrapped itself around the city outside, and the lights in his flat had switched themselves on, providing a warm glow to his study.

'So, the third tablet describes these entities as messengers from the gods, and not the gods themselves, as in the official transcript,' he summarised, before taking his drink back to his desk.

'And there is no mention in the official version of a group of villagers being taken from their families at this time. Why were these individuals selected, and for what reason?'

Sep-lee was even more convinced that these entities were not of a divine nature, and that the light itself was not a message from the gods. Still, the light must have come from somewhere, as must the creatures described in the tablets. As to their real intentions, the historian was none the wiser.

He felt his stomach rumble and realised that he hadn't eaten anything since breakfast. He contemplated making himself something to eat, but decided he would view the final tablet first. He could eat once he had got to the end of the story. The fourth tablet took shape, and once again Sep-lee started to take notes.

'The villagers tried to continue with their normal routines as best they could in the days that followed, but the people kept staring at Mount Rathkarn, worried that the messengers may return. Nothing more took place for a full week and then, one morning, three individuals were spotted descending from the mountain. As they got closer, the villagers could see that they were three of the youths taken by the messengers. As word was passed around the village of the men's return, a large crowd gathered and a huge cheer greeted their arrival. The families of the men rushed to meet them, taking their sons in their arms. The gods had been benevolent after all.

'However, it soon became apparent that those who returned seemed different to their families and friends. They had lost their energy and seemed pale and lethargic. Each had a reddish mark on their necks, and they kept staring at Mount Rathkarn, mumbling to themselves as they did so. They were unable or unwilling to say why the remaining two men taken by the messengers had not returned with them, or to explain what had happened to them during their absence. The men were taken back to their homes to rest, but within one day, two of them had died after a fitful sleep, and the third became incoherent and rambling after developing a raging fever.

'In the weeks ahead, more of the messengers descended onto the village, with more people taken from their families. Few of those selected were ever seen again, and those who did return suffered the same fate as the original three. Some died suddenly and others deteriorated in health so they became a burden to those who cared for them.

'Over time the village ceased to be a viable community. Crops remained unharvested and livestock died through lack of care and attention. Most of the strong and able had been taken by the messengers, and only the old or very young remained.

'In the end it was decided to abandon the village and try to set up a new home far away from Mount Rathkarn.'

Sep-lee read the final etchings on the stone tablet.

'This record of events is left for others to find in the future. Why the gods have treated us in this way we cannot say, but we have no choice but to leave our homes.'

The historian finished taking his notes and sat back in his chair, giving a deep sigh. *What really happened to those who were taken?* he pondered. *Why did some return, only to die or become ill? What happened to the others? Were the abductees subjected to some sort of experimentation and, if so, by whom?*

So many questions came to mind that Sep-lee felt he understood less now than he did before viewing the tablets. He was about to leave his desk and get something to eat when, by accident, his hand touched the red panel on the device. Suddenly, another image began to take shape on the wall, and he gasped as he saw another tablet come into focus.

'There's a fifth tablet,' he whispered, as all thought of food vanished in an instant.

# Chapter 11
# Lunch with Rel-do

Klop-tra reported the incident at Tellas through the official channels, and was promised that a squad of Imperial Guards would be despatched to the site as soon as possible. He sat down with Res-dor on a block of stone and surveyed the carnage around them.

'There's not much more we can do at the moment,' he said. 'We will have to wait until the guards arrive.'

'We won't be able to carry out any work on-site today either.'

The site manager added, 'I'll see if the builders can be transferred to another development.'

'Good idea,' Klop –tra agreed.

He did not want a day's pay for the construction workers to go to waste.

'Keep me informed,' he told Res-dor as he rose to return to his vehicle. 'We will also need to step up security at the other sites. I don't want a repeat of this vandalism anywhere else. Those damned insects may decide to attack again.'

Res-dor nodded.

'I'll look into it.'

Once back in the car, Klop-tra decided to continue on to the Windor village development as previously planned. *No point in wasting the entire day because of this setback*, he thought while driving off.

As the car moved across the rural landscape towards his new destination, he kept a lookout for any herds of Antis he could spot grazing in the fields.

'Perhaps the group who caused the damage to Tellas might still be in the area. If so, I'll let the authorities know, and they can send some Imperial Guards to wipe them out.'

The architect could feel the anger rising in him once again.

'These wretched creatures have cost us a great deal of money. They will live to regret what they have done – I guarantee it.'

His journey was uneventful, however, and he did not see a single Antis roaming the countryside. The sun had risen in a brilliant blue sky, with hardly a cloud to be seen. In fact, if it had not been for the traumatic events in Tellas, it would have been a very pleasant trip to the Outside. The vehicle soon reached Windor village, and Klop-tra parked near the Community Hall.

From what he had seen while driving through the streets, people seemed to be settling in nicely. Groups were standing talking, while others were shopping, and yet more were tending to their gardens, obviously proud of their new homes. Everywhere looked clean and well-kept and, although not yet completed, the village was already developing into quite a thriving community.

Klop-tra looked satisfied as he walked up the steps to the stone-built Community Hall to meet the new mayor of the settlement, a youngish man by the name of Stor-dal. The mayor was an enthusiastic and idealistic individual. He was totally committed to making the new village a success, and seemed popular with the new residents. He always made himself available to deal with any problems, however small, and he had quickly developed a reputation for hard work and getting things done. Klop-tra had met him a few times already, and even he was impressed with the "can-do" attitude of this local leader.

However, he was less keen on the young mayor's idealism. Stor-dal was determined to make Windor village a community which enhanced its rural setting, rather than simply being yet another blot on the landscape. He had insisted that tree-lined streets, parks and gardens would be a major feature of the village, with people encouraged to walk rather than drive whenever possible. To this end, a series of "green lane" walkways had been developed, joining the residential areas to the community, retail and employment sectors.

Klop-tra had no problem with any of this, but Stor-dal had also spoken about the need to try and instigate a dialogue with the insect Antis, in order to prove that the incomers wished to live in peace and were not a threat to the Antis way of life. The young mayor had even promised to set up a special reserve outside the village, where the insects could live in harmony with their Martian neighbours. Exactly how this "dialogue" would be accomplished was a matter for debate but, knowing Stor-dal, he would not rest until he had achieved his aim.

It was this particular passion of Stor-dal which Klop-tra was less enthusiastic about, at least until the village had been completed and all the residents had moved in. The architect had a lot of money tied up in the development, so the last thing he wanted was another Antis attack frightening off potential buyers and leaving properties unoccupied. This "touchy-feely" approach adopted by the mayor could lead to trouble, Klop-tra believed. If the insects realised that the Martian incomers were a soft touch, they may be tempted to make their claim on the area with another show of violence and destruction.

As he reached the entrance to the Community Hall, Klop-tra was met by the young mayor, who greeted him enthusiastically.

'Welcome back,' said Stor-dal. 'I saw you coming and thought you would probably want a tour of our little community. Refreshments first, perhaps?'

The architect shook hands with the younger man and declined the offer.

'No, I'm fine at the moment. Let's defer the drink until after the tour. I'm keen to see how things are bedding down.'

'Oh, I think you will be pleased with what you see.'

Stor-dal beamed jovially.

'People seem to have settled in well so far. We have a number of firms moving into the village already, and others are expressing interest, which is always a good sign. The school is open, and the medical centre, too.'

Klop-tra nodded as the mayor led them through the village centre.

'You seem to be doing a good job ensuring all is running smoothly. Have there been any problems with the new housing?'

'Not really,' replied Stor-dal, basking in the architect's compliment. 'A few snags here and there, but nothing major. The odd window not opening properly and a few settlement cracks appearing. The things you would normally expect in any new development. Our on-site team sorts them out without any problem.'

'What about the Antis?' asked Klop-tra.

'Any problems with them?'

'No, nothing like that,' the mayor assured him.

'We don't foresee any issues with our neighbours. We are keen to prove that we are not a threat to them and want to live in peace. That's a key part of our ethos here.'

'You need to be careful,' warned the architect. 'There has just been an Antis attack at the Tellas site. They demolished everything, and could try the same here.'

The mayor shook his head violently.

'Absolutely not,' he said forcefully. 'It won't happen here. For one thing, the Tellas development has no residents yet. It's just a building site. They probably see it as fair game. I don't think the Antis would try and attack a thriving community like ours. Also, we are much smaller than Tellas, and less of a threat to them. We've also gone out of our way to push the "good neighbour" message. As you know, we are establishing a large reserve just outside the village. Not wasteland, but good-quality grazing land for the Antis. They can set up home with no interference from us.'

'You sound confident,' said Klop-tra, sounding unconvinced. 'You have no proof that your neighbourliness will be reciprocated by the insects. This village is still built on open land, which they may see as belonging to them. I can't see them turning up with a bottle of wine and bunch of flowers to welcome you to the area. Just be careful, and make sure that your defences are operating properly. Do you check your plasma field regularly?'

'Yes, of course we do,' replied the mayor, a sense of irritation creeping into his voice. 'We're not idiots. We do take the welfare of our residents seriously. It's just that we don't want to make a big issue out of security. People living here are not living in a prison, or even a gated community. Too many barriers will frighten people off.'

Klop-tra shrugged his shoulders.

'Let's continue with the tour, shall we? I'm sure there's a lot more to see.'

The architect's remaining time in Windor village was fairly uneventful. The last few housing developments were taking shape and the two men chatted to the builders, who assured them that the houses would be ready for their new occupants on time. The village centre was a hive of activity, with some shops already open and others with signs in their windows proudly announcing that they would be "open for business soon".

The landscaping in the village gave a pleasant rural feel to the new settlement. There were parks, gardens and tree-lined streets, and even a sizeable pond near the temple. Local birdlife was already making good use of the facility, with a group of dark blue sennats enjoying the sunshine on the calm waters of the new lake.

Expressing his satisfaction with the village, Klop-tra was led back to the Community Hall by the mayor, who was clearly delighted with this positive reaction to his hard work. After a quick drink in the mayor's office, the architect took his leave following a final warning to Stor-dal to "be careful and don't take chances". He returned to his parked vehicle and checked the time on his wristband. He should be in time to meet up with Rel-do for his lunchtime appointment.

The solicitor had made a booking back in the city at Belos, a favourite venue for business lunches, not too far from the city gate. *I'll need to be careful not to overindulge*, Klop-tra reminded himself. *I must go back into the office afterwards, and I still have two other site meetings this afternoon before meeting my dear wife for dinner.*

He was well aware of the fact that his solicitor friend was a passionate advocate of the "leisurely lunch", believing that the best business decisions were made over a good meal and a bottle or two of delicious wine. Unfortunately, Klop-tra did not have the time for such luxuries today.

On arrival at the restaurant, he found that Rel-do was already seated at a table with a glass of wine in front of him. By the look of the near-empty bottle by his side, he had been there some time. The table was situated next to a large picture window, with extensive views of the flora outside. In particular, there was a small copse of banyar trees, with their leathery dark green bark.

These trees were amongst the strangest plant life on Mars. In fact, it was believed that the trees were a sort of hybrid between plant and animal. They had no leaves, but long, trunk-like branches which moved like a nest of snakes, writhing above the central body of the tree. The branches were similar to the trunks of elephants, completely flexible, and moving blindly in the warm air, hoping to catch tiny insects that ventured too close. If they were successful, the squirming branches would suck up the unfortunate insects, curling up to transfer the morsels of food back to the centre of the tree. If you listened carefully, you could even hear a satisfied sighing noise coming from the tree as it relished each new titbit. Legends even said that if the trees had exhausted the food supply in their area, they could lift their roots from the ground and slowly move to a more bountiful location. However, there was no hard evidence of this happening, and many dismissed the claim as mere conjecture.

Klop-tra shook hands with Rel-do and sat down. Menus were brought by an attentive waiter and pre-lunch drinks were ordered. Rel-do quickly emptied his glass and ordered a large flute of the locally produced vishto wine. His guest opted for a non-alcoholic drink, pleading that he had site visits on his agenda for the afternoon.

As they waited for their drinks to arrive, Klop-tra informed the solicitor of the morning's events, particularly focusing on the Antis attack on the Tellas development.

'Those bloody insects,' boomed Rel-do, his face reddening by the second. 'This time they have gone too far. All the pussyfooting around, trying to appease these creatures, has got us nowhere. It's time for some direct action. Otherwise, our profits will suffer – you mark my words.'

'The authorities have promised to send a contingent of Imperial Guards to examine the site,' replied Klop-tra, scanning the menu before making his choice. 'Although I'm not sure what they can do now,' he added.

'Round up the lot of them and blast them to eternity,' was his companion's helpful suggestion.

'They won't try anything like that again.'

'Ideally I would agree with you,' said the architect, finally deciding on his selection of dishes. 'However, I think it is highly unlikely such a response will gain support from the powers that be. You also need to remember that the Antis have their supporters in the city, and even in the new towns and villages. I've just been talking with the mayor of Windor village, who is totally opposed to any action against the Antis. He's all for mutual respect and peaceful coexistence. There are a growing number who think like him.'

A dish of savoury nibbles appeared on the table, together with the drinks. Klop-tra took a handful of wriggling weally grubs and popped them into his mouth, savouring the smoked meaty flavour as they dissolved on his tongue.

'Nonsense,' replied Rel-do, taking a large swig from his glass of chilled vishto wine. 'If we don't hit back soon, they will gain in confidence, and we could face further attacks elsewhere. I certainly don't want these damned creatures causing trouble in the Bolan Plain project. It's all going well at the moment, but if those insects interfere, the whole development could be delayed. Time is money.'

The two men stopped their conversation in order to give the waiter their orders. Rel-do chose a large dish of seema fish, a meaty, pink-fleshed creature, freshly caught in one of the large lakes outside the city. Klop-tra, mindful of his gut-busting meal to come at Marla's that evening, chose a salad with a small selection of local cheeses. Both chose vishto wine to accompany the meal, a large glass for Rel-do and a small one for Klop-tra.

'Well, let's see what the authorities conclude after the guards descend on Tellas,' said the architect, finishing the last of the weally grubs. 'I'll keep you informed.'

In the time it had taken Klop-tra to empty the bowl of tasty titbits, Rel-do had finished his first glass of vishto and had drained the rest of the bottle he had bought while waiting for his guest.

'It will all end in disaster if we don't retaliate firmly,' warned the solicitor. 'These Antis lovers make me sick.'

With that, he gave a large burp, and then eagerly eyed up the new glass of wine which the waiter had just deposited by his side, together with his steaming bowl of seema fish.

The two men tucked into their meal and moved the discussion on to other business matters of mutual interest. After the lunch ended with a large bowl of mixed fruits, which they shared, Klop-tra glanced at his wristband and realised that he had to take his leave. Rel-do was still in full swing, his tonsils by now well lubricated. Having ordered yet another bottle of wine, he was well into his second glass when Klop-tra made his excuses. The architect had business to attend to this afternoon, even if his friend was obviously in no rush to go anywhere. He offered to pay for his share of the lunch, but Rel-do waved him away.

'No, no, this is on me,' he announced, pouring his third glass from the new bottle. 'You can pick up the tab next time.'

The pair shook hands, although, sensibly, Rel-do did not attempt to stand up.

Just as Klop-tra was leaving the restaurant, he received a call on his wristband. It was Res-dor, the site manager at the Tellas development.

'Bad news, I'm afraid,' he reported, glumly. 'The authorities aren't going to send any Imperial Guards to examine the mess left by the Antis after all. They say it's our fault for not securing the site properly. That's rubbish, of course, as the security devices were working normally when we all left the previous evening. I can't understand it.'

'But they can't do that,' Klop-tra spluttered. 'A crime has been committed, and it's their duty to investigate it.'

'They're adamant they won't get involved,' replied the site manager. 'I don't see what more we can do.'

Klop-tra ended the call, promising to call back when he had more time to think through their options. *If the Imperial Guards won't protect us against the Antis, who will?* he thought while walking back to his car.

# Chapter 12
# First Day on Mars

Tom Fisher opened his eyes in the darkness, temporarily forgetting where he was. Then the truth dawned on him. He was waking up to his first morning on planet Mars. The sun would be rising soon, so he decided to quickly wash and dress and go out to the observation deck to watch his first Martian sunrise. Each accommodation pod had its own small shower cubicle, barely large enough to fit a reasonably well-built man like Tom, but sufficient for the purpose.

*God knows how Rob fits in his cubicle*, thought the astrophysicist as he showered in the hot water. *He must shower in stages.* He walked towards the kitchen, trying to be as quiet as possible so as not to wake the others. *We have a busy day ahead of us. Let them sleep in a bit on their first day.* He quickly poured himself a steaming mug of tea and wandered over to the observation deck.

Tom pressed a button to retract the night shield, which protected the viewing screen from any dust storms during the hours of darkness. As he looked out at the Martian landscape, he noticed an icy fog beginning to lift as the sun started to appear above the horizon. Although they had landed near the equator of Mars, and it was summer at their location, night-time temperatures could fall to about -75 degrees Celsius, rising to a balmy high of around plus 20 degrees at midday. As the sun continued to rise, the sky began to take on a rose-coloured hue, turning to a bluish colour surrounding the sun itself. As the sky lightened and the mist dispersed, he could see patches of frost on the rocks. These would quickly turn to vapour as the air warmed up with the approaching dawn.

Tom heard a noise behind him. He turned to see the New Zealand astrobiologist, Angela, approaching.

'I thought I heard someone moving around,' she said with a slight yawn. 'I thought we had mice!'

'Sorry to wake you.'

Tom apologised.

'I just had to see my first Martian dawn. It's quite something.'

Angela moved beside him and drank in the view.

'We are so lucky to be able to experience this,' she whispered. 'The first humans to land on Mars, and about sixty million miles from home. Unbelievable!'

Just then, Tom saw something over to his left.

'Look at that.'

He gasped, pointing frantically.

'Is that a puddle of water?'

Angela looked at the spot where Tom was indicating and laughed out loud.

'Oh yes, I think you're right. People have argued that as the frost melts in the warming air, water could condense in the early morning to form puddles. It will only be short-term, as the liquid will vaporise very soon in the thin atmosphere.'

'Well, here's the evidence,' said Tom excitedly. 'I'll need to add this to my first daily report. Should get the boffins in a spin back home. Doesn't that make the chances of finding life here much improved?' he asked, thinking about the consequences of discovering liquid water on the surface.

'It could do,' acknowledged the astrobiologist. 'The air pressure outside is equivalent to about twenty-eight miles up from the ground on Earth. Some have said that conditions on Mars are similar to the Atacama Desert in Chile, where life certainly exists. Tests have also shown that some kinds of Antarctic lichens can adapt to the Martian environment. We've found no evidence of this so far from the unmanned probes, but I certainly aim to try and find my first Martian daffodil if I can!'

Tom smiled.

'One big difference, though, is the harmful solar radiation. On Earth, we are protected because of the magnetic field, which doesn't exist on Mars. Goodness knows how anything could survive out there long-term, being constantly bombarded with heaven knows what. Would any life have had time to adapt to changing conditions on Mars? '

Angela shrugged.

'Who knows? On Earth, life is found just about everywhere, even in the harshest conditions. Once established, life tends to fight for survival. Perhaps the same is true here.'

Just then, they were interrupted by the sound of footsteps behind them. Jason, the Canadian medic, and Frances, the Australian chemist, walked towards them holding mugs of coffee.

'Thought we'd join you to welcome the new day,' said Frances, jauntily.

'Well, come and have a look,' urged Tom. 'It's certainly worth getting up early for.'

Within a few minutes, the rest of the crew had arrived at the observation deck, and Tom and Angela explained what they had witnessed so far.

'A real puddle on the surface of Mars,' repeated Robert. 'Perhaps I can go for a swim after all!'

By now, the sky was brightening rapidly, turning a rich butterscotch colour, with just a few wispy clouds above the horizon.

'I suggest we have breakfast and go through our work schedules for the day,' said Tom. 'You should all have received your detailed instructions for today by now.'

The others all nodded.

'They came through during the night,' added Martin, the Scottish engineer.

'Top of my agenda is to examine Mars Prospector and see what all the excitement is about.'

'I think we are all scheduled to go out to the probe,' agreed Tom.

'They want confirmation from all of us as to what Mars Prospector has found.'

'I can't wait to try out the spacesuits on the surface,' said Frances, her eyes turning to the panorama of rocks and dusty soil outside the craft.

The team had gone through extensive testing of the suits before the mission, including numerous EVAs on the even harsher surface of the Moon. The suits were not ideally suited to the extreme lunar conditions, where there is no atmosphere at all, and the gravitational force is even less than on Mars. The reasoning behind the tests, however, was that if the astronauts could cope with the Moon, things should be a lot easier when it came to working in the marginally kinder Martian environment.

The crew chose their selection of meals for breakfast and took their seats around the communal table. Most opted for a mixture of dried fruits, cereals and yogurt substitute, but Robert pleaded that he was ravenous, so chose the nearest he could get to a full English. The ingredients didn't look very appetising on his plate, being a combination of reconstituted egg, sausage and bacon, but the geologist did admit it tasted better than it looked.

Once they had finished their breakfasts and cleared away, they went over the arrangements one more time for their first excursion on Mars. The initial stage was to be beamed back to Earth and the Moon, where billions of people were eagerly anticipating the first views of humans walking on the surface of another planet.

Tom, as head of the crew, had to make a short statement to the waiting world back home as he stepped onto the stony ground, and there would be recordings of the astronauts as they pointed out features of interest to their eager audience. It was intended that all members of the mission would be involved in sending back messages to the viewers, explaining the different tests and experiments they were carrying out.

The authorities wanted to make this Mars mission as interesting and relevant as possible to the general public. The aim was to whip up a great deal of enthusiasm for the venture so as to build support for future trips.

Everyone was aware of the old Apollo Moon mission in the late 1960s and 1970s. Initially, people were glued to their television sets as the grainy images from the lunar surface were beamed into homes across the planet. However, this initial interest waned with later missions, and eventually the project was cancelled after Apollo 17.

This time the idea was to attract as many people as possible to the Mars expedition. Due to the enormous advances in technology, people no longer had to be tied to their armchairs watching television in order to get involved with what was happening on Mars. Members of the public could send messages to individual members of the crew, and they could also use three-dimensional goggles to experience the Martian surface for themselves, wherever they may be. Daily updates from Mars could be accessed by anyone at any time, whether at home of an evening, travelling to work or during their daily breaks.

However, there would be no public access to the reconnaissance with the Mars Prospector rover. The consequences of what had been discovered, once confirmed, would have to be seriously considered by the relevant authorities before deciding what, if anything, to put in the public domain.

The crew of New Endeavour moved towards the exit chamber, nicknamed the Robing Room, to put on their spacesuits, chatting to each other as they walked. They all felt a mixture of excitement and apprehension to varying degrees, but didn't want to admit that they were in any way nervous to their teammates. They had all prepared for this moment for many months, and now the time had finally arrived.

Jason, the team medic, was well aware of what everyone, including himself, actually felt. As they prepared to disembark, he kept a watchful eye on the crew members for any signs of panic which might prove fateful once outside.

The spacesuits were lined up in front of them, like a group of medieval knights waiting for the signal to charge. They were all a deep grey colour, but with bands of colour on the arms and legs. Each astronaut had a different band colour in order to make it easy to recognise who was who on the Martian surface. Tom moved behind his suit, which had bright blue embellishments.

The material used was incredibly tough but lightweight and flexible, making the suit much easier to work in than the old Apollo versions. Although the gravity on Mars was much stronger than on the Moon, being roughly one third of Earth's, the suits did have to cope with the potentially lethal doses of radiation along with the chemically reactive dust on the surface. The suits also had bubble-like helmets, with the visors featuring a wide field of view, offering near normal vision for the wearer when operating outside.

On the back of each spacesuit was an entry hatch, resembling a large backpack that walkers on Earth might wear. Each astronaut climbed into their suit from the back via the hatch, meaning that the suit was in effect a personally tailored mini spaceship. Once inside, an astronaut could make final adjustments using voice-enabled technology, including fine-tuning the integral life support system. This had an inbuilt carbon dioxide removal device, which operated continually once outside New Endeavour, where the rate of extraction would be synchronised to the astronaut's individual breathing pattern.

The crew all climbed into their suits, and then signalled that they were ready to disembark. Tom checked all the suits were fitting properly, and Martin carried out the same checks on him. Once completed, Tom gave the thumbs up signal and they moved in line towards the first of the two airlocks. Tom and Martin both pressed a pad either side of the hatch simultaneously in order to release the first airlock. The same procedure was adopted with the second hatch, after which the metal door drew back revealing the stark beauty of planet Mars. Frances looked at Robert, who gave her a reassuring smile.

Tom was first to descend, using the steps which had extended once the second hatch had been released. As his foot touched the surface, a cloud of dust rose into the thin Martian atmosphere. He was soon followed by the others, who made a semicircle, with Tom at the centre. When all was ready, the head of mission made his introductory comments, using the words he had been practising since they'd arrived.

'We arrive as emissaries from the blue planet to the red. Not to conquer, but to learn. We come in peace for all mankind.'

The last sentence of his message was borrowed from the stainless-steel commemorative plaque, which had been taken to the Moon by the first manned Apollo landing in July 1969. The plaque had been attached to the ladder of the descent module, and had been followed by similar plaques on the remaining missions. In fact, the phrase "we come in peace for all mankind" was itself derived from the 1958 National Aeronautics and Space Act's Declaration of Policy and Purpose. This was the United States Federal Statute that created NASA, and had been signed by President Dwight D. Eisenhower, ushering in the age of space exploration. Tom thought it appropriate to reuse the phrase, as a symbol of the continued progress of mankind as it ventured further out into the solar system.

He then introduced each member of the crew to the public watching these historic events back home on Earth and on the lunar bases. He asked each person to explain a bit about themselves and to give an indication of the work they would be carrying out while on Mars.

Martin explained how he would be concentrating on the Mars Prospector probe, trying to get it back into working order, and his responsibilities concerning the efficient running of the systems on New Endeavour. Angela told of her search for life on, or more likely underneath, the surface of Mars, where simple life forms would be protected from the harmful radiation. She also mentioned the discovery of the liquid water puddle earlier in the day and how this could improve the chances of finding living organisms. Angela had reported this find to mission control before they left the spacecraft, and she had been given the go-ahead to mention it in her first public broadcast. Finding life on the Red Planet was still the public's main interest, so anything that caught their attention was likely to boost viewing figures back home.

Jason explained his duties as medic for the expedition and the importance of proper exercise while the crew were living in a low-gravity environment. He even promised to share some of the exercises with the public so they could practise at home what the crew were experiencing on Mars. Robert and Frances pointed out the rocky nature of the Martian landscape and explained how they would be examining samples from different areas to try and learn about the events from the past which had shaped the Mars of today. They told how the planet was once much warmer and wetter than now, with rivers, lakes and even seas, and explained that Mars also had a much thicker atmosphere earlier in its history. These more favourable conditions, they suggested, could have been suitable for some forms of life to develop.

Tom mentioned that he was an astrophysicist by training and that, as well as his head of mission duties, he would also be studying the orbits of the tiny Martian moons of Phobos and Deimos. It was thought that they could have been asteroids, captured into Mars's orbit at some stage in the planet's past. Phobos in particular had a very odd orbit, travelling around its mother world three times a day.

Once the team had finished their introductory comments, Tom closed the session by promising that future broadcasts would give those watching a detailed picture of their work on Mars, with tours of New Endeavour and plenty of views of the fascinating Martian surface. One thing none of the crew mentioned was their quest to find what Mars Prospector had actually discovered while digging just below the dusty surface.

The probe was only a few hundred yards from where their spacecraft had landed, so once public transmissions had ended, the team set off to carry out a preliminary rendezvous with the unmanned vehicle.

By now, the sun was well above the horizon and the temperature was starting to rise. At this time of the year, at their location, the outside temperature could climb above freezing to a maximum of about 20 degrees Celsius, positively balmy by Martian standards. The earlier frosts had disappeared, and the puddle of water spotted by Tom and Angela at the observation deck had completely vaporised long ago. She had noted its location, however, and aimed to take samples to examine in the laboratory later on. The adage "where there's water there's life" made her quite excited about her forthcoming work on the supposedly barren Martian surface.

Walking on Mars was much easier than on the Moon and the greater flexibility provided by the new spacesuits made the whole process more enjoyable. All around the group, the landscape of rocks and dust spread out into the far distance. The horizon was marked by a range of low-lying hills, and a few wisps of cloud provided the only interruption to the otherwise endless expanse of butterscotch-coloured sky.

They could see the probe clearly in the distance and, as they approached the rover, they could start to make out details on its body.

'It looks to be covered in sand,' said Martin. 'No wonder it's not working properly. Its solar panels must be almost useless.'

The craft looked tiny, being no larger than a small bath. Its solar panels were outstretched, as they should have been, but were caked in the gritty Martian sand. At one end of the body a metallic arm was extended, like the trunk of a frozen elephant. At the far end of the arm was a claw-like appendage, which had been digging beneath the surface before the vehicle stopped functioning. The last images that reached mission headquarters had shown the arm picking up a rock which seemed to contain something unusual. It was difficult to make out what, but it had certainly stirred up immense interest; hence, the reason why New Endeavour had been despatched to Mars earlier than originally planned. It was also the reason for the naming of the mission as "MARS mission". In this case, the name did not relate to the destination itself but, unknown even to the crew, it was an acronym for Martian Artefact Retrieval Sortie.

Robert knelt down by the arm of Mars Prospector and peered at the rock still held firmly in the vice-like grip of the metallic claw. At first glance, it looked much like any other rock, but then he noticed something glinting in the mid-morning sunlight. He carefully eased the rock from the claw and stood up to show the others.

'There's definitely something lodged in here. I can't make out what it is, though.'

Gingerly, he moved the small object, trying to dislodge it from the crumbly rock in which it was encased. Suddenly, he let out a gasp, as the real reason for their journey across space broke free and revealed itself.

'It's a ring,' he announced to the stunned group of astronauts watching him. 'It's a bloody gold ring.'

As he turned the piece of jewellery in his hand, they could all see that it was indeed a square-topped gold ring, with a row of what looked like diamonds across its centre.

# Chapter 13
# The Fifth Tablet

Sep-lee sat back in his chair and started to interpret the symbols on the just discovered fifth tablet. The etchings were not as clear and distinct as on the other four, as if this final message was made in haste. He read the following.

'The people prepared to leave their homes for the last time, taking only what they could carry. As final preparations were being completed, two men were seen running from the summit of Mount Rathkarn towards the village.

'They arrived in a dishevelled state, with fear etched onto their faces. They were shivering, even though the weather was warm and sunny. The two men were helped by the villagers and offered food and water. The food was declined, but they drank huge quantities of water, as though they had not quenched their thirst in days.

'One of the men started to speak at great speed, his eyes never moving from the mountain from which he had just descended. Great terror could be seen in his eyes and as he spoke, tears ran down his cheeks as his story unfolded. The men had been taken earlier from the village by the messengers of the gods, dragged from the fields where they had both been tending their animals. They were taken across the mountain in silence, and thereafter reached a huge golden pyramid, where the gods had first arrived after their journey from the heavens.

'Inside the house of the gods, they were lined up with others, where they awaited their fate to be revealed. Suddenly, what appeared before them was not a god, but a devil of hideous countenance. The group of people cried out in fear, and some tried to escape. The messengers of the gods, or more correctly the demons from hell, moved to quell the disturbance. The narrator of the story and his friend, who were positioned at the back of the group, took the opportunity to escape amongst the ensuing chaos and ran away, hearing the terrible screams of the poor unfortunates who met their end in a most cruel and agonising manner. The two men managed to leave the place of terror; they did not stop running until they reached the village.

'Their captors will return to punish them both, along with others who harbour them in any way. We will all perish, not at the hands of the gods, but by the creatures of damnation who have arrived to plague our world. May the true gods take pity on us all and protect us from the nightmares to come.'

Sep-lee could not move from his chair. He sat at his desk staring at the image of the fifth tablet still projected onto his wall. He read through his notes again and checked the symbols inscribed onto the stone. It was often difficult to interpret exactly the meaning of the symbols used in the ancient Martian writings. The hieroglyphs did not correspond to individual words but their positions in a sentence, and their relationship to symbols both before and after gave expression to what the narrator really wanted to say. A few symbols could be interpreted by an expert like Sep-lee to give the same meaning as many sentences in modern-day writing.

He was happy that his translation appeared sound and was about to switch off the device, when it occurred to him that there may be a sixth tablet waiting to be discovered. However, this time he was unlucky. No further images appeared, so he was confident that he had gained access to all there was to see.

*We will probably never know what happened to the remaining villagers, or to the poor prisoners trapped in that pyramid of gold*, thought Sep-lee. As he mentally revisited the story as told on the tablets, he tried to summarise what he had read and give a scientific explanation to what had really happened all those centuries ago.

*It appears that this planet was visited by otherworldly beings, who landed their craft in the shape of a pyramid beyond Mount Rathkarn. They despatched servants, "the messengers of the gods", to kidnap the local inhabitants and return them to whoever or whatever controlled the spaceship.* Sep-lee rose from his chair and walked towards the large window as he continued his train of thought. *I assume that the "devils of hideous countenance" were the true masters of the alien force and, as the captives tried to escape their unknown destiny, the servant creatures moved in to stop them. What horrors awaited the villagers, we do not know, but there was obviously some reason for the capture of so many young and strong men from the village.*

Sep-lee stared at the throngs of people in the street below, oblivious to anything he had just discovered while busying themselves with the largely mundane routines of their daily lives.

*My real concern*, concluded the historian, as he turned back towards his desk, *is what this means for us all today. What are the consequences of these events for our current population? Did the alien ship leave the planet – and if so, did it or others like it return? Are we still being visited today?*

There were so many unanswered questions; Sep-lee did not know what to do next. He was not supposed to have seen the tablets, which were imperial property. He could hardly openly discuss his findings with anyone else, or they might both end up in great danger. On the other hand, he could not keep his discoveries a secret, as the story may have direct relevance to the population at large. *Surely people have a right to know about their past,* he thought, *and what it might mean for them both today and in the future. The Martian people are generally well educated and, even if many appear a bit naïve about some issues, they are not children. No one has the right to drip-feed the populace only with information deemed acceptable for public consumption.*

'What do you think I should do?' he asked Taya, who merely whistled at her owner, and then yawned as if bored with the whole topic of conversation.

# Chapter 14
# Inside the Palace

Aka-des could not move. The dreadful shrieking had stopped, but the sound echoed around the gloomy chamber in which he now found himself. As his eyes became accustomed to the semi-darkness, he realised he was in a small room with stone walls which was completely empty. Apart from the window he had just climbed through, the only other feature of the room was a door in one corner. He gradually regained his composure and his legs eventually agreed to move, although shakily at first.

All was now quiet again, so the young man moved towards the door. He realised there was a dampness in the chamber, as well as a disconcertingly musty smell. Not what you would expect from an imperial palace.

*Perhaps this part of the compound isn't used any more*, he reasoned. *No doubt things will improve as I move further towards the action.* Luckily, the door was unlocked. He crept into a corridor outside before quietly closing the door behind him.

*Which way now?* He pondered, before deciding to turn left. Slowly, he inched along the corridor keeping as close as he could to the walls.

There was some dim lighting in the ceiling, but still an aura of gloom enveloped him as he made his way further into the compound. The complex was a maze, and Aka-des lost count of the turns he made, moving from one corridor to the next.

*If I'm discovered now, there's no way I can escape*, he realised. *I haven't a clue where I am, and all these corridors look the same. And where is everyone? The place is deserted.* As he wound his way through the dimly lit passageways, he eventually noticed that the stone walls he had encountered so far were now replaced with walls of metal, cold to the touch. They were completely featureless, apart from the feeble glow from the lights in the ceiling marking his way. He also noted that the walls were now sloping at an angle.

Suddenly, he heard footsteps in front of him, and he just managed to press his body into the shadows as two Imperial Guards emerged from an adjoining corridor and marched past. They appeared to be carrying a large bowl of glass between them, like an enormous goldfish bowl, filled with murky-looking liquid. The container must have been about four feet across, but the guards seemed to carry its huge weight with ease. *How can two people carry something so heavy?* thought Aka-des in awe. *These guards must have superhuman strength. What do they feed them here?*

As the metallic *clomp, clomp* of the guards' feet faded into the distance, Aka-des turned into the corridor from which the guards had appeared. He crept along even further, and then noticed a large glass window on the right-hand side. He peered through, but all he could see was the same murky liquid as in the glass bowl.

*Odd*, thought Aka-des. *I seem to be looking into a huge tank of some sort. I wonder what they keep in here.* He then suddenly sensed the awful vinegary fishy smell, which he had noticed previously, becoming much stronger, so he tried to hold his breath.

'By the gods, what a stink,' he whispered. 'Whatever is it in there?'

As he continued to peer into the tank, he thought he could make out shapes moving in the liquid. They were indistinct, but there seemed to be a number of creatures of some sort swimming slowly through the murk. They appeared to be large, with a somewhat bulbous outline; but apart from that, he could not tell. Just then, something slapped against the glass, only inches from the startled Aka-des's head. He jumped back in alarm, as what looked like a tentacle slithered back into the gloom.

The youth had to stop himself from crying out aloud as he rushed from the corridor in a panic. He blindly ran for what seemed like an age, but was in fact no more than a matter of seconds, before he arrived at a second window looking into another large chamber.

Gingerly, he peered into the room beyond and was surprised to see rows of Imperial Guards standing to attention, probably more than one hundred in total. He watched for a few minutes, unsure whether to make a hasty retreat in case he was spotted. As he continued to look into the room, he realised that none of the guards were moving. They stood like statues, completely motionless, with no signs of life whatsoever. With a start, he then noticed that a group of guards in one corner of the huge room, standing apart from the others, had parts of their bodies missing. Some were missing hands, or even entire arms, and a few even lacked a head. Aka-des stared open-mouthed, unable to tear himself away from the macabre sight of these limbless metal giants.

Suddenly, a door at the back of the chamber slid open and two guards marched in, one of them carrying a metallic object in his hands. Aka-des couldn't make out what the object was, but then he saw the guard unceremoniously lock it into place onto the neck of one of the guards lacking a head. They were replacing the missing body part of one of their immobile comrades. The other guard who had entered the room then pressed a pad located on the arm of the now complete soldier. Immediately, the metallic body sprang to life.

'They're robots!' whispered Aka-des. 'The Imperial Guards aren't men in armour at all.'

The reality of the situation then dawned on him.

'If the guards are robots, what happens to all the people who are selected to join their ranks each year? Where do they go?'

He didn't really want to think about the consequences of his discovery as he thought about his friend Beta-vac.

*I've seen no people at all since I arrived here*, he realised. *I must try and find Beta-vac before it's too late. The more I see of this place, the less I like it. Something very odd is going on here, in the name of our "dear" emperor.*

At that point, the two guards who had entered the room, together with their newly completed and reactivated comrade, turned and left the chamber, the door closing behind them.

*The reason this lot aren't moving*, surmised Aka-des, still staring at the rows of silent sentinels in the room, *is that they haven't been activated yet. They are simply waiting until they are needed.* The young man shuddered, and then turned back into the corridor. *If I stay here much longer, I'm going to be found. If that happens, I'm done for. I don't think whoever is in charge here will take too kindly to a member of the public sneaking into the imperial compound in the back of a van and finding out what actually goes on here out of the public gaze. They are hardly likely to offer me food and drink before waving me off. If I'm discovered, that's it.*

He remembered the dream he'd had the previous night, when he was brought before the emperor after being found in the palace grounds. The words the divine leader had hissed at him ran through his mind once again.

'Death to those who defy my rules. Death to those who defy me.'

Determined to try and save his friend, but with no real plan to follow, he decided to continue following the corridor to see where it led. *Surely, I must be getting nearer the heart of this place by now*, he mused. *If there are people to be found, I must come across them sooner or later.*

Then Aka-des heard a swishing sound and another door slid open in front of him. He managed to slip into a narrow alcove, out of sight, and peered out to see what was happening.

He was overjoyed to see three men being led from a room, still dressed in the flowing white robes of a novitiate. He couldn't make out their features, as they were facing away from him, but the fact that they were still alive gave him hope. The three recruits were herded forward by a pair of Imperial Guards, or robots as Aka-des had now discovered their true identity to be.

*I wonder where they are being taken,* he pondered. *I'll try and follow them. They may lead me to others who have just joined up. Perhaps I might even find Beta-vac.*

The three young men in their white robes were marched along one corridor, and then down another, before arriving at an enormous door of what looked like pure gold. Above the door was the sunburst symbol of imperial authority.

*Perhaps they're about to meet the emperor*, concluded Aka-des, a strange feeling of dread passing over him as he again smelt the dreadful mix of putrid fish and vinegar. The smell seemed to be coming from the vicinity of the golden door.

The huge door swung open and the three novitiates were led into the room by the Imperial Guards. For some reason the door did not close behind them.

*Perhaps they're expecting more recruits to join them*, thought Aka-des as he crept nearer to the open door. He peered through the opening and saw a large chamber inside with sumptuous decorations in mainly gold and white, in stark contrast to the plain metallic walls of the corridors he had passed through so far.

There were a dozen men lined up in rows of three, all facing a stage on the far side of the chamber. On the stage was a large dish-shaped structure, similar to the one at the Emperor's Day parade, topped with a canopy emblazoned with symbols of imperial power.

*They're obviously here to meet the emperor*, concluded Aka-des. *Perhaps they will even finally get to see what he really looks like. And so will I.*

Aka-des remembered the image of the emperor in his dream. A tall, handsome, well-built individual dressed in a suit of gold mesh and wearing a mitre covered in diamonds. *I wonder if the reality will match the image?* he asked himself while still considering what would happen if he was now caught red-handed in the seat of imperial authority. The words the emperor had spoken to him in the dream, as those piercing blood-red eyes penetrated his very soul, returned to haunt him.

Aka-des moved silently into the chamber and crept down behind one of the huge pillars situated around the edge of the room. He noticed that the novitiates, all dressed in the same white robes, did not appear to be very excited about the prospect of meeting the god king. In fact, most had their heads down with their chins almost touching their chests.

*Surely, they can't be asleep, can they?* thought Aka-des in disbelief. *It's not the sort of image you want to present to your divine emperor.*

A few of the men did seem more animated than the rest, but they gave the impression of being more nervous than excited, their eyes darting around the room fearfully waiting for something to happen. There were six Imperial Guards hemming in the group of twelve, three on each side. Aka-des even though he heard one of the white-robed youths start to whimper, and a chill passed through his own body as he tried to remain hidden behind the ornate pillar at the back of the chamber.

Suddenly, part of the rear wall of the room, behind the stage, slid back and the brilliant imperial orb moved silently to take its place above the dish-shaped structure, under the canopy of white and gold. All twelve novitiates stood to attention in unison, even those who had previously looked to be asleep, and they stared in awe at the imperial presence before them.

The orb did not move, but Aka-des got the distinct impression that the twelve men were being watched by whoever was sitting inside it. He then felt a faint tingling sensation in his neck, which turned into a dull throbbing. He clutched at his neck with his hand, and saw that most of the novitiates were doing the same thing. Some of them started to look sleepy again, although others still stared transfixed at the emperor. Aka-des wondered if they were due to be blessed with another speech by the imperial leader, emphasising the great honour that had been bestowed on the young recruits by being selected to serve their god king. If so, he would need to find a more comfortable position, as his legs were starting to feel stiff from crouching behind the pillar.

Suddenly, the orb started to open. The top half parted gradually to present the divine god emperor in all his glory to his adoring subjects. The novitiates looked on in horror as the creature inside the orb was revealed, and Aka-des froze to the spot, his mouth wide open. What they saw was not a handsome well-built man in a suit of gold, but a pulsating blob of pure evil, a creature from anyone's worst nightmare. The grey-green head of the monster was enormous and covered in a mass of thin reddish veins, like a network of tiny canals, transporting blood to its vital organs. The creature had three large eyes, as black as the depths of hell, and a beak-like structure dripping saliva from its mouth, which was hidden from view. Beneath the head, large tentacles writhed in the air like serpents carrying out a macabre dance, beckoning the unwary to an embrace of death. Aka-des noticed that two of the tentacles were thicker than the rest and ended in claw-like hands. The abomination gurgled with fevered expectation as it stared with unblinking eyes at the group gathered before it. The fishy vinegary smell was almost overpowering.

A few of the novitiates, recovering from their dazed state sufficiently to realise their predicament, started to cry out. The others simply continued to stare at the emperor with glazed eyes, as if in a trance.

*It looks as though they are drugged*, thought Aka-des, grappling with what his next move should be. As adrenaline fired through his body, his stiffness was forgotten in an instant as his instinct for survival took hold.

Just then, the bottom half of the orb parted to reveal the rest of the creature. It had no real body, but underneath the grotesque blob of its head three legs appeared, more like trunks than tentacles, and each ending in a large webbed sucker acting as the feet of the monster.

The emperor moved slowly and awkwardly from the orb to the centre of the stage, where it surveyed the latest batch of recruits to be brought before its imperial presence. Aka-des realised that the creature was dripping with some viscous liquid, as if it had recently emerged from a bath of some unknown putrid fluid. It did not seem to be in its natural environment as it moved in laboured steps towards the front of the stage, with first one leg gingerly moving forward, then the next and finally the third bringing up the rear. The creature became more and more animated as it got nearer to the group of waiting men, gurgling more strongly, and with its tentacles writhing with ever-greater intensity as the saliva continued to gush from beneath its beak.

Then, in a nightmare vision which Aka-des would keep in his mind for the rest of his life, the emperor opened its mouth and three long worm-like translucent tubes uncurled from within and snaked their way towards the first line of novitiates below the stage. It was almost as if three immensely long blind worms were sniffing the air, trying to locate the scent emitted from the warm bodies of the petrified youths in their white robes of innocence.

Once these slender tubes reached their target – the bare necks of the unfortunate victims – tiny, pointed teeth at the end of each tube latched onto the succulent flesh and bit deep. Barely a whimper emerged from the trio of novitiates as their blood started to surge back up the tubes into the open mouth of the increasingly hysterical creature on the stage. The ecstasy the thing was experiencing was clear to see once it gorged on the precious liquid pouring into its obscene body.

Aka-des had seen enough. There was no way he could help any of the wretched youths awaiting their dreadful fate, so his only option was to try and escape. If he could get back to the city and let others know what their beloved emperor really was, perhaps they could be persuaded to take action. Doubts began to creep into his mind. What if people didn't believe him? Even if he could convince people that their emperor was nothing more than a bloodsucking monster, what realistically could they do? He immediately banished these thoughts from his mind, deciding to worry about such things later. First of all, he had to get away from the imperial compound, and return home.

Aka-des lifted his arm, pointed his wristband at the hideous nightmare on the stage and pressed a button.

'Perhaps an image of the divine emperor might prove useful,' he whispered to himself before quietly moving back from the column he was hiding behind and slipping out of the still open doorway. He didn't have a clue where he was, or even how close he was to a way out of the palace, so he just kept moving, listening intently for any clanking of metallic feet which would indicate the presence of one of the robot Imperial Guards.

He hadn't gone far when he saw a dim light coming from a large window. As he approached the source of the light, he noticed another large chamber filled with the same murky liquid as the one he had seen earlier. His blood turned to ice as he saw, swimming in the gloom, three creatures looking just like the emperor. They seemed much more at home in this watery environment, gliding across the tank with their tentacles laid out behind them, compared to the jerky movements of the god king in the chamber he had just left.

Aka-des could just make out some sort of console in the middle of the tank, and one of the creatures glided up to it, using its claw-like hands to manipulate various controls. *So, we have more than one emperor*, he noted with sarcasm. *We have an entire imperial family.* Not stopping to see what happened next, he continued to ease his way along the corridors, keeping as close to the walls as possible. They all seemed much the same, being totally featureless apart from the odd window and the dim lighting providing scant respite from the prevailing gloom.

*Why is everything so dark?* he wondered. *Perhaps these creatures can't tolerate bright light. If they spend most of their time in those dingy tanks, I suppose that makes sense.* After what seemed like an age, he found himself in front of a door, which automatically slid open as he approached it. He peered inside cautiously, half expecting to come face to face with one of the robots or, even worse, one of the stinking creatures, dripping wet as it made one of its occasional ventures outside its tank.

Luckily, the room was empty, but he noticed with utter relief that there was a small window with daylight flooding in.

*Thank the gods.* He sighed, silently offering a prayer of thanks to whichever divinity may be listening. *I wonder why so much of this complex is so empty, and so lacking in security*, he pondered. *Perhaps it's because they think it's so unlikely anyone would want to break in from outside, given the normal adoration showered on the emperor by his devoted subjects.*

With this thought in mind, Aka-des reached up to the window and pushed it. At first, he thought it was locked, but with a bit of effort it opened up sufficiently for him to squeeze through. His eyes took time to adjust to the daylight, and he took deep breaths of fresh air in order to try and erase the lingering smell of decaying fish and vinegar, which seemed to permeate his clothes.

*Only problem now is how do I get out of the compound without being seen?* He had jumped down into a narrow lane, similar to the one he had used to first enter the complex. *This might lead back to into the main plaza I arrived in earlier,* he hoped. The young man continued to walk gingerly along the passageway, trying to keep as best he could to the limited shadows available. The lane did indeed open out into the central plaza and, even better, there was another delivery van disgorging what looked like sheets of metal.

Aka-des could not believe his luck. Two men were unloading the goods, chatting to each other as they worked. Even better, the back of the van was open.

'I'm not going to get a better chance than this,' he said quietly, waiting for the right moment to take his chance.

The plaza was deserted apart from the delivery men, just as it had been when he arrived earlier in the morning. The two men stopped unloading the material and stood to one side laughing as they watched something on the wristband of one of the pair. Aka-des made his move and sprinted across the courtyard towards the van. He managed to jump inside as the men resumed their work, stacking the remaining sheets of metal with the others. There were still a number of boxes and packages in the back of the vehicle; Aka-des hid behind some large cartons, hoping that not all the goods were to be unloaded here.

Luckily, he heard the van door swing shut as the two men took their seats at the front. Aka-des's heart was pounding. *What happens if I was seen and some Imperial Guards turn up demanding to see what's in the back of the van?* he thought, *I'd be done for.* The thought of being brought before one of those hideous creatures with their writhing tentacles and worm-like tubes snaking towards his neck made him shudder. Fortunately, he did not hear the clanking of metallic feet on the stony ground outside, and in a few seconds, he heard the van start up and head towards the exit.

*I've made it*, thought Aka-des, starting to relax a little. *Let's hope they are returning to the city for the next delivery and I get a chance to hop out without being noticed.*

That was a problem for later. The young man was so relieved to be leaving the horrors of the palace behind him that nothing else mattered. He sat back and closed his eyes, trying to blot out the nightmare scenes he had witnessed earlier. *I didn't manage to find Beta-vac, though. He sighed with regret. He may not even still be alive. The best I can hope for is that he is still being held with others who haven't yet had the honour of meeting their emperor.*

He realised that the task before him was immense. He needed to prove to people at large that their leader is, in fact, one of a group of tentacled monsters who spend most of their time immersed in a murky liquid, emerging every now and then to feast on the blood of those chosen to serve their emperor. Not easy when those same people were only recently cheering their god king and waving flags with a level of enthusiasm verging on hysteria. Even if he could get people to listen, how could they ever manage to free the captives and defeat the armed robots protecting their loathsome masters?

He could hear the two men at the front of the van chatting to each other as they headed back towards the city.

'Where's the next delivery?' he heard one of the men ask. 'Somewhere near the library,' came the reply. 'According to the route planner we should be there fairly soon.'

Aka-des felt a wave of relief surge through his body. He had escaped from the hell of the imperial compound and would soon be back in the centre of the city. From there he could make his way back home. He needed to talk to someone about what he had seen, and his father seemed the obvious choice.

He felt a jolt as the vehicle came to a stop. The two men were still talking and laughing, and seemed in no hurry to make their next delivery. Aka-des inched his way to the rear of the van and pressed the small panel at the side of the door which, if all went to plan, should open the rear doors. The panel was a safety device, so it was impossible to get locked in the storage hold if the doors closed by accident.

Like a dream, the doors slid back immediately. The young man jumped out. He couldn't close the doors behind him without access to the control panel in the driver's cabin of the van, or by using a remote device which the two men would no doubt have with them. Aka-des didn't wait to see what their reaction would be when the men finally went to make their delivery and found the rear doors of the van wide open. That was their problem. He quickly merged with the people in the crowded street and disappeared into the throng.

As he walked through the city centre, he looked at the people going about their business, concerning themselves with their normal humdrum daily routines. *If only they knew what was happening*, he thought, feeling a mixture of anger and despair. *Things have got to change and people need to know the truth. The problem is going to be getting them to listen in the first place. They will probably think I am completely mad and send me somewhere for medical help.*

Aka-des finally arrived at his home and noticed that it was almost lunchtime. He walked in, only to come face to face with his mother.

'Oh, there you are,' she said breezily. 'I thought you were out with your friends. You'll have to make yourself some lunch as I'm in a hurry. I've got to meet Mrs Lou-ing for a bite to eat, and then we're going to hit the shops. Still haven't found my ring…' she shouted back as she reached the door. 'And your father's at work. He left early this morning as he had a meeting to attend. Have fun.'

With that, she was gone.

'Nice to be missed,' mumbled Aka-des sarcastically. 'I'll just have to wait until Dad gets home, I suppose.'

He was itching to explain all that he had witnessed at the palace, but it was no good spilling the beans to all and sundry. He trusted his father and valued his opinion. A loose tongue could prove dangerous, so he would have to bite his lip until his father returned.

Although it was time for lunch, he didn't feel hungry. Instead, he felt totally exhausted as the drama of the morning suddenly hit home. *I'll try and get a couple of hours sleep*, he decided before ambling off to his bedroom. The young man collapsed onto his bed and within seconds had drifted into a fitful sleep, dreaming of writhing tentacles, cold emotionless robots and the screaming faces of those who literally gave their lives for their emperor.

# Chapter 15
# The Antis

The insectoid Antis were an ancient race on the planet Mars. Some would say they were the original intelligent species, predating the humanoid Martians by many thousands of years. The two races developed separately, and for aeons there was very little contact of any sort between them. The Martians evolved to become predominantly urban creatures, gathering initially in small villages which later grew to become towns, and eventually into cities.

The Antis had always been nomadic, living in small colonies, with each colony or hive being ruled over by a queen. With an entire planet at their disposal, there was rarely any conflict between the two races in the past. The Martians kept to their urban centres, and the Antis roamed the countryside, which was designated by them into tribal areas. Rarely staying in one location for long, the Antis would move from one home to another, once the order had been received from the queen. Scouts would be sent out to locate a new base, sending pheromone messages to the rest of the colony once a suitable location had been discovered.

The Antis were large creatures, standing over seven feet tall, and were generally of a grey-green colour, although the exact hue varied somewhat depending on the particular role the creatures were born to fulfil in the hive. They had two large compound eyes made up of thousands of tiny lenses, which were excellent at detecting even the smallest movement. They also had three further eyes located on the top of their heads, called ocelli. The middle one of these simple eyes was in fact a deadly weapon, capable of emitting a piercing microwave field, which fried the internal organs of any unfortunate adversary.

The Antis were also telepathic, and communicated with each other through their antennae, which vibrated in the air as thought messages were transferred over large distances. At the heart of the communication hub of the colony was the queen. She could send messages to all the other Antis under her control, and could block any signals sent between other members of the hive if she so wished. The queen never left the colony. She remained hidden in a secure location and was protected by fierce soldiers who had the ability to bite and sting, injecting a toxic venom into any would-be assailant.

Apart from controlling the rest of her colony, the queen's sole role was to produce eggs in order to expand the population of the hive. In particular, she would produce a royal egg of a brilliant green colour, late in her life cycle. Once the royal egg was laid, it was time for the colony to move to a new home. The entire population would move en masse to a location selected by the scouts, with the precious cargo of the royal egg given absolute priority. The egg would be carried by a dark grey royal servant, with soldiers providing the escort guard. Winged versions of the soldiers would provide aerial support, and the whole colony would march in procession to their new home.

The only members of the population remaining at the former location would be the old queen and two loyal servants. They would tend to the queen until she died soon after the rest of the hive had moved on. Their job completed, the servants would face each other in front of the body of their old leader; and with their middle ocellus, each would kill the other simultaneously by emitting the deadly ray, in a final act of service to the old queen.

As soon as the queen was dead, the rest of the colony would instantaneously receive the message, and from that moment on their allegiance was transferred to the inhabitant of the royal egg. Once the group had arrived at their new home, the royal egg would be deposited in a safe location, with a guard placed at the entrance to the royal nursery. It was as if the embryo queen became aware of her new role as head of the hive as soon as her predecessor had passed on.

Rapidly, the new queen would hatch, avoiding the larvae stage of the other Antis offspring, and would grow to adulthood in a matter of a few days. The cycle had been completed and the new queen would take on her position as sovereign of the colony.

Although each hive lived independently from others, and each colony's allegiance was to its own queen, it had been suggested in the past that the entire Antis race was also ruled over by a Queen of Queens. No one had ever seen this supreme ruler, but certain behavioural characteristics of the Antis indicated that this was a possibility. On arrival at their new home, for example, the entire colony would not initially pay their respects to their own queen, but the insects had been seen to line up in rows, all facing in a particular direction, and then bow their heads as one, as if confirming allegiance to some unknown and unseen entity.

Also, on occasions when a queen had died unexpectedly without laying a royal egg, members of the colony affected would again line up, facing in the same direction, with their antennae vibrating, as if gathering instructions from elsewhere. The entire population of the old hive would then disperse, with members joining other colonies in the vicinity. Each creature, however, would seem to know which colony was to become their new home, as if orders had been received from a higher authority.

Some Martian scientists had even organised expeditions to the area considered to be the location of the Queen of Queens, but so far, such expeditions had proven fruitless. The region selected as the possible home of the supreme leader of the Antis was large, mountainous and completely uninhabited by the Martian race. Without firm evidence as to the exact spot where such a creature would exist, it was always going to be a difficult quest to make.

In many ways, the Antis race remained an enigma to the Martians. Some saw the insects as merely vermin, increasingly causing problems as the humanoids expanded their settlements into what was previously seen as tribal Antis lands. Others saw the insects as simply another intelligent race with whom they shared the planet and its resources. Such people were more willing to feel sympathy with the Antis, who were being pushed further out into the Outside lands. They were of the belief that compromise between the two races was desperately needed to avoid worsening levels of conflict in the future, and this would mean somehow creating meaningful dialogue between the two sides.

For many years the view that the Antis were vermin tended to hold sway, but increasingly some people were now accepting that the insects had rights as well; and if these rights continued to be ignored, the future for both races would be potentially bleak and uncertain. Perhaps both indigenous races of Mars could really learn to live in harmony, with each race respecting the rights of the other. It would take time and effort to achieve but, as increasing numbers of people would say, a task worth the perseverance.

# Chapter 16
# The Secret

The crew of New Endeavour returned to base, with the ring safely enclosed in a protective sample case, to be examined in the relative comfort of the spacecraft's laboratory. Angela, Robert and Frances were all eager to study the remarkable artefact in detail, each with their own particular perspectives based on their areas of specialism. Angela, the astrobiologist, saw the ring as evidence of a previous intelligent Martian civilisation, long ago made extinct due to the dramatic climatic changes the planet had suffered in the past. Could there be other artefacts to be discovered which could provide further information about the civilisation and what happened to it? Robert, the geologist, and Frances, the chemist, were eager to examine the composition of the ring and the rock in which it was ensconced. How long had the item been entombed in the sandy Martian soil?

Only Martin the Scottish engineer was reluctant to return to the spacecraft. His real interest was the Mars Prospector probe, still sitting patiently on the ground covered in sand and dust, and refusing to operate. He was itching to repair the machine so it could help them in their further exploration of the Martian surface, as well as the personal satisfaction of bringing this technological wonder back to life. But that would have to wait. Tom was adamant that their first priority should be to examine the ring and send a full report back to mission control. No doubt their work schedules would have to be adjusted in light of the new discovery.

On their return to New Endeavour, Tom immediately set about filing a preliminary report and requested details of the crew's revised priorities for the days ahead. All the other members of the team headed straight to the lab, taking the ring with them like a group of children about to open their presents on Christmas morning. Angela carefully opened the sample case and removed the ring. She held it gingerly in her right hand and turned it slowly, examining the piece of jewellery from all angles.

'It's beautiful.'

Frances gasped, admiring the square-topped object with its row of diamonds.

'It could do with a good clean,' Robert added.

'Goodness knows how long that thing has been buried under the surface.'

'An odd shape, though,' said Angela, as she lay the item on the lab table. 'It must be nearly an inch long, and the hole is very small. I can barely fit it on my baby finger. Whoever wore this must have had very long, thin fingers.'

'At least they had fingers, and wore jewellery,' said Jason, the team medic. 'So, they can't have been that different from us.'

'Just think,' gushed Angela, hardly able to contain her excitement, 'a race of intelligent Martians, probably humanoid, living on the planet in the distant past. How like us were they? Did they live in big cities? How technologically advanced were they, and what happened to them? I came to Mars expecting to find a few hardy microbes at best, and here we are examining jewellery worn by a long-dead Martian.'

Just then, Tom entered the room and walked over to the huddled group.

'Just heard back from mission control,' he said. 'Our previous work schedules go on the back burner for most of us, I'm afraid. Our new priority is to carry out a detailed examination of the area where the ring was found. We have machinery on board to help with the excavation.'

He turned to Martin before adding, 'You will need to carry on working to get Mars Prospector operational again, though. The probe can help with its digging equipment once it's repaired.'

The engineer beamed at this news.

'Righto, boss,' he replied with obvious glee.

Tom then looked at Jason.

'Your programme of tests and examinations will continue as previously scheduled. We still need to make sure we all keep as productive and healthy as possible, whatever work we may be doing.'

The medic nodded in agreement.

'That's fine by me.'

'Will news of our discovery be made public?' asked Frances. 'And how will all this affect our public relations work while we're here on Mars?'

Tom was quiet for a few seconds, before turning to face the group as a whole.

'Mission control will not be making the discovery public, at least for the time being. Apparently, they want more evidence before doing anything.'

'More evidence?' Robert queried in astonishment.

'What more do they want? Matching earrings, bracelet and necklace? We found a bloody ring. It had to have been made by someone. We're the first humans to set foot on Mars, so it must have been made by a Martian, or at least some alien from somewhere else, who just happened to be visiting wearing their Sunday best.'

'I'm just telling you what I have been told,' replied Tom defensively. 'As for our public relations work' – he paused and licked his lips – 'we won't be doing any.'

The rest of the crew stared at him open-mouthed.

'The authorities will be providing the public with a mock-up version of the Martian surface, which has already been set up somewhere in Australia. They also have a team of scientists who will pretend to be us. Apparently, they have been chosen because they look similar to us and have the same specialisms as we do. Their faces have been used in public broadcasts during our journey to Mars, so the folks back home won't notice anything different.'

'So, it's all a big con,' spluttered Martin. 'How can they get away with it?'

'What about our families?' asked Frances.

'How do the authorities explain the fact that the people being shown on public broadcasts aren't us?'

'They have all been sworn to secrecy,' said Tom, trying to sound authoritative while privately agreeing that this all sounded rather suspect and clandestine. 'They have been told that we are on a highly secret mission, which could be jeopardised if the truth gets out. They have also been told that they will be updated regularly about us while we are away, but our safety depends on the whole mission remaining a secret.'

'This has all been planned in advance,' bellowed Robert, his anger rising as he spoke. 'Mission control were well aware we could find an alien artefact here on Mars, but told us nothing. We're just puppets carrying out their instructions. We should have been told what all this was about at the outset.'

'I agree,' said Martin. 'We've all been conned from the start. All those broadcasts we made during the journey here were a complete waste of time.

Nothing we said or did was actually broadcast to the public at all. Instead, our doppelgangers back on Earth have been feeding the public a pack of lies.'

Tom looked at the faces of the group gathered in front of him. Their previous enthusiasm and excitement had been replaced with anger and despondency. This whole trip was in danger of falling apart. If he was faced with a mutiny, what could he do? The authorities on Earth might just forget about them. *After all*, he thought, *no one knows we really exist. As far as the population at large are concerned, the group of imposters in Australia are the real "us", so the public can be fed any cock and bull story as to what is happening on "Mars".*

Tom took a deep breath and tried to calm the troops.

'The fact is, though,' he began, 'we've just made one of the most important discoveries in human history. We have evidence that a race of intelligent beings lived here on Mars at some stage in its history. We're all scientists after all. Surely, it's our duty to find out what we can about this extinct civilisation, irrespective of what our orders are from Earth.'

Angela nodded reluctantly.

'At least we can now concentrate on exploring Mars without bothering about the reaction back home.'

'We still have important work to do here, so I suppose we might as well get on with it,' Frances added in support.

Jason kept quiet, and Tom secretly wondered if the medic was mentally taking notes about the reactions of the various crew members as material for some future report on the emotional well-being of the team.

'Well, I don't like it one little bit,' said Robert. 'I don't like being conned by a bunch of idiots back on Earth. How dare they put us in this position?'

'As I see it,' countered Tom, trying to remain as calm as possible, 'we have a choice. Either we pack our bags and leave, or we take the opportunity of a lifetime and buckle down to exploring this planet.'

# Chapter 17
# Revelations

Aka-mas had had a busy day, mostly consisting of meetings with his colleagues in the Earth Observation Team at the observatory, and with officials at the Imperial University, to which the observatory was attached. The meetings had not gone well. In light of the elders' response to the discovery of life on their neighbouring world, pressure had been exerted on the university to cut any further funding for Project Earth.

The arguments Aka-mas had put forward at the meetings, stating that this was a major discovery and warranted further detailed study, held no sway with the university authorities who controlled the purse strings.

The heads of the university were well aware that they held their positions under imperial patronage, and the elders were the mouthpiece of the emperor himself. If the university did anything to displease the elders, and hence ultimately the emperor, they would soon find themselves without a job, and without any prospect of obtaining another position elsewhere. In the end, Aka-mas had to admit defeat. Project Earth would be terminated.

The most difficult part of the day for him had been when he had to report back the decision of the university to his colleagues in the Earth Observation Team. Many of them, like Aka-mas himself, had devoted years of work to the project. Now, at the moment of their greatest triumph, everything was coming to an abrupt end. It all seemed so unfair, particularly as the authorities had given no reasoned argument as to why the project would be ended with immediate effect, apart from vague excuses relating to "funding issues". The team was to be disbanded; its members would return to other areas of research of a less controversial nature.

Aka-mas had left the observatory under a cloud, and his journey home was a complete blur. He had gone over the issues debated during the eventful day over and over again in his mind, but was totally unaware of any of the mundane matters relating to how he actually arrived at his front door.

However, as the familiar frontage of his home appeared before him, his thoughts seemed to snap back to the present. With a deep breath he entered his house. He immediately poured himself a decent sized glass of the highly alcoholic themox juice and slumped into a chair. The themox was a turtle-like creature, about the size of a small pig. It had the peculiar ability to hypnotise any would-be assailant with its seven enormous orange eyes, and it could also spit a foul-smelling dark blue substance at anything it saw as a potential threat. It was this substance that was used to produce the drink which Aka-mas now held in his hand. Unlike in its raw state, the themox juice actually smelt rather pleasant, but had to be drunk with caution. A couple of glasses would send most people reeling.

Aka-mas was not a heavy drinker normally, believing that a brisk walk in the Outside was a better way of clearing the head and reducing stress than relying on the contents of a bottle. However, today was an exception, and he relished the comforting warmth of the drink as he took his first sip.

He looked around and realised he was alone. *Nothing unusual about that*, he thought. His wife was normally involved in some social gathering with her group of friends, and Aka-des lived a fairly independent life these days, often only appearing at meal times. Aka-mas placed his glass on a table beside his chair and momentarily closed his eyes. *Just occasionally*, he thought, *it would be nice to return home to be welcomed by my wife so we could discuss the day's events together as a couple. Not very likely, though.* He sighed. *My wife has absolutely no interest in my work, and I probably care even less about her increasingly shallow life. A constant round of shopping, eating out and spilling the dirt on whichever unfortunate member of her group is this week's bête noire. How can she find that satisfying? Was it always like this?* he asked himself. *When we first got married, we were definitely in love. We have always had our different interests, but we loved each other, and that was all that mattered. Do I still love her, and does she love me?*

It was definitely true that in many ways they had grown apart over the years and were leading increasingly separate lives. But there was still something there in the relationship, he hoped, but what? *Perhaps we merely tolerate each other these days*, he considered, somewhat glumly. *We have just got used to each other being around, like a piece of well-worn furniture. Can that be true? Or deep down do we still really love each other?* It hurt Aka-mas to realise that he couldn't really answer that question with a definite response. Just then, a door opened and in came a dishevelled-looking Aka-des.

'Had a good sleep, have you?' asked his father sarcastically.

'Some of us have to go to work for a living.'

Aka-mas expected a quick-fire response from his son, but Aka-des remained silent, and looked very pale.

'Are you feeling ill?' asked the older man, wishing he hadn't jumped to conclusions with his earlier comment.

'No, I'm not ill,' replied his son quietly. 'But I need to speak to you.'

'Feel free. Come and have a seat,' said Aka-mas, wondering what Aka-des had been up to. 'Are you in trouble? Where have you been?'

'I've been to the palace,' was the brief reply. Aka-des looked as though he was about to break down, and his father looked concerned.

'The palace? Why have you been to the palace of all places?'

'I wanted to try and find Beta-vac and persuade him to return home. I was sure he didn't really want to join the Imperial Guard.'

'So, you just wandered up to the palace, knocked on the door and asked to speak to him, did you?' questioned his father incredulously.

'No, I hid in the back of a van which was making deliveries to the imperial compound and then sneaked into the palace without being seen.'

Aka-des shivered as he began to recall the events of the morning. It already started to feel like a bad dream.

'You did what?' spluttered his father with rising astonishment. 'What if you had been found? You could have been put in prison for trespass, or even worse. Whatever came over you? Have you completely lost your senses?'

'I did what I had to do,' replied his son, with a degree of firmness that surprised Aka-mas.

'And did you find Beta-vac?' asked his father.

'No,' came the reply. Aka-des stared at the floor. 'But I did find out quite a lot about what really happens in the palace.'

'What do you mean?' Aka-mas coaxed, concerned at the seriousness etched on the face of the young man sitting beside him.

'The emperor is not a man,' replied his son in a quiet, measured tone.

'You've actually seen the emperor?' gasped his father, unable to conceal his rising excitement. 'The actual emperor, not just the orb?'

'Yes,' said Aka-des. 'But he's not a man. He's a monster.'

Aka-mas found it difficult to take in what his son was saying. He almost expected Aka-des to suddenly burst out laughing and crack a joke. He was not used to the young man actually being serious, and it worried him.

'How do you mean, a monster?'

Aka-des took a deep breath and then poured out the whole story to his father, beginning with him stowing away in the delivery van. Aka-mas listened intently in utter amazement.

'The emperor is not of our race. In fact, there is a whole colony of these creatures, living in tanks of some liquid in the palace. They feed on the blood of the novitiates, literally sucking the life out of them through long tubes that snake out from the mouths of the creatures and then latch onto the necks of their victims. Whether they drain the poor devils dry or simply take enough to quench their thirst, I don't know. I left the room as soon as I could.'

'So, there is more than one emperor,' said his father, mulling over what his son had just told him. 'They probably take it in turns.'

The thought was almost funny.

'And no wonder we never get to see him in person.'

'And the Imperial Guards are just robots,' Aka-des added.

'No one chosen to go to the palace ever joins the guards. They are just food for these tentacled monsters.'

'That's why families have no further contact with their sons once they are selected to serve the emperor,' reasoned Aka-mas. 'The ultimate honour is, in fact, the ultimate sacrifice.'

'What can we do?' pleaded his son.

'We can't just leave all those people to a gruesome fate as fodder for the creatures in the palace. We've got to get them out of there.'

'And how do you propose to do that?' asked Aka-mas.

He realised his son was correct in what he said, but it was just not practical to turn up at the palace gates and set everyone free.

'We need to get people to believe your story first. And that won't be easy. We need some proof to show them, and perhaps start a rebellion.'

'I took an image at the palace, when the creature left the orb and lumbered across the stage,' Aka-des remembered.

. He immediately pressed a button on his wristband, but then flopped back in his chair in disappointment.

'The image isn't clear enough,' he moaned. 'It could be anything.'

He showed the picture of a fuzzy-looking lump standing on a stage to his father, but for some reason the image lacked any real detail.

'People would just laugh at us if we showed them this,' agreed his father.

'We'll have to think of something else. We need to find people who are sceptical about the imperial system to begin with, if such people exist.'

'We exist,' replied his son. 'If we are sceptics, there must be others who are the same. It's just a matter of finding them.'

His father sat back and took another sip from his still three-quarter full glass of themox juice.

'It's unbelievable,' he said after a few moments thought. 'We've been ruled for goodness knows how long by a race of apparently alien creatures. How have they got away with it? Are we all really that stupid?'

His son shrugged. 'People have never known anything different.'

'As long as most people have jobs and homes and can provide a reasonable standard of living for their families, they don't care who wears the crown. Why should they?'

Aka-mas sighed. He knew his son was right again. People were brainwashed from birth into the cult of emperor worship – and as far as most were concerned, the emperor was divine. Why would you turn on a god without good reason? *But that's the point*, he realised. *'Without good reason'. Surely what Aka-des has discovered is ample reason? The problem is making people realise that they have been conned all along. Their emperor is not a benevolent father figure, providing for his subjects, but a race of alien monsters who look on us as we would look at a herd of cattle. Nothing but a source of food.*

Suddenly, it came to him.

'I know who we should talk to,' said Aka-mas, rising from his chair. 'I know just the person.'

# Chapter 18
# The Message

The Antis roamed the lands freely, in harmony with the planet and its bountiful resources. The goddess Duma had provided them with a paradise, and they praised her munificence daily. The lush vegetation furnished them with as much food as they could wish for, and the many lakes, rivers and streams gave them ample fresh, clean water to quench their thirst.

The insect race made full use of these resources, but were careful never to take more than could be replenished by the natural cycle of growth and rebirth, which Duma had ordained. They used their fibrous, woody faeces as a material to build their nests, and over time, after they had moved on to a new location, these would decay, and the remains would nourish the soil on which they were built.

When feeding, they would never strip an area bare of its vegetation, but would take what they needed before travelling to another locality, thus allowing fresh growth to restock and restore at the original site.

The harmony between the Antis and their precious world had existed since time immemorial, with the continued health of their world at the heart of their everyday life and decision making. Anything else would be an insult to the goddess Duma.

However, things were changing. The humanoids had started to intrude further into Antis tribal lands as they built their towns and villages with no regard to the impact on the planet. The humanoids did not work in harmony with nature. They tried to enforce their ways on the natural world, with increasingly dire consequences. Their settlements were like sores on the fair skin of Duma's world. Every new building dug into the cherished ground, gouging out chunks of the surface, as if some animal had ripped the innards from a still living creature.

The planet felt the pain of these atrocities. The plants and vegetation cried out in fear as their roots were pulled from the protective soil, and the animals displaced, from the smallest insect upwards, would shout their anger and distress as their world was literally turned upside down. But no one heard their cries.

The Antis were a peaceful race, but ever mindful that the humanoids were posing an increasing threat to their own way of life, so they realised that things could not continue like this for much longer. Duma's anguish would need to be assuaged.

All over the planet, the colonies of Antis went about their business as usual, tending their crops, looking after their flocks of aphid-like Aphonas, building their nests and attending to their queen, while others would march in procession to set up new homes elsewhere.

On one particular day, without warning, they all stopped what they were doing, and the entire population of Antis across the lands turned together to face in the same direction. Every member of every hive bowed as one; their antennae vibrated as they all received the same message.

'It is nearly time, my children, for our race to stand against the humanoids. Their destruction of our beloved world cannot go unanswered any longer. Duma is looking to us all to avenge the violation of her domains, before it is too late for us all.

'Prepare to take action, my children. Await my command to retake the planet from the heathen humanoid intruders. We will emerge once again as the rightful custodians of our glorious world, and will renew our vows to the goddess Duma, in the certain knowledge that her legacy to us all is safe once again.'

The antennae of every Antis vibrated vigorously as a huge cheer was channelled telepathically between every member of the entire race.

# Chapter 19
# The Crew

A shaky truce hung over the crew of New Endeavour. In the end, their curiosity as scientists overcame their anger at being kept in the dark about the true nature of the mission, and they all reluctantly agreed to carry on with the revised programme, at least for the time being. After all, they reasoned, having journeyed for nearly five months to travel over forty million miles to reach Mars, they might as well take the opportunity to do something useful now they were here.

Angela was itching to get started on exploring the area where the ring had been found, and Martin was keen to start work on repairing the Mars Prospector probe. In fact, all the crew members had their own particular reasons for wanting to stay. There was a whole world to explore, and they were unlikely to get another chance if they simply packed up and returned home.

For Tom, this trip was the culmination of everything he had worked towards throughout his life. His desire to explore the Red Planet had been behind every major decision he'd made since applying for a place at university. He had been single-minded about reaching Mars, almost to the exclusion of everything else. He had never married, and even he had to admit that he was somewhat a loner. He'd had a few short-term relationships in his younger years, but nothing serious. 'Why get involved with someone,' he had concluded, 'when I don't intend hanging around on Earth in the future.' He was not the sort to find satisfaction in normal family life. Raising a family, going on holiday and tending to the garden did not appeal to his sense of adventure at all. Mars was where he had always wanted to be, and Mars was where he now was. For some reason he felt a strange affinity to the cold almost airless, bone dry world of sand and dust. Somehow, he felt at home here. Not that he would ever say as much to the other members of the crew, who would probably think he was crazy.

They all had their own reasons for wanting to be here, it was true; but for most, this was just an exciting adventure, at the end of which they would be happy to return home to family and friends. As for Tom, the mere thought of leaving Mars filled him with dread.

Martin, the only other crew member from the original UK, was very different. He had studied engineering at Edinburgh University, where he met his future wife, Sandra. She had studied Scottish history, and was now a senior lecturer at the same university, making quite a name for herself in the realms of academia. They had two young children, Scott and Amanda, and were the stereotypical family unit.

Martin had joined the UK Space Programme after completing his doctorate in spacecraft technology, and had spent a lot of his career to date in Canada and Australia, working on various projects for UKSA (United Kingdom Space Authority). Sandra and the children joined him whenever they could, and he returned to Edinburgh in between projects, but he and his wife accepted that sometimes there would be fairly long gaps when they didn't see each other. Luckily, both sets of parents lived quite close to the family home in the city, and were more than willing to help out with the children whenever they could.

Angela, the New Zealand astrobiologist, was the youngest member of the crew. Having studied biology at the University of Auckland, she had developed an interest in the relatively new science of astrobiology after meeting her now boyfriend, Simon Peake. He had been giving a lecture at Angela's university on the recent discovery of microbes living quite happily in the upper regions of the thick cloud layer surrounding the hellish planet, Venus. Although conditions on the surface of Earth's nearest planetary neighbour were unbelievably harsh, with temperatures exceeding 400 degrees Celsius, atmospheric pressure nearly a hundred times that on Earth, and with rain of sulphuric acid, the American Aphrodite probe had found microbes not just existing but thriving in the upper atmosphere of the planet. Angela had been enthralled with the lecture, so afterwards she sought out Simon to question him further about the discoveries.

One thing led to another, and their initial friendship gradually developed into a full-blown relationship. Ten years older than Angela, Simon looked much younger than he actually was, and he encouraged the biologist to branch out into the field of astrobiology. She obtained her PhD and spent the next four years working for UKSA in Australia, where she and Simon had set up home.

The new Mars mission was looking for an astrobiologist to join the team, and Angela just happened to be in the right place at the right time. The first choice for the position fell ill, and Angela was asked if she would be willing to step in. The young New Zealander leapt at the chance; thereafter, she underwent months of intensive training on Earth and the Moon before finally being accepted as a member of the crew.

Mindful that she was only second choice to take on the role, she was keen to show her true worth to the mission. Now, with the discovery of the Martian ring, she had the chance of a lifetime to really make a name for herself in her chosen field. She wouldn't just be studying microbes, but trying to uncover the past history of a race of long-dead intelligent Martians.

Jason Lombard, the only Canadian on the mission, had never really intended to travel into space. He was already well known in his home state as a dynamic young doctor of medicine who had written a number of well-received books on psychology. He was also a familiar face to the general public, due to his numerous appearances in the media dealing with medical issues and discoveries. In fact, in Canada he was known as "Mr Medicine" to his many fans.

The UKSA, keen to garner popular support for the forthcoming Mars mission, wanted the young medic on board. Jason was asked if he was interested. At first, he declined the offer. He was openly gay and in a relationship with his partner, Felipe Macron, a Quebec lawyer. They had never married but were in a long-term relationship, having opted for a civil partnership instead. Jason was a staunch Roman Catholic, even though he had often found the Church's teachings on homosexuality difficult to reconcile with his own lifestyle. Recently, however, the Church had modified its approach to same-sex relationships, although marriage was still forbidden for gay couples.

Whether this had any bearing on his and Felipe's decision not to marry, Jason wasn't sure. Felipe was happy with the arrangement they had, which was all that mattered to Jason. The lawyer was not a religious person, so he wasn't keen on a traditional church wedding anyway. Being together was the really important issue, whatever the formal relationship was called. But it was Felipe who had encouraged Jason to accept the offer of a place on the Mars mission, so finally the medic had agreed.

The remaining two members of the crew, Robert Franks the geologist and Frances Downes the chemist, were both from Australia. They had never met before joining the training programme for the mission, but had formed a firm friendship in the months leading up to the launch. Robert was the joker in the pack. He gave the appearance of being quick-witted and jovial, always ready with a humorous comment, whatever the situation. He could be relied upon to reduce the tension if matters became fraught, and his ability to put people at ease made him a firm favourite with the rest of the crew. The Australian gave the impression of being confident and in control, and someone you could rely on in times of difficulty.

In fact, as is often the case, his true character was quite different. Growing up in rural Atherton, in the Atherton Tableland of Queensland, as an only child, he had not found it easy to make friends. As a youngster, he was tall for his age, and quite skinny. He towered over his schoolmates, who often referred to him as "Beanpole Franks". Robert was, however, extremely bright, and had a passion for rocks and fossils, which made him stand out even more from his contemporaries, who were much more interested in sports and girls. As a result, he was often excluded from the various friendship groups which inevitably develop with young children. To make matters worse, his father, whom the young Robert adored, died suddenly when the youngster was only thirteen. Robert retreated into his shell, which only compounded his problems at school, where he became the victim of bullying. Eventually, he admitted to his mother that he was unhappy and wanted to leave his school.

Luckily, she had been aware that all was not right with her son, particularly since the death of her husband. She hugged Robert, telling him that he could move schools if he wanted to, but running away from a problem wasn't necessarily the best way of dealing with it. She pointed out that similar problems were likely to surface wherever he was, unless he tried to change the way he behaved in front of others. 'Be proud, and be strong,' she had urged her son. 'You have a great future ahead of you, so don't let these idiots get you down. If they try and bully you, try and laugh it off. Make a joke. If they see that you're not bothered by their taunting, they'll get bored and give up.'

Robert had taken her at her word – and to his surprise, the tactic had worked. The bullying didn't stop overnight, but Robert started to build friendships with some of the other children, and he soon began to make a name for himself as the class joker. His final years at secondary school were much happier, and realising that putting on an act could cover up his innate shyness, it soon became an integral part of his character, which he continued into university life and beyond.

He studied geology at the University of Queensland, where he excelled. His inquisitive mind and methodical approach to fieldwork had made him an outstanding student, which had led to an early career in research, working at the school of Earth and Environmental Sciences at his alma mater.

Frances Downes had also been a very bright youngster, and had developed an early interest in the sciences, particularly chemistry. She did very well at school, earning high grades in all her subjects, but it was in chemistry where she really shone. Frances had plenty of friends at school and, being a pretty if petite young woman, she was never short of male attention. She obtained a scholarship to study organic chemistry at the University of Melbourne, where she was noticed by her tutor as "one to watch".

She had expected to move into a career in industry after gaining her PhD, but was asked to join a team carrying out research into the composition of rocks brought back to Earth by various probes exploring comets and asteroids. The possibility of mining these celestial bodies for their minerals had been debated for many years, but the matter was becoming more urgent as Earth's supplies were drying up. Frances became totally absorbed in the work, rising to become head of the team.

Her growing reputation as an outstanding scientist brought her to the attention of the UKSA, who were impressed by her many published papers, which experts held up as prime examples of well-researched, well-documented and well-argued work. In fact, it was as a direct result of this research that UKSA made a commitment to begin mining operations in earnest, out in the asteroid belt between Mars and Jupiter.

Both Robert and Frances were asked to join the Mars mission as the final members of the crew, and both had willingly accepted. It was during training that the two Australians had formed a close bond. Robert found that he could open up to Frances in a way that he still found difficult with most other people, and she enjoyed the company of her tall compatriot. The fact that their areas of specialism in geology and chemistry were interrelated had helped nurture their friendship initially, but it was more than that. There was no romantic spark between them, but they developed a close "brother-sister" type relationship as the months passed by. As both had no siblings, and currently with no partner of their own, they found comfort and strength in meeting someone they could turn to for advice and companionship, with no baggage attached.

***

Six people whose destiny it was to become the first humans to travel through the cold depths of space to reach the barren, desolate Red Planet. Whether Mars ultimately proved to be welcoming or not, being forty million miles from home, they would all need to rely on each other completely in order to overcome the hardships they would undoubtedly face as they set out to explore the secrets of this ancient and mysterious world.

# Chapter 20
# Meeting with Sep-lee

Aka-mas had known the historian for a number of years. They had originally met at a social function at the Imperial University, where both men were working. Aka-mas had found the older man fascinating, with his stories of ancient Martian history. He also had an inkling that Sep-lee was not just another "emperor worshipper" who would never say anything out of line for fear of the impact on their position at the prestigious institution. The historian was, Aka-mas had decided, a sceptic like himself. In fact, Sep-lee was the first person he had ever met, apart from his son, who could reasonably be described as such. *Perhaps I'm not alone after all*, he had reasoned. *There really are others who feel as I do.*

Aka-mas had never questioned his colleague about his beliefs before, but now things had changed. He believed his son's account of what was happening at the palace completely, but they needed someone with which to share the discovery. Sep-lee's knowledge of Martian history may prove useful in providing a clue as to when these creatures actually arrived on Mars. *Were there any accounts or myths relating to the arrival of beings from the sky?* he wondered. *If anyone knows, it's Sep-lee.*

Aka-mas contacted the historian immediately via his wristband and arranged a meeting at Sep-lee's flat. Aka-des would also attend, so he could relate his story first-hand to his father's colleague. Aka-mas had not told Sep-lee exactly why he wanted the meeting, but he had obviously aroused the older man's curiosity. The meeting was arranged for early evening on the following day.

Aka-mas and his son arrived at Sep-lee's flat just before the agreed time. The sun was just setting as the historian opened the door and ushered the two younger men into his home.

'Can I get you a drink?' he asked, as Taya's long furry tail released its grip on its owner's arm so the creature could examine the two visitors more closely.

After the two men declined the offer, they were led to a comfortable-looking settee near the large picture window. Sep-lee sat at his desk, with Taya stretching out before him, the big green eyes of the animal firmly focused on the two strangers sitting opposite.

'How can I help you both?' asked a smiling Sep-lee.

'I must say, I found your call yesterday rather intriguing.'

'To be honest, I didn't know who else to turn to,' admitted Aka-mas, looking intently at the older man. 'I hope I'm not talking out of hand when I say' – he paused, searching for the right words – 'that you are not someone who is an uncritical admirer of our emperor.'

The historian looked somewhat puzzled at this line of questioning, but he kept calm and smiled once more.

'It's true that I am not a firm advocate of our imperial system of government,' he answered. 'Although, I surmise that I am probably in a distinct minority in my views.'

He chuckled softly while looking closely at the faces of the two men sitting on the settee. *They look worried*, he thought to himself. *Why are they really here?*

Aka-mas quickly spoke to try and dampen what he considered to be a growing suspicion in the other man's voice.

'You are not alone in your views,' he confirmed. 'I believe there are many of us who take a similar view, even though we may be reluctant to publicise our beliefs.'

The older man nodded, arching his fingers under his chin as he waited for further explanation.

'The fact is,' continued Aka-mas, 'my son has made some rather disturbing discoveries as to who, or what, our emperor may be.'

Sep-lee bent forward in his chair, resting his arms on his desk.

'What do you mean?' he asked, his curiosity overcoming any suspicions he may have harboured earlier.

Aka-des then described in detail to their host the events of the previous day. Sep-lee sat in silence as he listened to the story unfold. The smile on his face disappeared as he absorbed all that Aka-des had to say. The historian nodded at times and took some notes as the narrative continued. Finally, Aka-des finished what he had to say, and he looked at Sep-lee for some sort of reaction. Did the historian believe him or not?

'Well,' said the older man, pondering what Aka-des had just said, 'that's quite a story. Our emperor belonging to a colony of presumably alien invaders, who have ruled our civilisation for perhaps thousands of years.'

Aka-des and his father both realised how ridiculous this must have sounded, and were waiting for Sep-lee to tell them not to waste his time any longer and for them to leave his home. In fact, the historian did no such thing.

'I believe what you have told me. To be honest, it backs up a lot of what I have recently discovered through research of my own. Look at this.'

He picked up the device still sitting on his desk, and then projected an image of one of the Tablets of Skothath onto the wall. He explained the meaning of the ancient symbols and the story they told. He described how the craft had landed thousands of years ago beyond Mount Rathkarn, and how the messengers of the gods had appeared before the villagers, their bodies glowing in the setting sun. He told how some of the villagers were taken prisoner, and how a few had returned with reddish marks on their necks, tired and lethargic. The historian explained how some of those returning had mentioned "devils of hideous countenance" who they had encountered while being held, and how there was no mention of the supposed spacecraft actually leaving.

Father and son sat in awe as Sep-lee went through the tablets, vividly describing what had happened all those years ago.

'I had read about the official version of the tablets,' said Aka-mas, 'but always assumed it was just a myth carried down through the centuries.'

'As most do,' admitted Sep-lee. 'But, as you can see, the real story as told on the tablets ties in rather well with your son's description of what is happening even now at the palace. The key points of his narrative are remarkably similar to what I have just outlined to you.'

The historian stood up and paced the room with his arms folded behind his back, as if he was about to deliver a lecture to a group of waiting students.

'Take the description of the messengers of the gods according to the tablets, where their bodies were "glowing in the setting sun". Does that not imply the rays of the sun were glinting off the metal armour of the Imperial Guards? The robots Aka-des so vividly described have been around for a very long period of time. And the "devils of hideous countenance" would seem an apt description of the creatures encountered by this young man at the palace, don't you think?'

Sep-lee turned to Aka-des, who nodded his agreement.

'And what about the few prisoners who managed to escape from their captivity?' continued the older man.

'The description of them as being "tired and lethargic". I put it to you both that you would also be similarly indisposed if a large amount of your blood had recently been drained from your bodies by these monsters. And one final thing.' he added, standing directly in front of his two guests seated on the settee, as if admonishing a couple of students who had forgotten to hand in their homework.

'I am intrigued by the description of the escaped victims as having reddish marks on their necks. Did you not say in your narrative, Aka-des, that when you first saw the imperial orb, there was a tingling sensation in your neck, and the poor unfortunates brought before the emperor also clutched their necks before the creature appeared, which seemed to dull their senses?'

Aka-des nodded once more.

'I have been thinking for some time that the Egg of Imperial Splendour, which is inserted into the neck of every child as part of the citizenship ceremony, must serve some purpose. It is my view that this device somehow controls the individual and makes them passive supporters of the imperial system. No wonder so few people actually oppose or question our form of government.'

Aka-mas and his son sat in astonishment, trying to take in all that Sep-lee had said.

'Could this really be true?' asked Aka-mas, finally breaking the silence. 'That our race has been ruled over by a colony of alien creatures for thousands of years, without our knowledge? And that these creatures have controlled us all this time by inserting a tiny device in our necks while still infants, to make us all subservient to their demands?'

'I believe it is all true,' replied the historian. 'Based on what your son has told us, and my own findings from the tablets, I do not see any other possibility.'

'But why don't the eggs seem to work in us?' asked Aka-mas.

'Why aren't we affected in the same way as other people?'

Sep-lee shrugged.

'All people are different. A few may not be susceptible to the devices and do not fall under their spell, so to speak. We do seem to be in a very small minority, however, so the creatures are probably not too bothered about a few who fall outside the net. They obviously do not see the likes of us as a threat to them and their domination of our society.'

'They're probably right,' said Aka-mas with a sigh. 'What can we do to stop them? We are few in number, and most people would simply laugh at us if we tried to convince them of the truth.'

'Not only that, but I have no tangible evidence of what I saw, apart from a blurred image of something shuffling across a stage,' Aka-des added, sounding as despondent as his father.

'The only option is to try and break the control they have over the population,' replied Sep-lee. 'There may be some mechanism at the palace which controls the eggs once they are inserted into people's necks. If that were destroyed, perhaps everyone would awake, as if from a dream, and would then be willing to listen to our arguments. Maybe we could start a rebellion against these monsters and their robot guards.'

'But how would we find such a device, even if it existed?' asked Aka-mas doubtfully.

'It would mean returning to the palace,' answered his son quietly. 'It's the only way.'

'You're not going back in there,' said Aka-mas firmly. 'To escape once with your life is one thing, but to do so again is pushing the realms of credibility too far.'

'But I have to, Dad,' countered Aka-des, showing a degree of maturity his father had seldom seen in the young man. 'According to Sep-lee's translation of the tablets, people have escaped from the clutches of these creatures in the past. "Tired and lethargic" they may be, but that shows that the aliens don't completely drain their victims of their blood when they feed. That means that Beta-vac might still be alive, and I can't just forget about him.'

'Don't forget that those who did manage to escape in the past often died soon after from the experience they had suffered.' Sep-lee added.

'It is unlikely your friend would ever be the same as you remember him, even if he did survive.'

'I still have to try,' said Aka-des, defiantly. 'I must go back.'

The historian smiled at him.

'This Beta-vac must mean a lot to you if you're willing to risk your life again to help him escape. He is very lucky to have a friend like you.'

Aka-des blushed, but said nothing.

'If you are going to the palace, so am I,' interjected his father. 'I can't let you go back in there on your own. Two of us working together may have more luck in locating any control centre, if such a thing exists. We will also need to gather as much evidence as we can on the existence of these creatures. If people know what happens to their sons once they are taken to the palace, it may shake them from their stupor even if we can't shut down the power source of the eggs.'

'Another problem is how we get back in the palace,' said Aka-des. 'Two people hiding in the back of a van just seems too risky. We're bound to be found, even if we could find someone making another delivery.'

'In three weeks' time,' responded Sep-lee, moving back to the chair by his desk, 'it is the emperor's birthday celebration. As you know, crowds of people gather at the entrance to the palace, and the emperor appears as the gates swing open in order to watch the pageant and acknowledge the cheers of the people. I am too old for such a mission, so would only hold you back. However, if you both mingled with the crowds, there is a chance you could sneak into the palace compound without being seen. The creatures seem somewhat complacent about their domination of our society. I doubt whether they think it likely that a pair of miscreants would dare to penetrate their centre of power.'

Aka-mas nodded.

'You may be right. It will still be risky, but it's probably our best option.'

He turned to his son, who also nodded in agreement.

'You're always saying we don't spend enough time together. What better idea for a father and son bonding session?'

Aka-des's attempt to introduce an element of humour to proceedings helped to ease the tension in the room, and all three men laughed out loud.

'We must keep in touch over the next few weeks,' said Sep-lee. 'I would also like to bring someone else in on our little plan. Hak-tes, the Chief Librarian at the Imperial Library, also shares our views on the current system. It was he who gave me the device holding the images of the five tablets in the first place.'

'If you think that is necessary, that's fine with us,' replied Aka-mas, turning to his son, who quickly gave his consent.

'I just think that Hak-tes could be a useful addition to our little team,' said Sep-lee. 'He has many contacts who could help to smooth our pathway in the future.'

By this stage, Taya was getting bored. She had spent the entire time stretched out on Sep-lee's desk, watching the unfolding discussion intently, her large green eyes moving from one man to the next, depending on who held sway in the exchange at the time. She disliked being ignored, and wanted to be the centre of attention. Suddenly, she launched herself from the desk and jumped into the lap of a surprised Aka-des, where she made herself comfortable, curling her long tail around the arm of the young man.

'She likes you,' said Sep-lee with a chortle. 'You should feel honoured. Not all my guests get the same treatment.'

All three men laughed once again, and the historian rose from his chair, turning to his two visitors.

'Now, what about that drink?' he asked before ambling off towards his kitchen.

# Chapter 21
# Exploration

The crew of New Endeavour had started to settle into a daily routine as they began to explore the surface of Mars. Martin Robson had managed to clear the sand from the solar panels of the Mars Prospector probe, and had also fully cleaned some of the delicate electronics which controlled the tiny craft. This had involved dismantling part of the probe, thoroughly cleaning all the parts back at base and then reassembling them again on-site. Many of the components of the probe had become clogged with the grains of dust and sand thrown up by the numerous dust storms, a normal feature of the Martian weather. Once the operation had been completed, Mars Prospector was working like new again, much to the satisfaction of Martin, who had become surprisingly attached to the mechanical marvel now assisting with the excavations of the area close to where the ring had already been discovered.

He would never admit it to his colleagues, but Martin would always welcome the probe each morning as he arrived at the site with a silent "Mornin' to ya, my old friend" and similarly with a "G'night, sweet dreams" when he left to return to base. The other excavation equipment, which had been brought to Mars on New Endeavour, had also now been installed in situ, and was slowly burrowing beneath the Martian surface, examining the sandy soil for anything unusual.

The rest of the crew were also involved in periods of manual excavation, particularly in areas where it was difficult for the machinery to reach. This work was interspersed with projects from their original schedules, which had now been downgraded in order to prioritise the search for other artefacts beneath the surface of the Red Planet.

Robert and Frances were busy analysing the rock samples from the vicinity. They were surprised by the amount of water they had discovered, locked into these subsurface materials of the supposedly now dry planet. It had been known for some time that in the past Mars had been a blue world, much like Earth, with a substantially thicker atmosphere, and large parts of the surface had been covered in seas, rivers and lakes. The discovery of the ring also pointed to the existence of a highly developed Martian civilisation in the distant past. What had happened to that civilisation and the temperate climate of Mars was still a mystery, but the planet did not seem quite as dead today as everyone had expected.

Angela Trike was also heavily involved in the excavation. To her disappointment, no signs of any microbial life had yet been discovered, but she had not given up hope of finding some vestige of life still clinging on in the currently harsh environment of Mars. *Once life gains a foothold and becomes established,* she had reasoned, *it will fight hard to cling on when conditions deteriorate. We can see this happening on Earth, where life is found in the most unexpected places, from the frozen wastes of Antarctica to the burning deserts of the Sahara. Life has even been discovered in the boiling, acidic waters of Yellowstone's Hot Springs, where microbes don't just exist but thrive. Similarly, bacteria have been found living quite happily in a miles-deep gold mine in South Africa, eating sulphate in temperatures well over sixty degrees Celsius.*

She could also look to the recent discovery of microbes living in the upper atmosphere of the hellish world of Venus, and was still hopeful that Mars would also prove to be an abode of life, however simple that life may now be.

Jason Lombard, the Canadian medic, and Tom Fisher, the head of mission on Mars and astrophysicist, both split their time between work at the excavation site and work back at New Endeavour. Tom still had his daily reports to file with the authorities back home, and Jason was involved in a full programme of tests on the crew members. He had to monitor their physical and emotional well-being, and ensure that each member followed their personalised fitness regimes, which was an important part of everyone's daily routine. The impact of living and working for long periods in an environment where the gravity is only one third of that on Earth had to be monitored carefully and, in particular, the effect on muscle deterioration had to be determined.

Jason was also the only member of the crew who still had to periodically appear on public broadcasts made for the benefit of those on Earth. He had originally been selected for the team partly due to the fact that he was well known to the public back home in his native Canada which, it had been believed, would generate more interest in the mission to the audience watching developments from the Red Planet. Although the "substitute" team back home, pretending to be the Mars astronauts, were now the public faces of the mission, those tuning in to the broadcasts would still expect to see the "real" Jason from time to time. His doppelganger could deal with the outside broadcasts, supposedly being beamed from the surface of the planet, where his face would be hidden under a space helmet, but broadcasts from inside New Endeavour would still need to involve the actual medic.

One bright morning, Tom and Angela set off to the excavation site to take their turns at the dig. The sky was completely cloudless and there was a gentle breeze. The two tiny moons of Mars, Phobos and Deimos, had just set behind the range of hills in the distance. The rocky landscape spread out before them as they made their way the short distance to where Mars Prospector was already hard at work, sifting through the soil in search of anything noteworthy.

'What a beautiful morning,' said Tom, admiring the barren landscape bathed in the early morning sunshine.

'It certainly is spectacular,' admitted Angela as she walked beside the team leader. 'But just think what the view might have been like millions of years ago. How sad that the planet has become a desolate husk of its former self. We could have looked out at a landscape teeming with all sorts of life, with trees, grass, flowers, and running water, rather than just rocks and sand. Imagine the Martians going about their business, oblivious to what the future held for their home world. Think how annoyed the owner of the ring we found would have been when he or she realised it had gone missing.'

Tom smiled and gave a sigh.

'Just think what they could have told us. An ancient civilisation capable of producing something of such beauty would have been an amazing source of knowledge. I wonder how technologically advanced they were. Had they started to explore the solar system, just as we are doing now?'

'And where did they live?' asked Angela.

'Did they live in towns or cities – and if so, what happened to them? We've seen no evidence so far of any buildings.'

'Whatever dwellings they had would have crumbled long ago,' replied Tom. 'What was left would have been buried under layers of sand and dust during the millions of years which have passed since the end of their civilisation. Think of all the sandstorms Mars has suffered over that time. Hardly surprising there is nothing left today.'

Angela nodded.

'A whole race wiped off the map without a trace. No record whatsoever.'

'Almost without a trace,' corrected Tom. 'We did find the ring, remember. Perhaps we'll get lucky and find something else.'

'Well, that's what we're here for,' said Angela, her tone brightening as she contemplated a morning at the rock face. 'We might find something spectacular.'

Tom laughed as he looked at the young astrobiologist.

'Ever the eternal optimist.'

'I have to be in my field,' countered Angela while they both made preparations for the work ahead.

The two astronauts had been working for a couple of hours, carefully sifting through the Martian soil as they continued to dig. The excavation machines that had been set up at various locations in the area were also busily analysing the material revealed as they drilled ever deeper under the sun-blasted surface.

Suddenly, Angela let out a shriek.

'What is it?' said Tom, concern etched on his face as he walked over to where the astrobiologist had been working.

'Are you okay?'

'I saw something move!' she squealed. 'Down there in the hole.'

She pointed to the spot where she had been digging.

'You must have imagined it,' said Tom, relaxing as he realised his companion wasn't suffering from a fault in her spacesuit. 'The light can play all sorts of tricks, and you are probably tired after staring at piles of rocks for hours on end. Take a break.'

'I know what I saw,' replied Angela, somewhat miffed that she wasn't being taken seriously. 'Whatever it was quickly scuttled back down into the hole out of sight. I must have disturbed it while I was digging.'

'But complex life forms can't exist in these conditions,' reasoned Tom, as calmly as he could. 'It's just not possible.'

'Well, I saw something,' insisted the New Zealander. 'I think it was some sort of insect. Like an ant perhaps, but I can't be sure.'

Tom looked puzzled. He wanted to believe what Angela had said, but reason was telling him that it could not be true. There was just no way something as complex as an ant could survive in the harsh environment of Mars.

'Well, if there was something there, it has certainly gone now,' he said, deciding it was pointless arguing the case at the moment. 'We'll log what you saw, and I'll add it to my report later on.'

'It was alive.'

Angela almost shouted with excitement, ignoring what Tom had just said. 'There is life on Mars, even today. I knew that once established, organisms would do everything possible to cling on. This just proves it. Life has moved underground to escape the surface conditions. We know water exists down there, and where there is water there is normally life.'

Tom shrugged, not wanting to dampen Angela's enthusiasm for her discovery.

'Perhaps you're right,' he conceded.

'But we are going to need actual proof. Mission control won't accept an account of what you think you saw as sufficient evidence.'

'Well, let's carry on digging,' said Angela excitedly. 'We might find more of these creatures.'

'No,' replied Tom firmly, placing a hand on her shoulder. 'Protocol says we have reached the end of our shift. We need to go back to base. Another pair will come out this afternoon to carry on the search.'

'But the creatures may have moved on by then,' Angela protested. 'We may miss our chance.'

'We have to go back,' insisted Tom. 'I'm responsible for the well-being of the team, and I have to obey the rules. If the creatures exist, I'm sure we'll find them again later on.'

Angela reluctantly began to pack up her tools in readiness for the trip back to New Endeavour. She took one last look at where she had been digging, when her heart suddenly missed a beat.

'Look!' she shouted. 'Look there!'

As she pointed at the hole in front of her, the astronauts stared open-mouthed as two ant-like creatures stood before them. They seemed to be looking at the two humans who had dared to intrude on their domain.

Roughly an inch long, they were larger than terrestrial ants, with a grey-green hue. They had two large eyes at the sides of their head, with three further eyes located on the top. Each insect had long antennae, which started to vibrate in tune with each other, their movements perfectly synchronised. All at once, Tom and Angela felt as though they were being pushed back by some invisible force, and they both experienced a flash of brilliant light, which dazzled their eyes. A mental image of a tall, slim being dressed in long, flowing robes materialised before them, as if in a dream. The being looked humanoid, but with a large bulbous head. What they could see of its body was completely hairless, and it had thin arms, one of which sported an ornate bracelet, with each of its hands ending in six long, slender fingers. Its face had a small nose and mouth, and no obvious ears. Two large eyes stared into the distance, as if the being was deep in thought. As quickly as the image appeared, it was gone again, as had the two ant-like creatures in the burrow.

The two astronauts stood where they were, unable to move. Tom and Angela felt as if they had suffered an electric shock. Their bodies were trembling and their vision was blurred.

'What the hell was that?' said Tom as he started to regain his senses.

'Did you see that image of a tall humanoid being?'

'Yes, I did,' replied Angela shakily. 'It was dressed in a long robe and staring into space. What do you think caused it?'

'I don't know,' came the reply. 'But we both apparently experienced the same vision.'

'Do you think it was caused by the ants?' asked the astrobiologist, incredulously.

'The image appeared at the same time they did. Could they have projected it into our minds?'

'Telepathic ants,' suggested Tom in awe. 'Who knows? This planet just seems full of surprises.'

'Well, at least you know now that I did see something move earlier. These ants must live underground, and were investigating all the digging going on from above,' said Angela, satisfied that she now had a witness to her discovery.

Tom made brief contact with New Endeavour, saying that they were about to return to base. He didn't give details as to what they had witnessed, realising that they would probably be bombarded with questions if he did. The two astronauts could relate their adventure once they were safely back inside the spacecraft.

***

'Well,' said Jason, after Angela and Tom had described their experiences at the excavation site, 'small telepathic ants living on Mars. Who would have believed it?'

'Are you sure you two haven't had just a little too much of the ol' Mars juice out there?' asked Robert, only partly in jest.

'No little green men out for a drive as well?'

'It's all true,' said Angela, annoyed that the geologist was adopting such a flippant tone. 'This is probably the greatest discovery of all time. Not only have we evidence of a past civilisation on Mars, but we have proof that complex life forms still exist here today.'

'Not exactly proof,' corrected Martin. 'You both say you saw these ant creatures, but we have no physical evidence that they exist. I'm not saying that I don't believe you, but we will need more than a sighting to convince the boffins at mission control.'

'You're right,' said Tom, sighing in agreement. 'We're going to need tangible proof that these insects really do exist.'

'What puzzles me,' said Frances, 'is the image you both saw. A tall humanoid staring into space. What could that mean?'

'I've been thinking about that,' said Angela. 'The being we both saw had long, thin fingers, probably thin enough to wear the ring we found. We could have seen an image of someone from the extinct race of Martians.'

'But why would an insect on modern-day Mars project an image of a Martian, whose civilisation died out millions of years ago?' asked Jason.

'It just doesn't make sense.'

'I don't think any of us have any real answers to these questions at the moment,' concluded Tom, 'but as scientists it's our job to try and find them. I'll file a preliminary report to mission control and see what they want us to do.'

With that, the crew members dispersed and tried to get back to their scheduled work, although recent discoveries were putting the routine tasks into the shade. They all wanted to focus on answering the big questions such as

"What happened to the Martians?" and "How much life still exists today on the Red Planet?"

Outside the thin walls of New Endeavour, a soft wind moaned, caressing the strange intruder from the blue world, as if the ghosts of long-dead Martians were calling to the alien visitors, urging them to explore further.

'Come and find us,' it seemed to say. 'Come and find us.'

# Chapter 22
# Betrayal

Sep-lee awoke from a fitful night's sleep. He had been tossing and turning in bed, thinking of the proposed return to the palace, and he could not help but imagine all the things that could go wrong. *If Aka-mas and his son are found, there is nothing I can do to help them,* he had reasoned. *Are we stupid to think we can end potentially thousands of years of domination by these creatures? They have controlled us absolutely over that time, and people know no other way of life. To the vast majority, the emperor has always been there, and always will be. How do you get rid of a god and why would you want to?*

The historian rose from his bed and padded over to the kitchen to make himself a hot drink of peely. This reddish herb could be chopped and then stirred into hot water producing, when fully diffused, a delicious, comforting drink. It was said by some to have a truly calming effect on the drinker, and Sep-lee definitely needed something to soothe his shattered nerves.

As he sat cradling his cup in his hands, he tried to focus on the position. *We can't just ignore everything that Aka-des has discovered and what I have found when translating the tablets,* he argued to himself. *We have a duty to all the young people of our race, in particular, to try and destroy this evil regime, before any more become victims to these dreadful vampiric creatures. If these two brave individuals can, by some miracle, find the source of power these devils use to control us, and break their hold over people's thoughts and actions, we might just be able to turn the tables on these alien monsters. If enough people started to rebel against their masters, would these creatures be able to crush a growing revolution? They have never had to face any dissent so far. Would they know how to respond?*

Taya yawned and stretched as she greeted the new day. Such thoughts of rebellion and retribution were not important issues as far as she was concerned.

What she really needed now was her breakfast. She jumped down from the end of Sep-lee's bed, where she usually spent the night, and ambled over to her owner. Curling her tail around his leg, she stared at him with large imploring eyes.

'Oh yes, of course,' said Sep-lee, his thoughts returning to more mundane matters. 'You need your breakfast, and so do I.'

The historian arranged to meet Hak-tes in his office later that same morning. He could also take the opportunity to return the device with the images of the Tablets of Skothath, which his friend had earlier requested be returned as soon as possible. However, before giving the device back, Sep-lee decided to take a copy of the images of the five tablets which, he thought, may prove useful later on. He carefully recorded the historic record of those tumultuous events from millennia long past and stored them ready to download at his leisure later on. When all was completed to his satisfaction, Sep-lee left his flat and made his way across the city to the top-floor office of the Chief Librarian, in the magnificent edifice that was the Imperial Library.

The day was somewhat cloudy with a distinct chill in the air. The forecast had threatened rain, but Sep-lee had come prepared. The days of carrying an umbrella were long gone. Today, if the weather turned wet, an individual only had to access the relevant icon on the screen of their wristband to activate an invisible weatherproof shield, keeping the wearer warm and dry.

The streets of the city were busy, but no one took any notice of the elderly academic as he walked on towards his destination. He did not own a vehicle of his own, so sometimes relied on public transport to get about. More often than not, however, he preferred to walk whenever possible. He needed the exercise, it was true, but it was also a good opportunity to think things over. He found that walking helped to clear the mind and put things in perspective. The historian would sometimes walk for miles, lost in his own thoughts, before realising that he was completely lost, in an unfamiliar part of the city.

Today, though, he was focused on reaching the library as quickly as possible. He wanted to explain recent developments to his friend and seek advice as to how they should proceed. Sep-lee was still uneasy about letting Aka-mas and his son return to the palace on their own. *Aka-des had been lucky to escape unnoticed last time, but would the gods smile so favourably on the brave duo next time?* The old man shuddered as he thought of the consequences if the two of them were discovered. He had no doubt that the creatures in their tanks would be merciless in their treatment of the pair of intruders if captured. Their ultimate sentence would surely be death, but they would not be allowed to die without a full confession being extracted from them. As to how this would happen, Sep-lee chose not to think any further.

His train of thought was broken as he eventually arrived at the library and its imposing frontage of reddish stone. It was just starting to rain as he walked up the steps into the grand plaza, with its magnificent frescoes and the looming statue of the imperial orb near the ornate staircase. *If people only knew what hideous abomination actually resided in that orb, eyeing up the adoring crowds as sustenance for the next meal*, thought Sep-lee with disgust. *Well, perhaps, if things go to plan, they soon will.*

He quickly ascended to the top floor and was then ushered into the large, airy office of Hak-tes by the smiling receptionist.

'Nice to see you again,' said the Chief Librarian cheerily as he offered his guest a seat. 'What can I do for you?'

'Well,' said his friend, 'I would like you to give me your opinion concerning some rather startling recent discoveries, if you will.'

'Intriguing,' replied Hak-tes, settling into his seat. 'Please go on.'

Sep-lee then began to explain what he had discovered when translating the tablets, and also told of the visit to his flat by Aka-mas and his son, and of the events witnessed at the palace by the young man. When he had finished, he sat back and looked at the librarian, who had remained almost silent during his narrative.

'That's quite a story,' said Hak-tes finally, tapping his fingers on the large desk before him. 'Are you sure you can rely on these individuals? The whole thing does seem rather far-fetched.'

'Oh, absolutely,' replied Sep-lee confidently. 'I believe everything Aka-des said. I am convinced he was telling the truth, and his story ties in so well with my discoveries when deciphering the tablets.'

'Do you have the device with you?' enquired Hak-tes.

'We don't want it getting into the wrong hands.'

'Oh yes,' said Sep-lee before handing over the small box to his friend. 'To be honest, I'm glad to be rid of it.'

The librarian took the device and immediately placed it into a small drawer in his desk.

'I will need to ensure this gets back to its rightful owner.'

'Who is?' asked Sep-lee, still intrigued as to how his friend came into possession of such a startling artefact.

'I'm afraid that must remain a secret,' replied Hak-tes, a slight smile appearing on his face. 'My contact took significant risks to acquire the device, and I promised his identity would not be revealed to anyone.'

'So, what do you think we should do next?' said Sep-lee, anxious to hear his friend's views on how they should now proceed.

'Well, if what you say is true, we must remain vigilant and act with extreme care,' advised Hak-tes. 'If the authorities become aware of what you have found, they will do everything they can to stop your discoveries becoming public knowledge. You and your friends will be in great danger. For this reason, you must tell no one of your plans. I agree that the best course of action is for Aka-mas and his son to return to the palace, as it is vital we get tangible evidence to back up your claims.'

Sep-lee nodded, but looked worried at the thought of the pair sneaking into the imperial compound alone.

'They are either extremely brave, or extremely foolish,' he muttered finally. 'The risk of discovery is so high that it makes the venture reckless, at best. Are we just sending these two men to a near-certain death?'

'Perhaps,' replied Hak-tes, 'but is there really any choice? Without evidence, people will simply ignore what you have discovered. With evidence, we may at least have a chance of convincing some of them.'

'But with minds being controlled by these creatures, will we ever be able to convince enough people, and start a rebellion?' Sep-lee added glumly.

'That is another reason your friends must return to the palace,' said the librarian, sounding far more confident than Sep-lee actually felt. 'If they can locate and disarm the power source which you say controls the implants in people's necks, then success will be a lot easier to achieve.'

'If such a thing really exists,' countered the historian. He sighed and shook his head as he considered the gargantuan task that lay ahead. 'These monsters have dominated our race for thousands of years. Are they really going to allow two individuals to walk into their seat of power and destroy everything they have built up over aeons of absolute control?'

'That very much depends on how successful your friends are in hiding their presence,' replied Hak-tes. 'Don't forget that Aka-des has managed it once before. I will try and do what I can to help them gain access to the palace during the birthday celebrations. Perhaps a little prearranged disturbance could help divert attention from Aka-mas and his son at the crucial moment, allowing them to slip in unnoticed.'

'A disturbance?' asked Sep-lee.

'What do you mean?'

Hak-tes smiled once more.

'Just leave that to me. Remember, I have contacts.'

With that, the meeting broke up. Sep-lee agreed to keep his friend informed about what Aka-mas and Aka-des were planning to do, and it was also agreed that no one else would become involved in the arrangements for this daring escapade, in order to reduce the likelihood of information falling into the wrong hands.

Sep-lee left the library and noticed it was now raining quite heavily, the sky a dark sombre grey to match his mood. He switched on his weatherproof shield and started to trudge along the rain-lashed streets back towards his home. *Are we being ludicrously optimistic to think that this plan has even the slightest chance of success?* he pondered. *Isn't it much more likely that Aka-mas and his son will simply end up as prisoners of these vile creatures, with goodness knows what consequences?*

He couldn't answer that question, but as the rain beat down from the unyielding clouds, Sep-lee could not shake off a feeling of impending doom. He was not a religious man, but he did, this once, offer up a silent prayer to whatever gods may be listening, pleading for the safe return of his new friends.

***

Back in his office, Hak-tes sat in his chair watching the rain lash against the window as if in anger, like a caged animal furious at being unable to reach its prey. The librarian pressed a button on his desk's control panel, and a three-dimensional image of an elderly man dressed in robes of white and gold appeared before him.

'You have information for me?' asked the elder in a quiet, measured tone.

'We are correct in our belief that Sep-lee is a traitor,' replied Hak-tes. 'He and a couple of co-conspirators are planning an act of treachery against the imperial estate on the day of the emperor's birthday celebrations. The masters must be warned.'

The elder stared at the librarian, showing no signs of emotion.

'Your warning is appreciated, but the masters are already aware of this proposed act of treason against the state, and will be taking appropriate action against those involved. The miscreants will not succeed.'

With that, the image disappeared. Hak-tes remained staring at the blank wall in front of him considering what he had just done. *I have carried out my duty as a loyal subject of the emperor,* he argued, *even though it has meant betraying the trust of my old friend Sep-lee. I had no choice. Long live the emperor, and death to those who defy him.*

Satisfied with his actions, and aware that his loyalty would be well rewarded as usual, the Chief Librarian dismissed the matter from his thoughts. Bringing up an image of his diary before him, he noticed that he was soon due to meet with an architect concerning a proposed extension to the library. A wonderful new wing was planned, including an extremely generously sized and luxuriously furnished flat for his own private use, ideal for those occasions when work commitments warranted an overnight stay close to the office.

# Chapter 23
# The Satellite

'Have you heard the news?' Mrs Aka-mas gushed, breezing into the room.

'What news?' asked her husband, who was flicking through his messages on his wristband. He hadn't heard from Sep-lee since they'd met at the historian's flat, almost a week ago.

'Our beloved emperor is sponsoring the launch of a huge new satellite in celebration of his forthcoming birthday. It will be clearly visible from the ground and orbit the planet about three times a day. It will be a constant reminder of his magnificence and introduce a new star into the night sky. Isn't it exciting?'

'I haven't heard anything about a new satellite,' replied Aka-mas. 'Who is building it?'

'Oh, I don't know all the little details,' said his wife abruptly, 'but the launch is tomorrow, and Mrs Fel-por is holding a party to celebrate. I'll have to buy something suitable to wear.'

'You have a room full of outfits you hardly ever wear,' her husband said in exasperation. 'Can't you wear one of those?'

'Certainly not,' came his wife's indignant reply. 'They're all old stock. I need something to reflect the importance of the event. Just think, a new star to celebrate the emperor's birthday. It's just so exciting.'

She stopped momentarily to pour herself a drink, before disappearing into the bedroom with a parting shot to her husband.

'Have you found my ring yet? What's taking you so long?'

*That's very odd*, thought Aka-mas, as the bedroom door slammed shut. *Why would these creatures want to launch a satellite, and why now? There must be more to it than a simple vanity project to remind us how godlike our emperor really is.*

The huge spaceship was approaching the blue-green disc of the planet Mars, having journeyed through the frozen depths of space from its origin in the asteroid belt, situated between Mars and the giant planet Jupiter. It had been built, section by section, in orbit around the minor planet Ceres, where the tentacled creatures had a major base. Teams of Imperial Guards had toiled to construct the enormous ship, under the guidance of their liquid-based masters. The creatures had controlled the humanoid robots from their huge tanks located in their base on the surface of the asteroid. Food was delivered to the Ceres colony in huge tanker ships, with vats of blood brought from the nearest harvesting farms of the empire, providing the nutrition the cephalopods required.

The spaceship was vast, almost fourteen miles across, and the outside was camouflaged to look like any other asteroid. Inside was a true metropolis, with certain areas filled with the soupy liquid providing the environment needed for the creatures to live. Other areas were set aside for the Imperial Guards, together with laboratories and workshops. There was also a huge nursery, filled with thousands of eggs from which a new generation of cephalopods would eventually hatch, continuing the cycle that had repeated interminably for millions of years.

The creatures' home world was a planet orbiting a red giant star in a system hundreds of light years from our own. The world was much larger than any of the terrestrial planets of our solar system, and it was almost entirely covered in vast seas of the murky liquid where the cephalopods thrived. The few areas of dry land were home to a simple humanoid race, which was harvested by the creatures to provide the nourishment they needed. However, over the millennia, the humanoids had become weaker. The constant bleeding of the unfortunate beings, in order to satisfy the insatiable thirst of the vampiric monsters, had led to a thinning and diluting of their blood to such an extent that the humanoid race were no longer able to provide the nourishment demanded by their masters.

The cephalopods had developed space flight, with craft being built in their underwater cities, and they had started to explore new worlds in search of food. Over millions of years, they had spread throughout the galaxy, creating an empire of colonies, established wherever they found suitable worlds to conquer. When they eventually found the planet Mars, a world teeming with life and, in particular, home to a race of strong and healthy humanoids, the creatures quivered with anticipation. They had found a seemingly inexhaustible food source ripe for the picking and a people not so advanced as to put up a fight. Easy to control and full of nutritious lifeblood, Mars had proven to be an ideal settlement for the cephalopods.

The creatures had also discovered another race of intelligent beings inhabiting the new colony. These were large insects who roamed the planet at will and appeared to communicate telepathically, as did the cephalopods themselves. These insects had tough skins, and their blood was sour and totally unsuited to the needs of the tentacled creatures. As a result, the invaders ignored the insects, leaving the ant-like race in peace.

The creatures had arrived on Mars in a huge spaceship, which had become their base on the new world. They had started to harvest the humanoids almost immediately, using their robot servants to gather suitable specimens from the flock as needed. Over time, a more formalised system was devised to control the Martians and ensure that the humanoid crop remained compliant.

An imperial system of governance was instigated, where absolute loyalty to the emperor was demanded. Tiny electronic devices were implanted into each new-born child, controlled by the cephalopods, ensuring the humanoid race remained both loyal and malleable.

A small minority appeared to be immune from the effects of the devices, and fell through the net, but these miscreants were too few to concern the creatures. The humanoids developed through the centuries into an advanced civilisation, but one which accepted without question, almost universally, the dominant position of the god emperor in their society.

Of course, there was in reality no one emperor. Any of the creatures could take on the role for formal occasions, as the humanoids would never actually see their emperor in person. The populace was conditioned to accept that the imperial orb was the emperor, with each individual having their own mental picture of the god king's true image.

The system of novitiates meant that a constant supply of nutrition was provided by the strongest young humanoids to feed the growing colony of cephalopods. The fact that these food sources were willingly offered by their proud parents, basking in the ultimate honour that their sons had been chosen for a life of service to the emperor, made the Mars colony one of the most successful outposts of the cephalopod empire.

The newly constructed spacecraft would create a second moon for the planet Mars once placed in orbit. The plan was to create a new colony of cephalopods on the planet's surface, to benefit from the growing population of humanoids who were now building new towns and settlements outside the original city.

The new moon would also be able to maintain constant surveillance of humanoid activity in all the settlements wherever they were situated across the vast plains of Mars, something the creatures were currently unable to do, being tied to their original base.

One final part to the spacecraft was needed before it became fully operational, and this was to be provided by a launch from the imperial compound once the ship was in Martian orbit. The craft was, at the moment, totally invisible to anyone watching the sky from the surface of the planet. Only when the final segment was in place would the new moon become apparent as a wonderful addition to the inky black heavens. A new star to honour the divine majesty of the god emperor.

The following evening, as the silent and invisible spacecraft reached Mars's orbit, people below were gathering to watch the launch of the new satellite, heralding the start of the emperor's birthday celebrations. The night was clear, so the existing moon of Mars could be seen shining like a star as it moved across the sky, taking about thirty hours to travel on its orbit around the planet. This moon was very small, no more than eight miles across, and travelling at about twelve thousand miles above the Martian surface. The new imperial moon, once in place, would be much larger and brighter, orbiting less than four thousand miles above the planet and moving across the sky every four hours. A fitting and constant reminder of the emperor's glory to all those who witnessed the spectacle.

Excitement mounted as people chatted in groups, congregating in the streets and parks, not just in the city itself but also in all the settlements where the launch could be viewed.

Suddenly, at the allotted time, a huge roar could be heard and a bright flash of light announced the launch of the new satellite. It could be seen rising against the jet-black sky, like an angel returning to the heavens.

People gasped in awe and clapped their hands in appreciation of the breathtaking sight unfolding before them. The satellite rose higher and higher and then, with an almighty flash, the new moon suddenly became clearly visible to those watching from below.

'It's huge!' shouted animated voices from the crowds. 'Much larger than our existing moon!' Others cried out, 'Long live the emperor,' and a huge cheer rose from the assembled masses.

Aka-mas looked at his son and whispered, so as not to be heard by the loyal subjects nearby, 'That thing is enormous. Far bigger than the so-called satellite we just saw being launched. It must have already been in orbit.'

'Then why didn't we see it until now?' asked his son, mesmerised by the shining moon slowly making its way across the Martian sky.

'I don't know,' came the puzzled reply, 'but there's more to this than meets the eye.'

High above the city, the new moon was starting to become fully operational, and observations were already being made of the crowds gathered to witness the phenomenon. The images were being beamed to the cephalopods, who watched the behaviour of the humanoids from their tanks in the imperial compound, looking for any signs of dissent. They zoomed in on the cheering mass of people, but there was one couple not cheering, a man and a youth, who seemed to be whispering to each other. The creatures quivered violently and their tentacles lashed out in anger. A few of them opened their mouths to allow their snake-like tubes to unfurl, writhing towards the images of the two men, as if preparing to drain them of their life-giving blood.

# Chapter 24
# New Discovery

Tom had just woken from another restless night, one of many since he and Angela had experienced the powerful image of the humanoid while exploring the surface of Mars. Sometimes he dreamt of wide-open spaces, with green hills and patchwork fields. Rivers and lakes glistened in the warm sunshine, and all seemed at peace with the world. He could see creatures in the distance, roaming the lush grasslands, but could not make out their shape clearly. They seemed to be large and dark in colour, but they remained indistinct. On one occasion, he saw what looked like a town or village being built on the horizon, and he felt an inexplicable surge of anger against the unidentified builders of the new settlement. He also saw glimpses of humanoid creatures, similar to the image he had witnessed earlier. Their heads were completely hairless, and their large eyes looked somehow sad and distant. It was as if these beings were thinking back to events that had already happened, or were imagining with trepidation what was still to come.

Tom did not know what any of these dreams meant, but he was sure they were somehow connected to his earlier encounter with the small insect-like creatures at the excavation site. How things so small could have such a powerful telepathic hold on him he did not understand, but this planet seemed full of surprises, and appeared almost keen to reveal its secrets to the travellers from Earth.

He peered out of his window as the new day was dawning. The rocky landscape had a covering of frost while the remnants of an icy fog still clung in patches to the low-lying hills. The early morning sky gradually took on a pinkish-rose colour, with a few wispy clouds visible near the horizon. Tom checked the temperature. It was currently hovering at about -85 degrees Celsius.

*A relatively warm night*, he mused before flinging his legs onto the hard floor of his cubicle. As Tom showered and dressed, he recalled the images in his dreams of a lush green world, seemingly teeming with life. *Could this really have been a memory of Mars in the distant past?* he thought. *If so, when did it all change? What happened to the Martians, and did they leave any record of their history? What about their cities, towns and villages? Is it possible we could find any remains, even today?*

Tom thought this was highly unlikely, given that the Martian civilisation probably died out many millions of years ago. Any buildings would have been reduced to rubble aeons before, and the rubble gradually turned to dust, blown away long ago by the relentless Martian winds. He padded quietly towards the kitchen to make himself a mug of tea, and was surprised to see Angela already seated at the table, nursing a steaming cup of coffee.

'You're up early,' said Tom, making his drink. 'Having problems sleeping?'

'I had a dream,' she replied. 'A weird dream involving humanoids like the one we both experienced at the site. They seemed to be running away from something, but I don't know what.'

'I've had a similar dream myself,' admitted Tom as he took a seat next to the astrobiologist. He explained what he'd experienced while Angela sat quietly, listening intently to what he was saying.

'The fact that we've both had similar dreams, and only since we saw those ant-like creatures, suggests the two things are related,' she concluded. 'But wouldn't that imply the insects are intelligent in some way? Intelligent ants existing on Mars today.' She sounded incredulous, but Tom had to admit that she had a point.

'Perhaps they are trying to tell us something about Mars's past,' he suggested. 'But why, I just don't know.'

'Could it be a warning?' replied Angela, warming to her theme.

'A race of intelligent insects, who have somehow managed to survive the destruction of the planet's earlier environment by moving underground. We know that there are large quantities of ice captured below the surface. Perhaps there is liquid water as well.'

'What would they eat?' countered Tom.

'As far as we know there are no food sources on Mars.'

'Not on the surface,' agreed Angela.

'But who knows what exists underground.'

'And how do they breathe?' added Tom, trying to maintain a healthy scientific scepticism.

'Mars has practically no atmosphere.'

'That I don't know,' sighed Angela.

'However, we have seen them at the excavation site. We didn't imagine it, so somehow, they exist.'

'Life clings on,' replied Tom dryly, as he finished his tea.

They both decided to keep the content of their dreams to themselves for the time being, at least until they better understood their meaning. Angela was about to return her cup to be cleaned when Martin burst in.

'You'd better come quickly,' he announced excitedly. 'One of the excavation machines has made a discovery.'

The three of them hurried back to the control room, where Jason, Robert and Frances were already gathered, hunched over a screen. Frances turned to greet the new arrivals.

'We think one of the machines digging at the site may have found something of interest,' she said, trying to bring Tom and Angela up to speed. 'It's certainly not a rock, and it's bigger than the ring we found.'

'I told you we'd find the matching earrings and necklace,' joked Robert.

'I think we must have hit on an ancient Martian jewellery shop.'

The rest of the crew laughed at the suggestion.

'Shame we can't find an old pub,' he added.

'I could do with a few pints of the hard stuff.'

'I think Tom and Angela found that when they were out at the site earlier,' said Martin, still sceptical about the pair's claims concerning the ants.

'Don't start that again,' interjected Angela with a huff. 'We saw what we saw.'

Jason remained silent as he watched the other members of the crew interact, and Tom couldn't help but think that the Canadian medic was more interested in gathering data for his reports than integrating with the rest of the team. His general detachment from the others was beginning to worry the head of mission.

'We'd better get suited up,' said Tom, bringing the discussion to an end. 'Let's go and see what has been dug up.'

'Can we have some breakfast first?' pleaded Robert. 'Whatever the machine has picked up has been lying in the ground for thousands, if not millions, of years. Another hour won't make any difference, and I'm starving.'

Tom agreed, deciding they would all work better on the surface with a full stomach, so they trooped off to the kitchen to make their meal choices. Jason stayed behind for a few moments scribbling some notes in the pad he always seemed to carry with him before he, too, joined the others.

By the time they left New Endeavour, the sun was already well above the horizon, and the earlier frost and fog had disappeared. The pinkish sky was cloudless as they made their way along the now well-worn path towards the excavation site.

'Looks like it's going to be another lovely day,' said Robert jauntily. 'I should have brought my sun cream.'

Frances giggled and gently pushed him on the arm. The group soon arrived at the location, and Tom bent down by the excavation machine, which had a warning light flashing red to indicate that it had found something unusual.

Martin joined him and looked intently at the glowing light.

'It could be a fault with the electronics, I suppose,' he surmised, noting that a thin layer of dust was already accumulating on the solar panels of the machine.

'Perhaps it hasn't found anything at all.'

'I think it has,' replied Tom. 'Look at this.'

As the group peered into the deep hole where the arm of the device had been digging, they saw something glinting in its claw-like hand. Martin sat at the edge of the hole and gradually lowered himself down to retrieve the object. With the help of Robert and Jason, he scrambled back to the others and held out his hand.

'It looks like some sort of bracelet,' said Frances, peering at the dusty artefact.

'Similar to the one worn by the being in the image Tom and I experienced earlier, added Angela with growing excitement.

'It does look remarkably similar,' agreed Tom, taking the object and turning it in his hand.

Suddenly, Frances let out a shriek.

'I saw something move, just over there,' she said, pointing to a small ledge in the side of the pit where the excavation machines had been working.

'Don't you start,' said Martin, shaking his head. 'There's nothing there. Just a trick of the light and an overactive imagination.'

Just then, three of the ant-like creatures appeared on the ledge and stared ahead at the huge space- suited beings who had once again intruded on their territory. Their antennae vibrated, and the astronauts felt a strong invisible force push them back. A bizarre sequence of images flashed through Tom's mind in an instant. Tall, robed beings running in fear, huge insect-like creatures moving purposefully amongst them, as if on a mission, and even taller humanoids apparently dressed in suits of armour marching in step. Lurking in the background were indistinct shapes with tentacles writhing in anger. Just as suddenly the images vanished, and Tom could hear someone cry out in anguish.

'It's Jason!' shouted Angela in panic. 'He's collapsed!'

Martin and Robert, having recovered from the impact of the force before the others, helped the still dazed Jason to his feet and supported him as the crew made a hasty retreat away from the excavation site.

'What the hell was that?' said Robert in disbelief.

'Perhaps now you'll all believe what we told you,' added Angela, a hint of satisfaction in her voice.

'Okay, okay, I believe you,' admitted Martin as he tried to steer the groggy Jason in the right direction.

Tom was still clutching the bracelet as he turned back to face the excavation site. He could see no sign of the insects now, but could vividly recall the barrage of jumbled images which had flashed before him only seconds earlier.

'Those insects are trying to tell us something, I'm sure,' he ventured, peering again at the ancient artefact he was holding.

'Then why can't they sit us down and tell us over a nice cup of tea, rather than trying to blast us to kingdom come?' Robert queried, his voice reflecting a mixture of shock and anger.

'Perhaps they don't realise their own strength,' suggested Frances.

'They certainly pack a punch for such tiny critters.'

'Did any of you see anything just then?' asked Tom. 'Any mental images, even if just for an instant?'

Most of the rest of the crew shook their heads.

'The only thing I saw was the inside of my helmet as I fell back.'

Robert moaned.

'Now I've got a sore head.'

Tom noticed that Angela did not shake her head and had remained silent. Had she seen anything this time? He didn't push the matter, but decided to have a quiet word with the astrobiologist later.

On returning to base, Frances, who had undergone basic medical training before the mission in order to act as an assistant to Jason should the need arise, gave the shaken Canadian a quick check over.

'I think it's just a matter of shock,' she announced. 'I can carry out some further tests if he doesn't improve, but with rest I'm sure he'll be okay.'

'What's that mark on his forehead?' asked Robert, pointing to a small, almost perfectly circular, red mark above Jason's eyes.

'It could be a result of him hitting his head when he fell. I don't think it's much to worry about,' replied Frances, breezily. 'I'll keep an eye on it.'

Jason was now fully conscious and complaining of a bad headache. Frances gave him some water and painkillers, and Martin helped him to his cubicle to get some rest. The others turned their attention to the bracelet, which Tom retrieved from his pocket and placed carefully on the table in front of them.

'It looks like gold again,' said Frances, peering at the intricate designs ingrained on its surface, which were partly obscured by dust and sand. 'It needs a good clean in order to give us a clearer view of it.'

'I wonder if it belonged to the same being as the ring we found,' said Angela. 'Both artefacts were found in much the same area.'

'Not a very careful person if it did,' added Robert with a grin.

'To lose a ring is one thing, but a bracelet as well? I hope they had insurance.'

After the bracelet had been carefully cleaned and photographed, the crew gathered once again to examine the artefact. Jason, now feeling much better, joined the others as they considered the piece of Martian jewellery.

'You can see the designs much clearer now,' said Tom. 'I wonder what they mean.'

'It reminds me of a circuit board,' replied Martin, noticing the geometric pattern with small dots at the intersection of the various lines.

'These Martians had very thin arms,' commented Angela. 'I couldn't get that over my wrist.'

Frances nodded.

'Tall, thin, hairless, with large eyes, no ears, and six long fingers on each hand. We're starting to build up a picture of what these people looked like.'

'What about the insects?' asked Robert. 'Where do they fit in? Do you think they were around at the same time as the Martians?'

'They could well have been,' answered Tom, thinking back to his vision. The Martians were running away from something, but the insects were much larger than the ones they had just encountered, although looking strikingly similar. Had the ant-like creatures somehow regressed over the millennia, devolving into much smaller versions of themselves as they moved underground to escape whatever catastrophe had hit the planet? But who were the humanoids in suits of armour, and what significance were the tentacles he also saw in his vision?

Suddenly, Jason started to shake violently and stared at his companions, his eyes wild and distant.

'Come and find us,' he said quietly. 'Come and find us.'

'What are you on about?' asked Martin, worried that Jason might be about to collapse again.

The medic stopped shaking and looked at the other members of the crew, one by one.

'Oh, nothing,' he said. 'I'm all right now. Just a little tired, that's all.'

With that, he left the room and returned to his cubicle.

'We'll need to keep an eye on him,' said Robert. 'He's suffering from more than a bit of concussion if you ask me.'

'I'll watch him,' promised Frances.

'I'll do some more tests when he has rested.'

The group then dispersed to carry on with their duties. Tom had to make a full report to headquarters and await further instructions. However, before he left the now empty room he returned to the bracelet and picked it up.

'What secrets do you hold?' he asked, turning the object in his hand. 'How long have you been buried in the rocks? Thousands of years, or is it millions? What was the planet really like when you were made?'

Tom jumped back, almost dropping the ancient artefact. Was it his imagination, or was the bracelet becoming warm in his hand?

# Chapter 25
# Birthday Celebrations

The day of the emperor's birthday celebrations had arrived, and people were already making their way to the imperial palace to witness the festivities. As the official events were not due to begin until early afternoon, many were taking the opportunity to enjoy a picnic or eat at one of the many restaurants nearby.

This time of year seemed to be filled with imperial celebrations. The Emperor's Day parade had already taken place, where the god king gave his annual state of the nation address, and new recruits to the Imperial Guard were formally admitted into the service of the emperor. In many ways, this was a formal state occasion. The birthday celebrations on the other hand were more informal, a party thrown in honour of the great leader. It was a family event, full of pageantry, laughter and games. A chance for the population to relax and enjoy the late summer sunshine before the colder and wetter weather started to take hold.

All along the route to the imperial compound, street sellers were offering their wares to the throngs of people passing by. Some were selling tubs of freshly roasted inmel nuts, from the tree of the same name. Harvested from local orchards, the pea-sized nuts were a great delicacy in this season, and a nourishing and tasty snack to be eaten on the move. Other stalls were offering plates of lightly fried windrez fish. These star-shaped creatures had an aniseed flavour when cooked, and were eaten in great quantities by aficionados. It has to be said that not everyone was enthusiastic about the taste, but for those who relished the delicate flavour, there was simply nothing to compare to a plate of these intensely yellow-coloured sea creatures. Yet other stalls were selling a variety of fruits in every shape and colour, while some were peddling glasses of chilled juices of every imaginable hue.

Children gathered around vendors of the huge blue feathers of the serpent-like xaxxa birds. These creatures, about four feet long, had bodies covered in orange scales, but with a row of enormous bright blue feathers along their backs. Young males of the species would hump their bodies to display their plumes to the best advantage as a means of attracting a mate. As the birds matured, the feathers would simply drop off, to be collected mainly by children, who would run around holding the quill of the feather in their hands, squealing with delight as the air would move through the barbs of the vane and create a soft humming sound.

Enterprising individuals, however, would regularly scan the parklands in search of the largest most colourful feathers, which could then be sold to young children, or rather their parents, at fairs and parades such as the one being held today.

The birthday celebrations were one of the few occasions when the public had access to the Forbidden Zone, the area of parkland nearest to the imperial compound. This area was normally patrolled by Imperial Guards, and even today some members of the elite troop could be seen keeping a watchful eye on the families making their way to the venue for the parade. People were enjoying the spectacle of the enormous zaspi trees, with their deep yellow trumpet-like flowers giving off an intense perfumed aroma. Soon these blooms would glide to the ground at the end of the flowering season, so some people were taking the opportunity to enjoy the last few weeks of the stunning floral display. Many would return in the following weeks to witness the famous Lullaby of the Zaspi Trees, as thousands of flowers would emit a soft whistling sound as they gently wafted to the ground below.

Ebu-rum was a very fastidious individual, and he had made scrupulous preparations for his picnic. A single man, he was extremely careful when it came to making friends. Anyone who made the grade between acquaintance and friend had to be similar to himself in every way. He could not abide slovenliness or tardiness in any shape or form. As such, he had few friends, but today he had invited two of the chosen band to join him at a picnic before the parade began. He had arrived early so everything could be set out perfectly before his guests arrived. A large blue cloth was laid out meticulously, ensuring it was exactly parallel to a row of similarly coloured flowering plants behind him. In fact, he had chosen this spot after an earlier reconnaissance because the flowers matched the colour of his rug almost exactly.

He then measured out precisely where the plates and glassware should be placed, before centrally positioning on each plate a box containing the meal he had chosen for this auspicious occasion. Each box was a different shade of blue to complement the colour of the cloth and the flowers behind. He had also selected three bottles of a yellowish juice to provide a bold contrast in an acceptable accent colour. Ebu-rum was not going to provide any alcoholic drinks for his picnic, as he did not want to encourage any possible relaxation of the strict code of behaviour he expected from his guests. When all was ready, he sat back, satisfied with his endeavours.

He glanced at his wristband. His guests should be arriving in precisely four minutes and thirty-seven seconds. It was then that he noticed, just to his left, a small weed growing in the grass a short distance from his blue rug. He started to panic. He must remove the offending object at once because it had a small orange flower, which in no way coordinated with his carefully chosen colour scheme. He reached over to pick the misplaced weed, when suddenly he felt a sharp stabbing pain in his left wrist just underneath his wristband. He let out a yell and immediately removed the band to reveal a nasty bite from the wasp-like trugga. The venom from these insects was not dangerous, but it caused a painful reddish blotch on the skin of the unsuspecting victim.

Always ready for such eventualities, Ebu-rum placed the wristband carefully on the grass to his side and then pulled out a vial of ointment from his travelling medical box. He dabbed the cooling salve onto his skin and waited for the soothing mixture to take effect.

Just then, a green and brown alfix bird swooped down and picked up the shiny wristband in its beak, before rising again into the deep blue sky. The alfix bird was attracted to bright, shiny objects, and was a constant threat to the often ornately adorned Martians. Ebu-rum screamed in frustration as he stood up in a vain attempt to catch the bird. As he did so, his foot accidentally trod on his plate, catapulting his box of thoughtfully selected food items across the rug, knocking over the equally thoughtfully positioned bottle of juice for one of his guests. His display was ruined. Ebu-rum felt the panic rising within, made worse by the sight of his two guests strolling across the grass towards him, exactly as the four minutes and thirty-seven seconds were about to expire.

The alfix bird returned to its nest, high up in the foliage of a nearby zaspi tree, where it dropped the gold wristband next to a square-topped gold ring with a row of diamonds across its centre.

Aka-mas and his son mingled with the crowds as they approached the imperial compound. They could clearly see the huge pyramid at the centre of the complex and the high walls surrounding the entire estate. The moat, separating the compound from the surrounding parkland, was sparkling in the morning sunshine, with numerous bridges spanning the gap. They would need to cross one of these bridges to gain access to the palace through one of the many gates.

Luckily, Sep-lee had contacted them the previous evening with some more information gleaned from one of Hak-tes's informers from within the imperial household. One of the bridges spanning the moat at the rear of the compound would be unguarded, and the gate unlocked. Aka-mas and Aka-des were to make their way to this bridge at the height of the birthday celebrations, when all attention would be focused on the emperor and the parade taking place at the front of the palace.

Mrs Aka-mas was not with her husband and son, preferring to join other members of a group to which she belonged for a celebratory picnic elsewhere in the park. The group, incongruously called Women for Imperial Satisfaction, was one of many imperialist organisations that were both encouraged, and partly financed, by the state.

Aka-des felt his stomach churning as he waited with his father amidst the growing crowd of enthusiastic people, all eagerly anticipating the arrival of the emperor on his birthday. Of course, no one knew exactly how old the emperor actually was, or how long he had been on the throne. To most people these mere details did not matter. The emperor was, always had been and always would be, a divine and benevolent ruler who took care of his people. To question these facts in any way would be an outrage, nothing less than treason, and anyone mouthing such misgivings would rightly be dealt with severely by the authorities.

High above the throng of people, in the newly installed imperial satellite, malevolent eyes scanned the crowds from their tanks of liquid. At last, they came to rest on a man and his son, seemingly innocently watching proceedings together with the other humanoids. However, the sight of these two individuals caused the cephalopods to erupt with seething anger, lashing at the images of the miscreants with their tentacles and feeding tubes. Soon these traitors would be brought to justice. They would pay for their treason with their lives, as every ounce of their precious blood would be drained from their loathsome bodies, leaving mere husks to be disposed of by the robot guards.

At that moment, a huge roar rose from the crowd as the familiar imperial orb glided from the gateway, crossing the bridge to take its place on the ornately decorated stand erected on a swathe of grassland in front of the moat. Obviously, the adoring crowd was unaware that the occupant of the orb was just one of a colony of repulsive creatures living in the confines of the palace, whichever monster having drawn the short straw being selected to play the role of emperor at today's festivities. The god king was accompanied, as always, by a contingent of Imperial Guards, resplendent in their brilliant golden armour, and was preceded by a troupe of imperial musicians, heralding the arrival of the divine presence with fanfares, marches and anthems.

At the playing of the emperor's birthday anthem, the people began to sing with gusto, clapping and cheering as the orb sat motionless, hovering just above the gold and white covering positioned over the base of the stand.

'Doesn't he look wonderful?' gushed a woman standing near Aka-mas.

'He never seems to age at all.'

Aka-mas simply smiled at the woman, biting his lip to prevent him saying what he was actually thinking. *But you can't see anyone. You don't know what is sitting inside that orb, and nor does anyone else here. If you did, you wouldn't be standing here cheering.* As a procession started to march in front of the emperor, with people waving flags and some dancing in time with the music, Aka-mas looked at his son. It was time to make a move.

They quietly made their way to the back of the crowd and, using the trees as cover, moved towards the rear of the compound. All was deserted as they approached the bridge they were to use to gain access to the palace.

*Strange that there are no Imperial Guards on duty*, thought Aka-des. *Perhaps the creatures have discounted any idea of people trying to break their way into the compound in what, after all, would be an act of pure madness.* The only thing that stopped him taking his father by the arm and running away as fast as he could was the thought that Beta-vac could still be alive. As long as there was even a remote possibility, he couldn't abandon his friend to those bloodsucking creatures.

Father and son crept slowly across the bridge, keeping as low as possible, until they faced a wooden door in front of them. To say that the door was sturdy would have been a huge understatement. It was as solid as a rock – and if it was indeed locked, there was no way of breaking in. Aka-mas turned the handle cautiously. He gave a sigh of relief as the door effortlessly swung open. They were in.

# Chapter 26
# The Spider and the Fly

In front of them were two narrow passageways leading into a maze of buildings at the edge of the compound. They could see the top of the golden pyramid in the distance, rising high above the rooftops of what looked like rows of factories or warehouses, whose function remained a mystery. They decided to take the left-hand passageway and crept along looking for some way to enter one of the buildings, which spread along either side of the alley like an old-fashioned industrial estate. Aka-des was completely disorientated. He had entered the imperial compound from the front entrance last time, and all the buildings looked the same to him. It was impossible to try and retrace his steps.

Aka-mas noticed how run-down and shabby most of these outer buildings looked. *Hardly what you would expect from the seat of imperial power*, he thought to himself. *It looks more like a shanty town.* Then he glanced up at the apex of the gleaming golden pyramid ahead of him. Solid, defiant and, he had to admit, majestic. *That's the real centre of power*, he realised. *That's where these creatures live, and from where they control the lives of every person on this planet. We need to get inside that pyramid.*

Just in front, on the right-hand side, Aka-des saw that a door to one of the buildings was ajar.

'Look,' whispered the youth to his father. 'That's our way in.'

'Very convenient, don't you think?' replied Aka-mas with a niggling sense of foreboding.

'Perhaps it's been planned for us by Hak-tes's mole in the imperial household,' said Aka-des hopefully.

'Maybe,' said his father, unconvinced. 'Just be careful. It all seems too easy.'

The room they entered was large and dark apart from the beam of sunlight penetrating from the open door. Along the walls at each side of the room were stacks of canisters, each being about three feet tall. There seemed to be hundreds of them packed high, almost to the ceiling.

As Aka-des peered more closely at one of the containers, he saw that it contained a darkish liquid.

'It looks like blood,' he gasped to his father.

'Be quiet,' replied Aka-mas sternly. 'We don't want to attract attention. This must be a storeroom where the creatures keep their food supplies. Notice how cold it is in here compared to outside.'

'A bloody fridge,' said Aka-des, aghast. 'We're in a fridge.'

'I think that's it exactly,' agreed his father.

'That's disgusting,' replied the youth. 'How many people must have died to fill these vats? We've got to do something.'

'Well, that's why we're here,' said Aka-mas, somewhat startled by his son's sense of purpose.

He felt very proud of Aka-des and the way he had behaved these last few weeks. It had taken a great deal of guts to come alone to the imperial estate to try and rescue his friend in the first place. Some may say it was a rash act by someone who hadn't properly thought through the consequences, but Aka-mas disagreed. It had required courage and a sense of duty to his friend to do what Aka-des had done. Now he had agreed to return in what may well turn out to be a hopeless mission, with both of them forfeiting their lives, having accomplished nothing. But at least they would have tried to do something to end the tyranny of these creatures. No one could do any more. No, it was definitely pride he felt for his son. Aka-des had grown up a lot recently – and for that, his father would be eternally grateful.

They left the storage room by another unlocked door at the far end, having passed the columns of canisters filled with the blood of untold numbers of the youth of Mars, like sentinels gloating at the hopelessness of the task these two interlopers faced.

'*Do you really think you can beat us?*' they seemed to say.

'*We who have travelled the galaxy for aeons, creating the largest empire ever known. Do you think two unarmed humanoids can change the course of history, when armies have tried and failed in the past?*'

The callous laughter of a race at the height of their power swirled silently around the two men as they departed, quietly closing the door behind them.

Aka-mas and his son decided to turn left into the dank corridor they had emerged into, and then headed in the direction they thought most likely to lead them to the pyramid of gold. The two men were totally unaware that their every move was being monitored by the cephalopods, squirming in their tanks at the heart of the imperial palace. The loathsome bodies of the monsters pulsated and quivered as they waited for their prey, like spiders preparing to pounce on any unfortunate insects who happened to become entangled in their webs.

'Why is it so cold and damp in here?' whispered Aka-des, shivering as he tried to keep warm.

'I don't think the creatures are too bothered by a bit of damp,' replied his father. 'After all, they live in liquid. Why waste time heating buildings for no purpose?'

'And the people held captive here?' said Aka-des.

'I'm afraid they are nothing more than a crop to be harvested to these creatures,' answered Aka-mas gravely. 'Making their short lives comfortable is hardly going to be a high priority. Those people are a source of food and nothing more.'

'We've got to find Beta-vac,' said his son with determination, clenching his fists with frustration. 'We've just got to.'

Deep in the heart of the pyramid were the pens where the young men of Mars awaited their fate. Most of them were still in a state of shock. They had set out to join the Imperial Guard as novitiates, leaving behind their proud families as they marched purposefully towards a new life devoted to the service of their emperor. If only they had known what really lay ahead for them as prisoners of those vile creatures in their tanks of liquid.

They were treated as mere cattle, to be farmed ignominiously to provide the nutrition their alien masters required. The expected lifespan of a prisoner was a matter of months at most. If you were lucky, the creatures would not suck you dry of blood at the first feed. In fact, up to about fifteen per cent of an individual's total blood volume could be taken without significant effect. The body could naturally work to replace the lost blood over time, and so a victim would live to face another day. If the cephalopod was particularly hungry, and drained more than about twenty per cent of blood volume, this could lead to hypovolaemic shock, with symptoms such as weakness, confusion and perhaps unconsciousness in the poor victim. Taking much more than this meant that the heart of the person could no longer maintain adequate blood pressure or circulation, leading to a failure of major organs, coma and, without treatment, death.

However, if the cephalopod was ravenous, the person had absolutely no chance of survival whatsoever. In cases such as this, the tiny fangs at the end of the creature's feeding tubes would bite into the neck of the unfortunate victim, shooting poison into the body which turned the innards into a liquid mush. This would be sucked out by the monster to provide an à la carte meal of the most exquisite taste. To the cephalopods, this was known as a "rapture". Luckily for the prisoners, this extreme type of feeding was relatively rare, as it reduced the size of the humanoid crop far too quickly.

Beta-vac had been fortunate so far. His bleeding sessions had been of the least severe category, and he had escaped from the experience with little more than the odd bout of nausea and tiredness. He was concerned, however, that his luck could not last for much longer, and that his body would not be able to compensate for the feeds indefinitely.

The food provided for the prisoners was unappetising, but nutritious. The reddish-coloured paste they were given to eat contained plenty of iron and vitamins, which helped to replenish the red blood cells lost in a feed. Twice a day, bowls of the foul-smelling food would be brought to the pens by the robot guards. Whether the prisoners decided to eat it or not was up to them, but there was no other choice. Many refused to eat to begin with, but most succumbed in the end, as hunger started to bite.

Beta-vac had thought about trying to escape in the early days of his captivity, but had now resigned himself to his fate. He could see no way of ever leaving the confines of the imperial compound. The prisoners were watched over day and night by the Imperial Guards, who themselves needed no breaks to eat or sleep. Anyone trying to break free would be dead in seconds, if they were lucky. He had considered making an attempt, in the belief that a quick death at the hands of the guards would be preferable to a slow, potentially agonising death in front of the tentacled monsters. But, in the end, Beta-vac had decided against certain death, however quick. There was always a slim chance that rescue might arrive somehow, before he finally met his end, with the last of his blood being sucked along a snake-like tube into the fetid mouth of a quivering cephalopod.

Aka-mas and his son continued to make their way through the maze of passageways, hoping they were heading in the right direction. They aimed to capture as many images as they could, which would provide evidence of the horrors existing in the imperial seat of power.

So far, apart from the vats of blood stored in the fridge-like building they had originally entered, there was little to be seen except dank, featureless and gloomy corridors. They also needed to try and locate, and jam, the equipment that controlled the mechanisms inserted into the necks of the Martian populace, if such a thing existed. For that, they would need to penetrate deeper into the heart of the citadel.

The entire complex seemed completely deserted. They hadn't seen or heard anything since leaving the storeroom, and Aka-mas was becoming increasingly worried. They had entered the compound through an unguarded gate and been confronted by an open door giving access to the interior of the estate. Not a single Imperial Guard had so far been seen to impede their progress.

*Are we walking into a trap?* thought Aka-mas, *and if so, how did the creatures know of our plans?* No one knew of their intentions apart from Sep-lee, and Aka-mas was convinced that the historian was truly on their side. That left the librarian, Hak-tes, who Sep-lee had been so keen to include in the plan, in order to make use of his contacts. *Could Hak-tes have informed on his friend to the authorities?* argued Aka-mas. *Or could one of the contacts have double-crossed them all?* He had no way of knowing whether the two of them were heading for a prearranged confrontation with their imperial masters, or whether they had just been extraordinarily lucky, being part of a well-organised plan, with the help of brave allies from within the imperial household. Either way, it was too late to turn back now.

Eventually, the two men noticed that the damp stone walls of the corridors gave way to equally cold but sleek walls of metal. The light level had increased, and some of the walls were covered with deeply engrained symbols, which meant nothing to Aka-mas or his son.

'I think we might be getting nearer to the centre of operations,' whispered Aka-mas, as he recorded images of the symbols on his wristband. 'If this is a language of some kind, I've never seen anything like it before. Sep-lee might be interested to examine it if we manage to make it out of here.'

Aka-des nodded before pushing his father back into the shadows. He could hear the metallic clanking of the Imperial Guards' feet approaching from a side corridor. The two men held their breath as they waited. Had they been seen by the creatures, who were now sending their robot servants to apprehend the humanoid spies, who had dared to intrude where they had no right to be?

The mantra spoken by the emperor in his earlier dream flashed into the mind of Aka-des.

'Death to those who defy my rules. Death to those who defy me.'

Aka-mas could hardly believe his eyes when he saw what came into view. A sedan chair type contraption consisting of a clear cylindrical container filled with liquid, mounted on two supporting poles of gold, appeared before them. The ends of the poles were held by four Imperial Guards, and the cylinder contained a squirming nightmare of a creature, just as his son had described. Greyish-green in colour, with an enormous head laced with pulsating reddish veins, the monster had three black eyes which darted left and right, as if searching for something to kill. The creature radiated pure evil and hate as it lashed its tentacles against the sides of the container. There appeared to be some sort of control panel located within the cylinder, and the claw-like hands of the monstrosity seemed to be manipulating some levers. Its three trunk-like legs were latched to the base of the container using the large, webbed suckers which acted as the feet of the abomination.

Aka-mas quickly took an image of the creature before the retinue moved out of sight.

'Where do you think it is going?' asked Aka-des in a hushed tone.

'It didn't look very happy.'

His father managed a weak smile as he placed his hand on his son's shoulder.

'Shall we follow and see if we can find out?' he replied.

'That's what we're here for,' said Aka-des with a shrug, and they both moved back out of the shadows.

Keeping their distance, they quietly followed the macabre troop, which soon turned left into an adjoining room. A metallic door slid open to admit them, and then quickly closed once more.

Aka-mas and his son approached the room and peered through two of its porthole windows into the chamber beyond. It was filled with rows and rows of what looked like large green eggs or pods of some sort. At the centre of the room was a circular pond filled with the ubiquitous murky liquid. At one side of the pond was the creature in the container, still moving some dials on the control panel. The Imperial Guards stood silently behind the monster, like suits of armour in a museum. Aka-des noted that some of the eggs on the lower shelves were starting to pulsate, and he watched open-mouthed as small grey tentacles slowly appeared from a gap at the top of the eggs, like worms blindly searching for any signs of movement. Gradually, the gap increased in size and the tentacles latched onto the edges of the now sizeable hole. With a final heave, the body of the creatures within the eggs broke free. With three jet-black eyes and quivering bulbous bodies, the baby cephalopods made their entrance into the world.

The adult creature pressed a button on its control panel, and part of the wall at the back of the room slid open. A long metallic bench silently extended into the room, and the two men were horrified to see three youths laid flat on their backs, attached to the bench with metal straps.

As soon as the bench appeared, the baby cephalopods squealed with delight, opening their mouths to extend their worm-like feeding tubes, ready to enjoy their first ever meal.

The youths gave out a pitiful cry as they realised their hopeless predicament. The tubes wriggled towards the necks of the poor victims while the infant tentacles lashed with childish excitement.

Aka-des closed his eyes as he heard the screams of the youths, the feeding tubes latching onto their necks as the baby cephalopods started to suck wildly. Once they'd had their fill, the tubes retracted and the infants, bloated and replete, pushed themselves into the pond to begin their lives in the watery world of adulthood.

Aka-mas and his son had seen enough. They crept further down the corridor, wondering what further horrors awaited them. They didn't have to wait long before they heard footsteps approaching from a side corridor. Not the metallic clunking of the Imperial Guards, but the measured steps of a flesh and blood creature. Hiding behind a column festooned with ornate symbols, they saw two elderly men dressed in white and gold robes talking to each other.

'Two of the elders,' whispered Aka-mas, straining to see the faces of the approaching men.

The couple seemed to be in animated discussion, and then one of them stopped, pressing a pad on a wall of metal. Immediately, a hidden door slid open and the two elders entered. The door did not slide shut behind them, so Aka-mas and Aka-des crept up to the opening, peering into a magnificently gilded chamber. At its centre was a cylindrical container containing a cephalopod, its black eyes expressionless as the creature stared ahead. It was flanked by four robot guards, standing motionless, as if to attention.

In front of the container were rows of high-backed chairs arranged in a semicircle, and in each chair sat one of the elders, about thirty in all. The two men who had just entered the room took the two vacant chairs remaining, and all eyes turned to face the creature in its vat of liquid.

The elders stared intently at the malevolent eyes of the cephalopod and then, as if in a trance, each picked up a metallic band from a small table beside their chair and placed it on their head. Each headband had a small white jewel-like insert at its centre, giving the impression that the seated elders were wearing tiaras. The container at the centre of the room started to glow with a bluish light, and the white jewels in the headbands promptly turned a similar colour. No one in the room moved while the ghostly light bathed the faces of the elderly men. All eyes remained fixed on the hideous creature still writhing in its tank.

The eerie light washed over the elders for about five minutes, before gradually diminishing in intensity, and then finally extinguishing altogether.

'What do you think is happening?' asked Aka-des, as he and his father captured further images on their wristbands.

'I'm not sure,' admitted Aka-mas. 'Some sort of brainwashing exercise perhaps, or maybe the elders are receiving orders from their masters. The creatures must communicate with them somehow. My guess is that it's done telepathically, and the headbands may be part of the process.'

The seated elders then removed their headbands simultaneously, placing them back on the tables. They rose from their seats and, with a bow to the tentacled demon in front of them, the ministeriales of the cephalopods started to file silently out of the room.

Aka-mas and his son took their cue to leave and sprinted as quietly as they could away from the chamber before the first of the elders reached the exit.

The two men turned left and right, with no idea where they were in the complex. Aka-des noticed a small empty room just off the corridor they now found themselves in. He pulled his father inside, closing the door behind them.

'What did you do that for?' questioned his father, panting with the exertion of their sprint.

'We don't know where we're going,' replied Aka-des, 'and we can't keep running forever. Let's catch our breath and think about where we go from here.'

Aka-mas nodded his agreement while inhaling a few large gulps of air.

'I think we must be in the pyramid already,' said Aka-des, looking around the empty room. 'The walls and floors are all metal rather than the damp stone we encountered earlier, and some of the walls are angled.'

'Perhaps the outer walls of the pyramid?' suggested his father. 'If so, we must be getting near the control centre of the complex.'

Just then, the door to the room started to open. The two men held their breath. There was nowhere else to run; the room only had one door. They were trapped.

'No, it can't be!' cried Aka-des as he saw, standing at the entrance to the room, his old friend Beta-vac. Thinner and paler than he could remember, but it was definitely Beta-vac.

'You're alive… I-I can't believe it,' stuttered Aka-des as he approached his friend. Then he noticed the look of fear etched across his face.

'I'm so sorry!' he cried out. 'You shouldn't have come!'

'What do you mean?' blurted Aka-des, moving closer to his friend.

'They made me do it,' came the anguished reply.

Beta-vac was then pushed into the room by two Imperial Guards who stood at the doorway, their red eyes staring impassively at the three humanoid captives huddled together, with no means of escape.

The robot guards abruptly left the room, closing the door firmly behind them. The three men heard the clunk of metal on metal as the footsteps of the Imperial Guards receded into the distance.

Aka-des rushed to the door and pressed the pad on the wall. Nothing happened. The door was locked.

'We're prisoners,' he said, the tone of helplessness in his voice reflecting what the others were feeling. 'No way out.'

'Somehow the creatures knew of our plans,' said Aka-mas. 'We should have guessed. We entered the compound through an unlocked and unguarded gate, only to find an open door into the storeroom. We have moved around the maze of corridors without any resistance from the guards. It has all been just too easy.'

'I bet it was Hak-tes,' replied his son, bitterness replacing the helplessness in his voice. 'He must have passed on our plans to contacts inside the palace.'

'You shouldn't have come,' repeated Beta-vac, his eyes wild with fear. 'The elders found out that you were both intending to try and rescue me, and have been questioning me about you ever since. That's why I'm still alive.'

His eyes looked down at the floor, a look of complete despair enveloping the distraught youth.

'Now there's no need to keep any of us alive. They can kill us all without anyone finding out.'

'It's not your fault,' comforted Aka-des.

'We're here because we wanted to come. We realised the chances of success were pretty small, but we had to do something. We wanted to get some evidence as to what really goes on here to show people outside.'

He looked at his friend, concern etched on his face, before adding, 'And to get you out of here, if you were still alive.'

Beta-vac gave a weak smile and patted Aka-des on his shoulder.

'I'm afraid it has all been a waste of time,' he said quietly. 'They'll never let us go. You know too much. We'll end up as a meal for the monsters who control this place.'

'They must have a weakness,' argued Aka-mas, desperately trying to think of some way out of the mess they now found themselves in. 'For one thing, the creatures can only live inside their tanks of liquid, so their movements are restricted.'

'They can exist outside the liquid, at least for short periods of time,' corrected Aka-des, thinking back to the creature lumbering across the platform to face the terrified novitiates during his previous incursion into the palace.

'But they rely on the Imperial Guards to carry out their commands for most of the time,' added his father.

'If we could somehow jam their power source so they were shut down, the creatures would be helpless.'

'Nice idea, Dad,' said Aka-des, 'but how do you intend to switch off the power to hundreds, maybe thousands of robots in this compound? There's not likely to be one huge on-off switch, is there?'

'Then there are the elders as well,' Aka-mas added, deep in thought.

'I'm sure they are in some sort of hypnotic trance. The ones we saw being bathed in that blue light earlier, for example. Perhaps they have to go through a process of regeneration periodically to keep them compliant. Without that, they may wake up to reality and realise how they have been manipulated by these creatures over the years.'

'It's good of you both to come here and risk your lives,' broke in Beta-vac, resigned to his fate.

'I do appreciate your attempt to rescue me, but I don't think that three of us stand much chance against an empire which has ruled this planet for possibly thousands of years. As far as they are concerned, we are nothing more than a minor irritation. Like an insect settling on your face on a summer's day. Something to be swatted away with hardly a moment's thought.'

The simile struck home with Aka-des.

'You're right.'

He sighed as he sat down on the floor of the room, his back against the wall.

'It's hopeless. All we can do is just sit here and wait for the guards to return. We'll find out our fate soon enough.'

The other two men joined him on the floor, and the three of them sat silently, deep in their own thoughts. *I wonder if my wife will even realise we have gone*, pondered Aka-mas. *Probably not, at least for a few days, or until she wants a job doing.*

After what seemed like an age, but was in fact only a matter of some ten minutes, the three men were startled back to reality by a noise outside the door. It slid open to reveal a man dressed in the white and gold robes of the elders, flanked by two Imperial Guards.

'It's Cru-lem, the baker,' cried out Aka-des. 'He's an elder.'

Cru-lem smiled at Aka-des, but there was no warmth in his expression.

'I have only recently been elevated to this auspicious position, in recognition of my unstinting loyalty to the emperor. We have known about you and your treasonous intentions for some time,' said the baker. 'In fact, I even provided you with a means of transport for your first visit to the palace.'

'The delivery van,' spluttered Aka-des. 'You knew I had stowed away in the back.'

'Of course,' replied Cru-lem upon entering the room. 'We were interested to see what you would do and who else was involved in your feeble attempt to sabotage the state.'

*Sep-lee*, thought Aka-mas. *I hope he is safe.*

Cru-lem turned to stare at him, seemingly aware of his thoughts.

'The historian is in custody,' snapped the elder, his voice a cruel sneer. 'He has been arrested as an enemy of the emperor. His fate is sealed.'

'No!' shouted Aka-des. 'Leave him alone! He can do you no harm!'

Cru-lem simply smiled and, moving back, ushered the robot guards into the room with a wave of his hand.

'Take them to the reception suite,' he ordered, almost hissing the last two words of the sentence. 'I'm sure our guests would like to meet their masters.'

The three men were herded along the corridor and then pushed through the open door of a larger, more ornately decorated room. Aka-mas noticed that the walls were covered with intricately carved friezes made of what looked like gold. Some of the panels seemed to depict wars or battles of some sort, involving races of various kinds, some humanoid and some not. In each panel, tentacled creatures held sway, crushing the opposition with ruthless efficiency.

One panel at the centre of the wall showed what appeared to be a solar system, but its configuration was unlike the planetary system of which Mars was a part. There seemed to be six planets orbiting their sun, with the fourth planet highlighted in a blue colour.

'Perhaps it's the home world of the creatures,' surmised Aka-mas, marvelling at the size and detail of the friezes.

'You are correct,' said Cru-lem, glancing at the depiction. 'That is the home planet of our masters. The centre of their empire, if you like. Some of the other panels show famous battles in the history of their race. They have subjugated many worlds across the galaxy over the aeons. Mars is but one corner of a vast imperial family.'

'Family.'

Aka-mas spat in disgust.

'These monsters have stampeded their way across space, crushing any opposition they encountered, to create an empire of feeding colonies. The inhabitants of these planets aren't part of a family. They are mere cattle, or crops to be harvested. Their home worlds are just farms to provide the nourishment these creatures need to survive.'

'A little dramatic, don't you think?' replied Cru-lem quietly, as though admonishing an errant child.

'The masters have brought many benefits to their dominions, as will be explained.'

The three men were each led to a metallic chair facing the central panel of the frieze, showing the home world of the cephalopods. As they sat down, metal grips clamped around their wrists and ankles, making escape impossible. They heard a soft humming sound, and from the floor in front of them rose a cylinder containing one of the creatures, thrashing its tentacles in the brackish liquid surrounding it. Its three black eyes seemed to burn into the very minds of the prisoners, as if seeking their innermost thoughts. The monster appeared to radiate hate as its claw-like hands repeatedly thumped against the sides of the container, like the solemn beating of a drum when convicted criminals are led to the scaffold. The cephalopod anchored itself to the base of the container with its suckered webbed feet, while its protruding beak would periodically open and close, allowing the repulsive worm-like feeding tubes to dart in and out of its mouth, toying with the three terrified men.

Aka-mas could not take his eyes off the grotesque creature. This was the closest he had been to one of the cephalopods, and every detail of its loathsome body was clearly visible. The web of thin pulsating veins covering its bulbous head seemed to be getting more and more prominent as the monster squirmed and writhed, lashing its tentacles in a frenzy.

'The master is pleased to make your acquaintance,' said Cru-lem in a sneering, mocking voice as he rubbed his hands together in glee. 'He will certainly relish the experience. You could even say that it will provide him with a degree of rapture.'

The elder let out a muffled snigger; his ample body shaking in his robes of office. At the mention of the word "rapture", the creature in the tank seemed to become hysterical. Its feeding tubes thrashed violently against the container as if trying to reach the succulent flesh of the three prisoners sitting in the room beyond.

The creature pulled a lever on the control panel in front of it, and a helmet of the same metallic element suddenly appeared above the heads of the three men, gradually descending from a gap in the ceiling, being lowered into place at the end of an extending pole of the same material.

Aka-des looked at his father, and then at Beta-vac. *This is it*, he thought. *We're done for.* Just then, a similar helmet was lowered onto the head of Cru-lem, whose cold eyes glared at the prisoners. The elder immediately fell into a trance, and the three men simultaneously felt a dull pain in their heads, which vanished within seconds. Cru-lem opened his mouth, and the captives heard a strange gurgling voice filling the room.

'You have trespassed where you have no right to be,' said the voice, the words flowing around the men like waves lapping around rocks on a beach. 'Why have you come here? What did you hope to achieve?'

Aka-mas realised that the words were not those of Cru-lem; they had come from the creature in the tank. It was using the elder as a sort of conduit, conveying its thoughts to the three captured humanoids.

'We came to find my friend,' blurted Aka-des, his voice sounding more confrontational than was probably wise. 'We also wanted to gather information to prove to the inhabitants of this planet that their beloved emperor does not exist. They have been conned for thousands of years, and it has got to stop.'

The young man accepted that none of them would leave this place alive, so saw no reason to hold back. The creature stared at Aka-des with contempt.

'Your race is primitive,' said the voice. 'What you think is of no consequence to us. We allow your species to survive merely to provide us with what we require. We take what we need, and the rest of your miserable race can carry on with their wretched lives as they see fit. For the honour of providing us with sustenance, your people should be eternally grateful. You are serving a civilisation that has existed for millions of years. We have spread throughout the galaxy harvesting inferior species wherever they are found. It is our right to rule, and your duty to serve.'

'So, the benefit to us from your rule is that you allow us to exist as a species, as long as we are of use to you. Some deal.'

Aka-mas spat out the words with disdain.

'Enough,' replied the voice, the creature squirming restlessly in its tank. 'Your mission was fruitless. You have achieved nothing, but you will pay the price for daring to threaten our hegemony of this small and insignificant planet.'

# Chapter 27
# Ghosts of Mars

Tom was convinced that the bracelet did emit some form of heat, but the sensation was short-lived. Within seconds, it returned to normal, just a piece of jewellery lying on the table. He carefully placed the artefact in a box and put it next to the ring for safekeeping.

'Unless I am going mad, that thing definitely became warm in my hand,' he muttered to himself. 'But how could it? It must be millions of years old. It just doesn't make sense.'

The crew busied themselves with their tasks during the remainder of the day, and no more was said about the strange Martian bracelet. Even Jason felt well enough to undertake some light duties, although he was still experiencing a dull headache from time to time. *Must be the result of my fall outside*, he reasoned. *Nothing a good night's sleep won't fix.* He glanced at a mirror and noticed that the odd red spot on his forehead was getting darker.

'Must be the bruising coming out,' he commented, without any great concern. 'It'll probably fade in a day or two.'

Dinner that evening was a fairly relaxed affair, with each member of the team giving a brief rundown of what work they had been involved in. Tom reported that he had been in touch with mission control, who wanted a full analysis of the bracelet, and also firm evidence of the existence of the insects.

'They want us to capture a few of them,' he added.

'Nothing like a live specimen to keep the sceptics quiet.'

'How do they think we are going to do that?' asked Martin.

'If we get anywhere near those critters, they will blast us with their force field.'

'Perhaps we could put a pot of jam in front of them and wait until they take the bait,' suggested Robert helpfully.

Most of the others laughed.

'It could well come to that,' agreed Tom, with a smile on his face.

'Do you recommend strawberry or apricot flavour?'

Jason did not laugh. He looked at the others before adding quietly, 'The insects are indeed powerful. They must pay for their past interference and obtrusions.'

'You what?' said Martin, becoming irritated by the medic's increasingly erratic interventions.

'What do you know about them?'

Jason sat calmly at the table and simply repeated his warning.

'The insects are powerful creatures. We must be wary of any attempt to subvert them without careful planning.'

'You're crazy,' said Martin, rising from the table in a huff. 'I'm off to bed. Perhaps the oracle would like to take a stroll outside without a spacesuit.'

With that, he left the room.

The others looked at each other before turning to face Jason.

'Are you feeling okay?' asked Frances.

'It's just that you've been coming out with some odd comments since you bumped your head.'

'I am perfectly well,' assured the medic. 'I'm just concerned that we do nothing untoward to antagonise the creatures unnecessarily.'

'I can promise you that we will do nothing that could risk the well-being of any member of our team,' said Tom, who was sitting next to Jason.

The Canadian suddenly felt a burning thirst, unlike any he had ever felt before. He grabbed a jug of water from the centre of the table and poured the contents down his throat, splashing Tom and Angela who were sitting on his other side in the process. But it was no good. The water did nothing to quench his thirst. He stared wildly at his shocked teammates, as water dripped from his still open mouth, soaking his shirt. He focused on Tom, and then Angela, taking deep breaths.

He felt the warmth of their bodies, so close to his, and could sense the pulsing of a precious liquid as it coursed through their veins and arteries. A liquid rich in nutrients, he could smell the salty sweetness of it. This would quench his thirst, he realised, and nothing else would do.

With that, he lost consciousness and collapsed, his body slumped over the table, knocking the now empty jug of water onto the floor.

'I don't like this at all,' said Frances. 'There is something seriously wrong with him. It can't just be the result of concussion.'

'But we don't have the facilities here to look after him properly,' added Angela, as Tom and Robert carried the motionless body of Jason out of the room.

The two women looked at each other.

'We are going to have to return to Earth,' said Frances. 'We have no other choice.'

Outside, as the night drew in, the winds of Mars tightened their grip on the fragile craft from planet Earth. Tiny grains of sand and dust seemed to be knocking at the walls of the ship demanding entry, as the ghosts of forgotten civilisations made their claims on the travellers within.

# Chapter 28
# The Command

Across the plains of Mars, the Antis race went about their daily lives as they had since time immemorial. Grazing their lands and tending their flocks of pinkish-grey Aphonas, who fed themselves by sucking the sap of the cactus-like zegrona plants. The Aphonas would use their mandibles to pierce the tough skin of the plant, before sucking the sweet liquid through their stylets. The creatures stood on long, thin legs, their bodies almost translucent, and some were born with wings. In the wild, if the host plants became weak due to overfeeding by the Aphonas, the winged members of the herd would disperse in search of new food sources.

However, domesticated Aphonas would have their wings clipped by the Antis, so they were unable to leave the herd. The Antis would move their flocks of Aphonas to a new feeding area of their choosing whenever the zegrona plants in a particular locality showed signs of distress. The Antis would milk their herds of Aphonas for the creamy sweet liquid they produced by stroking the bodies of the creatures with their antennae. This liquid was a staple part of the Antis diet, and every colony protected its herd from possible attack as a primary duty.

Other members of the hive concentrated on building new nests or repairing existing ones, while some attended to the needs of their queen. Another major role in the colony, however, was that of looking after the young.

The worm-like larvae of the Antis had no limbs, and no antennae, so they were reliant on the adult workers who tended to them. The larvae would signal their hunger to the adults by pulsing their soft bodies in a unique way and also by emitting a low-pitched moaning noise. Their bodies were covered in tiny hairs, each ending in a hook-like appendage. The workers would use these hooks to attach the larvae to the walls of the nurseries to organise the offspring and determine feeding times. Feeding the offspring was almost a full-time occupation in itself. The larvae would digest insects and other small animals brought to them via the workers by secreting saliva, which dissolved the food almost instantaneously. The resulting mush would then be ingested through a series of feeding holes, before the remains were regurgitated by the larvae into the mouths of waiting workers. This was then passed to the queen of the colony, who used it as a vital source of nutrition to produce more eggs.

Female larvae would also produce a fine silky material, which adults then used to help build their nests. As a result, the offspring of the Antis had a crucial role to play in the long-term viability of the colony, and tending to their needs was one of the most important jobs in the hierarchy of Antis society.

The new day dawned, as had all previous days throughout the history of the Antis race, with a gathering in each hive to welcome the new day, and to give thanks to the goddess Duma, and the Queen of Queens, the unseen ruler of the entire civilisation.

\*\*\*

In the new settlement of Windor village, the young mayor Stor-dal arrived at his office early, intending to clear his in tray before the events of a new day added to the already heavy demands on his time. He poured himself a cup of freshly brewed masona leaves, to give himself the kick-start he needed at the beginning of every working day, as he stared out of the window of his office to the fields outside the village. Here was the reserve specifically set aside for the Antis, and Stor-dal was pleased to see that a colony of the insects had already moved in.

He was fascinated to watch their normal morning routine, as the insects massed in a large group. *What are they up to?* he pondered while observing intently. *Are they receiving their orders for the day, or is it merely a social gathering of some sort? If only we understood more of the Antis culture, we might be able to make contact in some meaningful way.*

He then noticed behaviour not normally associated with the insects' routine. The whole group suddenly turned to face in the same direction and then bowed their heads. Their antennae vibrated as a new message was received, unheard by anyone but the members of the Antis race themselves.

'The time has arrived, my children, for our people to rise up against the humanoids and their masters, and retake our planet from those whose actions, if unchecked, will destroy it. We must overthrow their leaders and destroy any who stand in our way. Their towns and settlements, built on our sacred lands, must be turned to rubble, and the lands reconsecrated in the name of the goddess Duma. We undertake this crusade, not just to avenge the desecration of our world at the hands of the humanoids, but also to honour our ancestors who did much to build a civilisation in harmony with its surroundings, and to ensure a sustainable legacy for future generations of our race. Rise up, my children, rise up.'

The same message was channelled telepathically through the entire Antis race, wherever they were located across the planet, and the resulting cheer of acceptance of the challenge similarly reverberated throughout their colonies as the insects started to make their plans.

Stor-dal wondered what this new behaviour meant, but he had no time to dwell on the matter. With a sigh, he returned to his desk and started to plough his way through the list of tasks which were part and parcel of his role as mayor of a thriving community.

Later that afternoon, as he was returning to his office after attending a meeting with the head of the new local school, Stor-dal received a call on his wristband, flashing red for "urgent". The mayor pressed the button to answer the call and listened as a very flustered Tag-wel, mayor of the nearby settlement of Remsal, gave a dire warning to his young colleague.

'The Antis are on the march!' he bellowed. 'They have already ransacked our neighbouring settlement, the village of Panloor, and they are heading towards us. Make sure your plasma fields are switched on and take all necessary precautions. The Imperial Guards have been notified, but this is an emergency. Do whatever you can until help arrives.'

Stor-dal thanked Tag-wel for his warning and then gave the order to turn on the plasma field. As he looked out of his office window, there was no sign of the giant insects. *Would they attack us here?* he wondered gloomily. *Am I being naïve in thinking that both our races can exist side by side? If that really is the case, there is no future for either of our species on this planet.*

# Chapter 29
# Attack

Within an hour, a large group or "raid" of Antis had arrived at the outskirts of the town of Remsal. It was an established settlement of some thirty thousand inhabitants, but had recently undergone a significant expansion into the surrounding area, with two new satellite settlements adjoining the existing urban area.

Unlike Stor-dal, the mayor of Remsal was not a fan of the Antis race. He was definitely someone who saw the insects as nothing more than vermin, to be eradicated from the area if at all possible. Setting up a reserve for the Antis just outside his town was the last thing Tag-wel would have contemplated.

He gathered with a group of civic dignitaries at the edge of the town, watching the Antis as they approached. There must have been thousands of the insects as they swarmed over the nearby hills, down to the valley where Remsal was situated.

'The plasma field is switched on,' Tag-wel assured his companions. 'Those creatures can't get inside the town. I'm just curious as to what they do.'

As the insects neared the settlement, they spread out into a large arc, with the creatures facing the town presenting an almost unbroken wall of dark green to the people watching from within the boundaries of Remsal.

These were soldiers of the insect race, standing at well over seven feet tall. They were larger than other types of Antis, and had huge mandibles which could capture, crush and disassemble prey easily. The thick armour-plated bodies of the creatures were a much darker colour than the generally grey-green hue of the workers of the species.

Suddenly, the advancing army stopped moving forward, and those at the front of the arc seemed to stare at the buildings of the town set out before them with their two large compound eyes, perfectly engineered to detect the smallest of movements.

The middle eye of the three ocelli on the tops of the insects' heads began to glow with a strange orange light, and the soldiers started to create a high-pitched sound by slowly rubbing their antennae together. The procedure began with those soldiers fronting the arc, but soon rippled back through the ranks, like a huge Mexican wave. An enormous pulse of sound of the correct pitch, matching the resonant frequency of the equipment controlling the protective plasma field, caused the components of the intricate machinery to respond with movement, eventually leading to violent oscillations, and ultimately to the equipment ceasing to function at all. The plasma field instantly switched off as the insects started to move forward once more.

Tag-wel and his associates stood open-mouthed as the huge creatures approached the very edge of the town, an unstoppable army now arriving at their open and undefended door. Word soon spread throughout the population, as people ran shrieking through the streets in search of shelter.

'Where are the Imperial Guards?' shouted Tag-wel, while the group of dignitaries accompanying him broke ranks, abandoning their exalted positions of dignity and honour in the community, fleeing in all directions, joining the general throng of people attempting to escape from the marauding insects.

'Why are the guards not here to protect us? Why have they left us defenceless against this plague of insects?'

Unlike his pusillanimous colleagues, Tag-wel refused to flee. He was mayor of Remsal and proud of his position. He had a duty to stand his ground against the invaders, whatever the consequences.

As the Antis marched into the town, they once again produced the high-pitched sound, creating a shock wave and an enormous amount of heat energy, which caused buildings to implode and collapse into rubble. People screamed and ran to escape the falling masonry. Some were unlucky, their dead bodies sprawled across the streets as they succumbed to the barrage of rock and stone.

Tag-wel remained rooted to the spot watching a group of dark green insects moving towards him. One of the creatures stood in front of the determined mayor, who remained resolute and unwavering in his commitment to the town. The strange orange glow of the huge creature's ocellus strengthened. Just then, an intense burst of microwave energy hit Tag-wel head-on.

'Long live the emperor!' cried the mayor defiantly, his words just managing to escape his lips before his internal organs were fried to a crisp by the fierce beam of radiation. Tag-wel and the town of Remsal were no more.

The Antis swept through the ruins of the settlement, mopping up any people unfortunate enough to have stayed behind, before turning their attention to the symbol of Martian authority every town or village was legally obliged to have; the statue of the imperial orb. There it stood, like hundreds of others across the land, a constant reminder of imperial power.

The golden image was surrounded by Antis soldiers, who rubbed their antennae to create the destructive wave of sound. The ground beneath the statue shook violently, with cracks appearing beneath the foundations of the simulacrum. The golden orb teetered on its base and then the imperial effigy itself cracked and broke into a thousand pieces.

A huge telepathic cheer washed through the assembled ranks of Antis as they left the devastated remains of the once proud Martian town, moving on towards the city itself.

***

High above the Martian surface, in the newly launched satellite, the deep black eyes of the cephalopods stared intently at the images of the destruction below, the Antis laying waste to settlement after settlement. The creatures writhed in their tanks, the veins on their bulbous heads ever more intense with anger surging through their bodies. The insects posed a threat to the power and domination of the tentacled creatures; this could not be allowed to continue. Dead Martians meant less food for their colony, as though intruders had set fire to a field of ripening crops. Like any farmers, the cephalopods had to protect their investment, so a message was sent to their kindred in the imperial compound below, instructing them to "act now and destroy the insects".

# Chapter 30
# The Advance

Aka-des looked at his father, accepting that they would never leave the room alive.

'Love you, Dad,' he said, his voice tinged with sadness.

'Love you, too, son,' replied his father, realising how close the two of them had become.

The love between them had undoubtedly always been there, but to express it openly was just not the "done thing" between a father and his adult son. *A shame that we have to be seconds away from death before we're willing to acknowledge our feelings*, thought Aka-mas.

Aka-des then turned to his friend Beta-vac, who was gripping the edges of his chair, almost catatonic with fear.

'Love you, too,' said Aka-des, a faint smile crossing his face. 'I don't regret trying to rescue you for one minute. My only regret is that we didn't make it.'

'I know,' replied his friend quietly. 'I can never thank you enough for what you've done for me. If only things had turned out differently.'

Just then, what sounded like an alarm resounded throughout the compound. The creature in the tank turned its head as if listening to a message or command, before focusing its eyes directly on the three men. Its tentacles thumped against the walls of the container, as if to express its anger and frustration at being deprived of a meal, and then the entire tank descended slowly from view beneath the floor of the room.

Cru-lem awakened from his trance and promptly commanded three Imperial Guards to take the prisoners to the cells.

'The masters will deal with these miscreants later,' he called out and swiftly left the room, his robes billowing behind him like washing hanging out to dry on a windy day.

Aka-mas and his two companions were led from the room by the guards and ushered towards yet another undistinguished metallic door further down the corridor. The three men were unceremoniously pushed inside by the guards, with the door quickly closing behind them, only to find that the room was not empty.

'Sep-lee!' cried out Aka-mas. 'They told us you had been captured!'

'I'm afraid so,' replied the historian with a nod. 'Two men came to my flat and told me that I was being arrested for crimes against the state. Taya was not impressed. She gave one of the men a nasty scratch across his face with her claws. I do hope she's all right.'

'Have you seen the creatures yet?' asked Aka-mas, desperate for some third-party verification as to the existence of the monsters.

Even at a time like this, when the best any of them could hope for was a stay of execution, it was still important to Aka-mas that his son's story be substantiated.

'No, not yet,' replied Sep-lee. 'I was brought straight here, and a gentleman in a white and gold robe told me that I would meet "my masters" shortly. I must say that I was looking forward to meeting the creatures your son so vividly described in the flesh, so to speak.'

Aka-des looked at the historian with incredulity.

'You really want to see these tentacled nightmares. Why?'

'Because I wanted definitive proof, before I died, that the story narrated in the Tablets of Skothath was true. I have spent my entire working life studying the amazing history of our people, but here is living evidence of one of the most important episodes in the long history of our race. I would die a contented man if I could at least see one of these creatures for myself.'

Aka-mas gave Sep-lee a knowing smile and patted him on the back.

'Well, I think we will all have the honour of meeting our masters one more time,' he said. 'Although personally, I am quite happy to forego the pleasure for as long as possible.'

'What do you think that noise was?' asked Aka-des.

'It sounded like some sort of alarm. What could it mean?'

'I don't know,' his father admitted.

'But anything that delays the inevitable is fine with me.'

\*\*\*

200

Han-doe was enjoying the sunshine as his shift at the Povas Gate entrance to the city was coming to an end. It had been an uneventful day's work for the young gateman, checking the details of people entering and leaving the city, but he was looking forward to a quick drink at his favourite hostelry before returning home to see his family. His wife had recently been blessed with a gorgeous baby daughter, and the couple were enjoying making plans for the obligatory Citizenship Ceremony, which was to be held in the next few weeks. Family and friends would gather to witness the infant being formally welcomed into the imperial family to which everyone belonged, and then there would be a party afterwards to celebrate the occasion in style. Han-doe grinned at his good fortune.

Just then, he happened to look out from his post across the undulating pasturelands that lapped up to the city walls, and to his astonishment he saw in the distance a dark green patch emerge from between a row of hills. As he continued to watch, he noticed that the indistinct patch of green was actually a large group of Antis, which seemed to be heading straight for the city.

*It can't be*, thought the gateman, staring at the approaching army of giant insects. *What are they up to?* He was about to contact his superiors for advice when he turned to see a battalion of Imperial Guards advance from within the city towards the gate he was manning. Deciding that his shift was finished for the day, Han-doe hurriedly got down from his chair and quickly left his sentry box, disappearing into the streets of the city with unseemly haste. Hardly appropriate behaviour for an employee of the state, he had to admit, but at times like this his desire for self-preservation superseded his sense of loyalty to anyone else.

The Imperial Guards, looking resplendent in their golden livery, purposefully marched through the streets of the city, creating quite a spectacle for the intrigued onlookers. Wondering whether this heralded an official ceremony they knew nothing about, crowds began to gather, with some people waving and cheering as the guards trooped by.

Then, a rumour began to circulate amongst the throng that an army of Antis had been spotted heading towards the city, and the guards were marching to defend it from any attack by the insects. Quickly, the cheers turned into screams as people started to flee. Some stood their ground, convinced that their brave soldiers would be more than a match for the primitive creatures

201

advancing on the city, but others were not so sure. There were no recorded instances of the Imperial Guards and Antis clashing in anything but the odd half-hearted skirmish outside the metropolis. The insect race had never attempted to make a concerted attack on the heart of the Martian civilisation before, so what, people asked, had changed their minds?

The Martian people, as a peaceable race, carried no weapons themselves. In fact, it was against the law to do so, with harsh penalties for anyone found contravening the regulations. Defence was entirely a matter for the Imperial Guards under the direct control of the emperor himself. The populace could only hope that their trust in the imperial forces was well-founded.

High above the growing melee below, the cephalopods in their orbiting space station watched as the Antis continued to advance on the city. The creatures controlled the deployment of their robot guards, bringing in further reinforcements from the palace compound to bolster the battalions already preparing to meet the insect menace. The tentacled monsters were incandescent with rage at the impudence of these insects who dared to interfere with their absolute dominance of the Martian race. The cephalopods had largely ignored the Antis since their arrival on Mars. The tough skin of the insects, together with their rancid-tasting blood, meant that they were not a suitable source of food for the creatures.

This mutual disregard between the cephalopods and the Antis had worked well for both races for thousands of years. The insects were left alone to run their colonies in the Outside, while the alien invaders concentrated on the Martians in the city and other settlements. It was only when the Martians started to expand their territories significantly that conflicts began to surface. The cephalopods had largely ignored any incursions by the insects into the new settlements, refusing to send out squads of Imperial Guards to resolve disputes, accepting that Antis hegemony of their tribal lands was a fait accompli.

However, this lack of response by the guards in clashes with the insects caused increasing concern and anguish to the Martian settlers affected. They could not understand why the imperial authorities had apparently abandoned them, but most accepted that it was not their position to question the decisions of the emperor. Attacks by the insects were simply acknowledged as one of the risks of moving outside the safety of the city in order to begin a new, and potentially life-changing, future in a more family-friendly environment. Many were willing to accept that risk was evident by the number of new settlements being constructed.

As more and more of the Imperial Guards marched through the city, the inhabitants began to regain their confidence at the sight of this redoubtable army. People cheered on the troops, waving flags and throwing flowers at the feet of the soldiers. Many now believed that it would be the Antis who would suffer ignominious defeat in any battle with the imperial forces, and the streets started to fill once more with the convinced and the curious.

Some of the Imperial Guards took up position at various points of strategic or civic importance within the city, such as City Hall, the law courts and the House of Elders. A large contingent stayed to protect the approaches to the imperial compound itself, while others marched towards the numerous city gates, exiting the city and fanning out to provide a protective cordon encircling the city walls, ready to face the Antis army.

As the insect forces got nearer to the city, their pace slowed until they eventually came to a complete halt. The uncountable rows of dark green soldiers posed a formidable sight to anyone watching from a distance, but here the Antis were not confronting an army of living creatures, inhibited by the full range of emotions experienced by beings of flesh and blood. The cold, emotionless warriors of the imperial forces were not subject to feelings of fear and exhilaration, brotherhood and purpose, or anxiety and pain, as would their living counterparts. They stood facing the insect army, unfeeling and dispassionate, unmoved and unmoving, until ordered into action.

# Chapter 31
# At War

They did not have to wait long. Suddenly the Antis army began to move forward, their antennae vibrating as the telepathic order to advance was transmitted to the soldiers from an unseen source.

'Advance, my children, in the name of the goddess Duma. Your time has arrived. You must now retake our planet to save it from the desecration inflicted by the humanoids and their alien rulers. You must restore to us what is rightfully ours, so we can undo the wrongs committed in the past, and heal the wounds that our beloved world has suffered at the hands of those who care nothing for the well-being of our mother planet. Advance! Advance!'

The frontline troops of the Antis army focused their middle ocelli, glowing a deep orange, on the silent sentinels of the Imperial Guards standing before them and emitted their deadly beams of radiation directly at the androids. Within seconds, the heat generated had melted the complex mechanical innards of the robots, rendering them completely immobile. The heads of the automatons affected slumped forward onto their chests and flames engulfed the bodies of the guards, as if in divine retribution for all the evils committed in the past in the name of the emperor.

More guards moved forward to replace their fallen comrades and, as one, they raised their arms, firing bursts of powerful energy of their own at the advancing insects. The death rays incinerated anything in their path, until they reached the Antis troops themselves. The beams of radiation did not meet their target, being deflected by the individual force fields activated by each of the Antis at the command of their invisible leader. Some of the giant insects did succumb to the death rays, their bodies instantly reduced to cinders, but for the most part the force fields prevailed, and the Antis forces continued their advance towards the gates of the city.

The insect creatures rubbed their antennae together, like greedy money lenders rubbing their hands with glee at the sight of a pile of cash recently extorted from their hard-up clients. This produced the usual high-pitched sound, sending a powerful wave of noise directly at the city walls. The heavy stone walls began to crack and collapse as the shock wave caused the stone blocks to break apart, with rubble falling onto the Imperial Guards below, crushing them like toys.

The sound wave also had the effect of interfering with the delicate mechanics of the robot soldiers, with some spiralling out of control like spinning tops about to topple in a violent last wobble due to increasing precession.

The cephalopods, unaccustomed to defeat, ordered their android warriors back inside the city to regroup and prepare for a counter-attack. The watching crowds in the city streets became nervous at the sight of their soldiers retreating at the onslaught from the Antis. The Imperial Guards were, after all, their kith and kin. Many had sons who had joined the guards and were now in the service of the emperor. As rumours of the destruction inflicted by the insects on the imperial troops outside the city passed through the crowds, nerves were replaced by fear and apprehension.

A woman at the front of the crowd rushed up to a contingent of guards, standing motionless and awaiting orders, and flung her arms around the neck of one of the soldiers, desperate to find her only son who had joined the force at the last initiation ceremony at the recent Emperor's Day parade.

She tried to remove the metallic visor at the front of the soldier's helmet, in the vain hope that she would find her beloved son, but was rebuffed by the robot, who pushed her aside roughly. The woman fell to the ground and hit her head. She cried out in pain and shock, before being helped up by others in the crowd. The onlookers could not believe what they had just witnessed. This was not the way a member of the elite Imperial Guards was supposed to behave. The unthinkable happened, and a series of boos rang out from certain sections of the crowd, hesitantly at first, but gaining in strength as people responded to this unwarranted attack on a grieving mother.

The guards did not respond to the disturbance. It was as though the crowd of people did not exist. The countenances of the troops were hidden behind their rigid and unreadable masks of metal, providing an inscrutable barrier between the protected and the protectors.

The people wanted to see some sign that their troops were truly with them at this time of peril, and that the soldiers understood their fears and concerns. They wanted to see in the faces of their defenders signs of strength, bravery, determination and, yes, even fear. Evidence of emotions such as these would prove a true connection with the populace, and also provide confirmation of an agreed responsibility for those they were pledged to protect.

It was hard to respond positively to a group of unresponsive and impassive warriors, hidden inside their suits of armour, and this was the first time many in the crowds had experienced such feelings. Some felt guilty that they found themselves strangely detached from the guards who were, after all, being sent into battle on their behalf. Such feelings of doubt had to be shelved, however, as the troops readied themselves for the expected arrival of the Antis inside the city itself.

'They're here!' someone shouted, as the first of the insects broke through the ruins of the city walls and made their way into the heart of the Martian metropolis.

The eerie cacophony of sound emitted by the insects resonated around the narrow streets of this, one of the older parts of the city. The houses of the neighbourhood were smaller than their more modern counterparts elsewhere, but they were full of character. Terraces of individually styled buildings tumbled down the steep hills leading to the city walls, their window boxes filled with lovingly tended flowering plants of all descriptions and colours. People living in the area in the past tended to be mainly elderly, cherishing their homes and reliving times gone by as they chatted with their neighbours while sitting by their open doors of an evening. Well looked after and now subject to a preservation order, these dwellings were now much in demand. Recently, more young professional people had started to move in, attracted by the historical significance of the location and keen to set up home away from the drab functionality of some of the more modern developments.

Strangely, the destructive wave of sound emanating from the insects suddenly reduced as they marched through the ancient streets, as if they were somehow aware of the cultural importance of these winding alleys, built at a time when the two races were able to coexist with a degree of mutual respect. It seemed as if the Antis forces had made a conscious decision to reduce, as far as possible, possible damage to these historic dwellings.

However, this apparent respect for the old town did not apply to any Imperial Guards the insects encountered as they moved forward. Relying on their deadly beam of radiation, the Antis met little in the way of real resistance from the imperial forces while making their way towards the modern centre of the city.

A small group of Antis encountered a line of Imperial Guards standing in their way as they steadily progressed through the city. A crowd of people were standing behind the line of guards, unable to escape. They were trapped at the rear of an imposing square, full of ornately decorated buildings constructed in an age when aesthetics took precedence over modern practicality. The crowd backed away as far as they could, realising that the only route out of the square was the street where the giant insects were now advancing.

The orange glow of the Antis's ocelli signalled as the forerunner of the lethal beams of radiation, and were now aimed directly at the line of soldiers ahead. The guards aimed their own death ray at the approaching threat, and a few of the Antis, lacking sufficient strength in their force fields, were obliterated into clouds of dust. However, a sufficient number of their comrades survived, and the full force of the insects' radiation beams hit the Imperial Guards full on. Some of the robots exploded into a thousand pieces on the spot, whereas others simply ceased to function, their workings fused by the intense heat. A few were decapitated by the force of the impact, their metal heads falling to the ground and rolling towards the crowd of terrified onlookers, while the remainder of their bodies continued to stand, upright and motionless.

People in the crowd screamed, realising their fate was sealed. Others looked more carefully at the remnants of the Imperial Guards and stared in amazement.

'They're not people!' shouted a man nearest to the scene of devastation. 'They're just robots. The Imperial Guards are machines.'

It was true, others agreed as they peered at the carnage in front of them, momentarily forgetting that they now faced the contingent of Antis totally unarmed and unprotected. The soldiers of the emperor were not their sons and brothers, but mere androids.

'Then where are our boys?' cried out another man. 'What have they done with them?'

Many in the throng of people simply watched the enormous insects, resigned to their impending deaths at the hands of the dark green creatures.

Then, without warning, the Antis troops turned and retraced their steps out of the square, leaving the baffled but thankful crowd to stand and stare at the flaming and smoking remains of the imperial warriors.

The cephalopods watching the trail of destruction below, from their vantage point some three thousand miles above the Martian surface, were aghast at the inability of their robot troops to penetrate the force field defences of the Antis. The insects were indeed formidable foes, justifying the policy of appeasement adopted by the alien race towards them since their arrival on Mars.

But the Antis now posed a direct threat to the cephalopods' rule, and this could not be tolerated. Some of the Martians in the city were now aware that the Imperial Guards were not an elite force composed of their offspring, but an army of metal puppets. If the people started to ask too many questions concerning the deception, even questioning the role of their emperor as head of the armed forces, the tentacled creatures could face a potentially insurmountable problem. The insects must be defeated and the green shoots of rebellion stamped on before being ground into the fertile soil of their Martian colony. The empire must prevail at all costs. The Imperial Guards were unable to contain the problem, so the cephalopods themselves would have to become directly involved in the fightback against the Antis attack.

At the heart of the imperial compound on the edge of the city sat the enormous golden pyramid, marking the very centre of cephalopod power on Mars. The palace, as the structure was known to countless generations of Martians, was the dominating and audacious presence that had come to symbolise imperial dominion to the deferential and effacing subjects of the divine emperor. The palace represented continuity and stability, strength and glory to the Martian people, as did the emperor himself. As far as the vast majority were concerned, the edifice had always been at the heart of their civilisation, and always would be. An empire on which the sun never set.

In fact, the pyramid was far more than just home to the emperor and administrative centre for the imperial household. It was the craft in which the alien cephalopods had arrived all those thousands of years ago, when a brilliant light descended behind Mount Rathkarn, as recorded on the Tablets of Skothath. The creatures had claimed Mars as their own, a new outpost of their ever-expanding empire. The area around the pyramid had developed over the centuries to provide the additional space required to run their burgeoning colony, and the walls of what had become the imperial estate were constructed to keep prying eyes well away. Now the unquestioned rule of the cephalopods was under attack, and the creatures had no option but to answer that outrage with the full force at their disposal. Sections of the gleaming outside walls of the pyramid slid open, as hundreds of imperial orbs, each piloted by a cephalopod, took to the air.

People in the city looked up in astonishment as the golden orbs moved across the sky, resembling so many bubbles created by a child's toy. Yet more of the orbs were released from the orbiting satellite, so that soon the sky was full of the gleaming objects, like thousands of diamonds glinting in the Martian sunshine.

# Chapter 32
# Freedom

In their cell within the pyramid, Aka-mas and his three fellow prisoners were aware that something important was happening outside. Imperial Guards were marching to and fro in the corridor and voices could be heard shouting orders. Aka-mas assumed these belonged to the elders, who were instructing the robots while the cephalopods dealt with more pressing matters.

Suddenly, the door of the cell opened and Cru-lem stood at the doorway facing the prisoners. Aka-des was convinced that this was the end for them all. They would be taken before the creatures and killed. The thought of the feeding tubes of the monsters snaking forward and latching onto his neck, the blood flowing back towards the open mouths of the creatures, filled him with horror. He then noticed that Cru-lem was not accompanied by Imperial Guards and also that his previous sneering countenance was replaced by one of growing fear.

'You must leave quickly, while the masters are otherwise engaged. Here, take this.'

The elder handed a small metallic disc to Aka-mas, which had a row of tiny lights around its edge.

'This will guide you out of the palace and back into the compound. If the lights glow green, you are on the correct route. Turn left here and don't look back. This is your only chance to escape. Go quickly.'

'Why are you doing this?' asked Aka-mas, taking the small device in his hand.

'Why are you helping us?'

The elder looked directly at Aka-mas, his eyes reflecting a deep sadness.

'I hate what I have become, but I had no choice. This is my one chance to do something right. Please forgive me.'

With that, he turned and hurried back down the corridor, his robes flowing behind him like a monk who was late for prayers.

'Come on,' said Aka-mas, 'let's go.'

His companions needed no persuasion, and soon the small group was making its way along the passageway, keeping a look out for Imperial Guards.

Aka-des glanced at his father, his friend and the elderly historian. Would they really escape from this hell?

*Do I trust Cru-lem?* Aka-mas asked himself as they followed the route indicated by the metal disc. *Why would he suddenly change his behaviour like this? Are we simply walking into another trap?*

They soon found themselves leaving the pyramid, the walls now turning from metal back to stone. So far, they had encountered no signs of life at all on their route, nor any Imperial Guards. It was as if the entire structure was empty.

'It's this way,' said Aka-mas, moving in the direction of the green lights. 'We must be back in the outer compound by now.'

The group followed, passing through one door into an empty storeroom and then another which led outside into a small courtyard.

Aka-des took a deep breath when he felt the warm sun on his skin.

'We've made it,' he whispered as he inhaled the sweet-smelling air. 'We did it.'

'We're not out of this mess yet,' replied his father. 'We've still got to get out of the compound and back into the parkland, without being seen.'

Sep-lee mopped his brow with a handkerchief.

'We've got to make it, he wheezed, while resting against a wall.

'We must get evidence of these creatures' existence to the outside world.'

Aka-des put his arm around Beta-vac's shoulders.

'Are you okay?' he asked his friend.

'Can you make it?'

Beta-vac nodded, still looking fearful.

'I can't believe we've managed to get this far without getting caught. I never thought I would see the sky again.'

He smiled at Aka-des, who responded with an affectionate hug.

Just then, Aka-mas pushed the others out of view as he pointed skywards. A stream of golden globes was flying out towards the city, apparently originating from the pyramid itself.

'What's going on?' Aka-des queried.

'They look like imperial orbs.'

'Fascinating,' said Sep-lee, having recovered his composure. 'Not one emperor, but hundreds. How will the authorities explain this to the population at large?'

'It could mean that not all is going to plan for some reason,' said Aka-des. 'Why else would the creatures be willing to expose their existence in this way?' he added.

'At least it's given us a chance to escape. We can work out what it all means once we're outside the compound.'

Making their way towards the walls of the imperial estate, following the green light pointing the way, the four men finally saw a gate in front of them.

'Let's hope it's unlocked,' said Aka-mas as they headed towards their potential exit to freedom.

\*\*\*

In the city itself, the battle between the Antis and the imperial forces was continuing apace. The golden globes flashed across the sky, aiming intense beams of radiation at the insects below. The force fields of the Antis were no match for the power of the cephalopods, and huge numbers of the creatures simply vaporised on the spot. However, the cephalopods did not care about the accuracy of their targeting. If Martians happened to be in the way, they met the same fate as the insects. The creatures in the orbs did not discriminate. Anything that moved was destroyed, whether that be Antis, Martian or Imperial Guards.

It seemed as if the tide had turned as the cephalopods pounded the insect forces below with their beams of destruction. Yet, in their hour of need, a voice appeared in the minds of every member of the Antis race.

'Do not fear, my children, we will prevail. It is time for us to sing the "Song of Destiny".'

The "Song of Destiny" had not been heard for thousands of years, yet knowledge of its existence had been passed down through the generations. Legend had it that the song would only be heard at times of great peril for the Antis race. Hundreds of miles away, in the heart of the Antis tribal lands, where no Martians had ever ventured, the Queen of Queens started to sing.

The haunting song washed over the mountains, hills and valleys of Mars, across the miles with a sea of undiluted sound. Martian farmers tending their fields stopped and listened to the song as it passed them by. Many fell to their knees; some started to cry at the indescribable beauty of the melody. Animals in the fields bowed their heads in acknowledgement, and even the trees and plants seemed to sway their branches and stems, urging the sound further and further on.

The song gained in strength as it continued on its path, eventually reaching the Martian settlements themselves. It passed through the ruins of those targeted earlier by the Antis, soon reaching Windor village, which had been completely bypassed by the advancing army of insects.

Stor-dal heard the song and joined other residents as they gathered in the streets. Tears ran down the face of the young mayor as he joined in with others who began to sing the bewitching melody, one just released from the subconscious recesses of their minds. For the "Song of Destiny" was not just a song of the Antis race, but a song of Mars itself. People fell to their knees and pointed to the sky above as the sound moved ever nearer the city.

It crossed the ruins of the city walls and passed through the narrow streets of the old town. As the Antis troops heard the song, they rubbed their antennae together, adding to the mesmerising strains. The song grew louder and louder when many of the city inhabitants joined in, too. The Antis looked skywards at the golden orbs hovering above the streets, and they also sang and sang. The Martians pointed at the orbs, the sound now reaching a crescendo.

At first nothing happened, but gradually some of the orbs started to wobble, and a few fell from the sky, crashing to the ground below. More and more fell as the sound jammed the power source of the orbs, causing people to run for cover. Like a sudden storm of hail, the golden orbs crashed downwards, turning buildings into rubble, with some cracking open upon impact. The cephalopods tried to steady their craft but were powerless to do so. The rich, haunting song seeped through the cracks and crevices of the orbs, finding its way into every component and device. The unique pitch of the sound caused the mechanisms to vibrate with such intensity that they broke apart, leaving the stricken vehicles with a complete lack of power.

Curiosity overcame the fear of the crowds who were watching the orbs plummet to the ground. Some of the braver souls crept forward to observe the broken craft at closer quarters. They were aghast to see writhing tentacles slither from the stricken ruins, as the cephalopods inside attempted to crawl from the wreckage.

\*\*\*

The door in the wall of the imperial compound was indeed unlocked, and the four men made good their escape, heading for a nearby clump of trees in the surrounding parkland. Up above they could see the golden orbs, but their destination appeared to have altered.

'They're returning from the city,' ventured Sep-lee, watching the craft change direction. 'They seem to be coming back to the palace.'

The cephalopods, realising they had no answer to the power of the mysterious song, retreated back to their pyramid, a structure which had symbolised their dominance for many thousands of years. Now it provided a refuge for the tentacled creatures as they confronted something almost unknown to their ancient race; the trauma of defeat.

Aka-mas and his companions made their way into the centre of the city only to be confronted by destruction and chaos. As they walked through the ruined streets, they saw people peering into the shells of the grounded orbs, their faces a mixture of terror and disgust as they witnessed the death throes of the cephalopods trying to emerge into the open air. Their huge heads pulsated as the creatures desperately sought in vain to breathe, their broken tanks seeping their precious liquid cocoon into the city streets.

Aka-mas approached a group of onlookers and pointed at a dying creature giving a final lash of defiance with its tentacles.

'Meet your emperors' he said, the voice a mixture of command and entreaty. 'These monsters have ruled our lives throughout recorded history. Take a good look at them.'

People stared at the hideous creature; its black eyes still filled with hate. It made a final attempt to eject its feeding tubes as a statement of defiance, but the snake-like appendages merely flopped onto the ground as the cephalopod closed its eyes and died.

While the crowds had been totally absorbed with the crashed orbs, they'd almost forgot about the Antis still milling around in the background.

Suddenly, someone shouted, 'Look, they're leaving!'

People turned to see the huge insects lumber off the way they had come, leaving the city and returning to their colonies. Their job was done, at least for now. The Martians would be allowed to make their own choices in the future, within reason. But, if the humanoids insisted on following their existing path of building more and more settlements in the sacred Antis lands, they would suffer the consequences. The power of the Antis race had been clearly demonstrated and, if the need arose, the "Song of Destiny" could always be heard once more.

A massive roar filled the air as people looked skyward.

'Look at that,' said a man standing near Aka-mas.

A brilliant light rose into the sky coming from the direction of the imperial compound as the golden pyramid of the cephalopods left the ground it had occupied for thousands of years. The creatures had realised that the illusion was broken. A relatively small group of cephalopods confined to their tanks of liquid relied on the unquestioning loyalty of the Martian race in order to rule. The mystique of the imperial system had been smashed, just like the golden orbs scattered across the streets of the city. Like a torch shining into the dark recesses of a cupboard, the reality had been exposed.

'Have they really gone?' asked Aka-des, unable to believe what he was witnessing.

'Will we be able to run our own lives in the future and learn to live in peace with the Antis?'

'Who knows,' replied his father, watching the craft rise higher and higher into the sky.

Just then, he felt someone slap his back. Turning around, he saw that it was his wife.

'There you are,' she said abruptly. 'I've been looking for you everywhere. I've arranged a little get-together with Mr and Mrs Rol-min this afternoon at our house. Don't be late.'

With that, she rushed off, picking her way through the wreckage of golden orbs as though it was just discarded litter.

Aka-mas watched his wife disappear into the crowd and then turned to his son.

'Somehow, I still think we have some way to go.'

# Epilogue

The day dawned on the planet Mars much as any other. The sun rose above the hills on the horizon, the mists of the previous night slowly dispersing. Tom yawned as he checked the time before making his way to the kitchen for his first cup of tea of the day. Upon entering the room, he was shocked to see Jason sitting at the table, tucking into a plate of reconstituted eggs.

'Good morning, dear leader,' said the medic between mouthfuls. 'Looks like it's going to be another lovely day.'

'Are you okay?' asked Tom, unable to comprehend the change in the Canadian's demeanour.

'You were acting very strangely last night, and then you passed out at dinner.'

'Just a touch of sunstroke,' replied Jason, laughing. 'I'm fine now.'

Tom had to admit that Jason did look much more like himself. Even the spot on his forehead had faded.

'Well, good to see you're feeling better,' he said. 'Just don't do too much today.'

As the others filed in, they were relieved to see the "old" Jason sitting at the table, smiling at one and all.

'Perhaps we won't need to return to Earth after all,' whispered Frances to Angela.

After breakfast, the crew dispersed to settle into their jobs for the day, and Jason returned to his cabin, on Tom's orders, to get some rest.

Frances, in her role as Jason's assistant, went to the small medical centre to check on supplies as part of a scheduled internal audit. She opened the refrigerated cabinet where vials of blood were kept in case transfusions were needed during their stay on Mars. She carefully counted the row of containers lined up in front of her.

'That's funny,' she said, noting the total. 'There appears to be one vial missing…'

## TO BE CONTINUED….